THE SOUL-DRINKER
AND OTHER DECADENT FANTASIES

JEAN LORRAIN (1855-1906) was the pseudonym of Paul Alexandre Martin Duval. He was one of the leading figures of the Decadent Movement and the author of numerous novels, volumes of poetry and short stories. At one point he was probably the highest paid journalist in France. Though mostly remembered today for his famous duel with Marcel Proust, he might be seen as the true chronicler of the *fin-de-siècle*. His short story collection *Nightmares of an Ether-Drinker* was previously published by Snuggly Books.

BRIAN STABLEFORD has been publishing fiction and non-fiction for fifty years. His fiction includes a series of "tales of the biotech revolution" and a series of metaphysical fantasies featuring Edgar Poe's Auguste Dupin. He is presently researching a history of French *roman scientifique* from 1700-1939 for Black Coat Press, translating much of the relevant material into English for the first time, and also translates material from the Decadent and Symbolist Movements.

JEAN LORRAIN

THE SOUL-DRINKER

AND OTHER DECADENT FANTASIES

Translated and with an Introduction by

BRIAN STABLEFORD

THIS IS A SNUGGLY BOOK

ISBN: 978-1-943813-09-4

Contents

Introduction   *vii*

Sonyeuse   *3*
The Unknown Woman   *56*
The Lover of Consumptives   *89*
The Soul-Drinker   *95*
Ophelius   *152*
Hylas   *172*
Day's End   *179*
The Legend of the Three Princesses   *187*
A Bohemian Tale   *195*
Princess Ottilia   *203*
The Marquise de Spolête   *211*
The Princess Under Glass   *228*
The Mandrake   *248*

Introduction

THIS is the second collection of translated short stories by Jean Lorrain that I have undertaken, following *Nightmares of an Ether-Drinker* (2002; Snuggly Books edition 2016). Whereas the first collection focused entirely on the author's shorter works, mostly produced in order to fit the regular *feuilleton* slots that many late-nineteenth century newspapers offered to writers as a tempting market, and therefore had to be adapted to a standard length of between 1,500 and 2,000 words, I have included a number of longer stories in this one, the greater scope of which allowed the author to develop his fascinations in more depth.

That decision has sharpened the distinction between the two sets of works included here: on the one hand, his psychological studies of amorous perversity broadly accommodated to the Naturalist tradition founded by Émile Zola and the Goncourt brothers and carried forward by the "neo-Naturalist" school whose principal exemplar was generally reckoned to be Paul Bourget; and on the other hand his *contes*, mock-folktales of a species central to the prose fiction of the "Decadent" Symbolist school, which some commentators saw as a contradictory rival to Naturalism in the last two decades of the nineteenth century.

In fact, there was no real opposition between Naturalism and Symbolism, and no writer illustrates the overlap of their parallel causes better than Jean Lorrain. The apparent distinction between the two schools had much to do with the fact that Symbolism was initially a school of poetry, whereas Naturalism was intimately bound to the evolution of the novel. In fact, Naturalist writers never spurned symbolic devices in their fiction, and when Symbolists elected to write in prose rather than verse, they naturally adopted many of the narrative techniques developed in the course of the novel's gradual technical sophistication. Although the kinds of short fiction known as the prose-poem and the *conte* remained closely associated with Symbolism because of their ostentatious artificiality, longer short fiction, even if it maintained many Symbolist affectations, inevitably acquired a closer resemblance to Naturalist fiction, especially when it was naturalistic with a small 'n', shunning the supernatural devices that were part of the basic stock-in-trade of the *conte*.

What writers of both schools had in common, from the very beginning, was a fascination with the seamier side of life, and with the aspects and peculiarities of amorous attraction and fixation. Although the "decadence" of which Symbolist writers were often accused was primarily a matter of ornate and contrived style, that often went hand in hand with an intense interest in various species of "moral decadence"—and in that regard, Naturalist fiction very often manifested a similarly intense interest, albeit from a narrative standpoint that was usually more obviously disapproving. As Zola's personal example, with its pseudoscholarly interest in the hereditary factors supposedly involved in moral decadence, gradually gave way to

Bourget's equally pseudoscholarly interest in psychological roots that were both more general and more individual, that kind of fiction crept up, as it were, on the mysteries of the unconscious mind, whose conscious echoes could only be represented, in the mind as well as in literature, in symbolic terms. It was, in consequence, in examining the psychological roots of amorous attraction, and particularly its apparent paradoxes, perversities and abnormalities, that Naturalism and Symbolism overlapped extensively, to the point of apparent fusion. No other writer of the *fin-de-siècle* period undertook a more elaborate exploration of those apparent paradoxes, perversities and abnormalities than Jean Lorrain, and no one else went as far afield in the search for discoveries of that curious kind than he did. Perhaps, given the variety of actual human behavior, it was not possible for him actually to invent perversities that no one actually practiced, or were even tempted to practice, but what is certain is that no one—including the practitioners and the psychologists who followed in the wake of Richard von Krafft-Ebbing's *Psychopathia Sexualis* (1886)—ever examined the anatomy of eroticism, including its wilder extremes, with a greater analytical fervor.

The first five stories in the present collection, the first three of which are taken from the collection *Sonyeuse* (1891) and the other two from *Buveurs d'âmes* (1893), are all examinations of erotic obsession; all of them are distanced from the supposed narrators, being placed within frames in which the victims of obsession are either observed from a distance, or narrate their stories to the notional teller. Sometimes the displacement is doubled, but even when the accounts appear to be given directly to the notional narrator and faithfully reproduced, they are usually uncertain and manifestly unreliable, and whenever the ultimate narrator intervenes in them as a commentator, his reliability immediately becomes suspect too. The stories are deeply ambivalent as well as deeply ambiguous, and the fact of fascination, on the part of the hearers within the stories as well as the reporters, is always fascinating in itself, inevitably questioning both the fascination of the author and the potential engagement of the reader.

In consequence of their narrative strategy, the most remarkable thing about the stories is, at least arguably, not the bizarrerie of the psychological syndromes they describe and detail, but how very engaging they are. They can certainly be regarded as case-studies in abnormal psychology, but they are also insidiously seductive literary works, inviting from the reader, if not identification, at least a sympathetic disturbance. If they are to be perceived as horrific, as they intend to be, the horror that they engender is uncommonly intimate and subtle, and scrupulously uncertain as to what the appropriate objects of that kind of horror ought to be, and where their boundaries lie.

It is perhaps not surprising that Jean Lorrain should have dedicated so much of his efforts to fictions of that kind. He was a homosexual who never "came out" in the sense that he made an explicit declaration of his homosexuality, but in whom it was sufficiently manifest for no one who knew him to be in any doubt about it. His attitude to his own sexuality was, however, deeply problematic; he did not know how to cope with it, and honestly did not know whether he ought to loathe and despise himself for his attractions, or to what extent. Relatively few of his studies in perversity focus on homosexuality *per se*, but those

that do—"Ophelius" is the obvious example herein—
address the subject with a tortuously confused obliquity.
He felt that he was on much safer ground when conduct-
ing analyses of much stranger attractions, and considering
in a more seemingly objective manner the problem of how
they might be adapted into lifestyles, if any such adaptation was possible. He rarely treated his characters any
more mercifully than he treated himself, but he really did
try hard to understand them, to make them comprehen-
sible, and to take them seriously, always refusing to write
them off as simply evil or mad.

In terms of their narrative strategy, the other eight stories in the collection, the first seven of which are taken
from the collection *Princesses d'ivoire et d'ivresse* (1902) while
the last was presumably omitted from that otherwise-
definitive collection of his *contes* because it had been published separately as an illustrated volume, *La Mandragore*
(1899), are quite different from the first five, all of them
being related by a supposedly-objective narrative voice
external to the tale, with no apparent ambiguity or possibility of unreliability, although their very laconism might
seem a trifle suspect to sensitive readers. For the most
part, they relate sequences of events without any delving
into the minds of the characters, and when the narrators
report what the characters are thinking they rarely attempt
to penetrate very deeply thereinto—although the actions
of the characters, of course, frequently speak volumes.
Nevertheless, their subject matter, whether apparent or
subtextual, very often displays the same fascination with
strange and wayward amour.

In *contes*, that waywardness is often represented in
frankly supernatural terms, but the supernatural terms in

question are inevitably symbolic of the same covert forces and urges that are the ultimate objective of analysis in the Naturalistic stories, which attempt to go inside the heads of characters to reach the same hidden depths by a different route. In the same way that the naturalistic stories intend to be horror stories, so do the *contes*, and if the *contes* often supply the kind of *deus ex machina* endings to which such fictions are hospitable, almost to the point of making them compulsory, it is very obvious that Jean Lorrain's notion of what might constitute an apt *deus ex machina* is just as conscientiously perverse and challenging as his notion of what might constitute an appropriate conclusion for a psychodramatic analysis.

"Jean Lorrain" had been born Paul-Alexandre-Martin Duval in 1855, in Fécamp, a small coastal town in Normandy, which is featured extensively herein, in lightly transfigured form, in both "Sonyeuse" and "The Soul-Drinker." His father, Amable Duval, was an apparently-prosperous but secretly profligate ship-owner whose vessels were involved in trans-Atlantic trade. Paul's love of fiction developed at an early age, encouraged by his mother. He was very fond of *contes* and chivalric romances, and particularly fascinated by the idealized princesses that often featured as their central characters. Having been educated at home for a while, Paul was sent to complete his schooling to a Dominican seminary, which left him with a lifelong antipathy toward the clergy, although he was not as inclined to give extravagant vent to that antipathy in his writings as many other writers who cultivated a similar detestation.

The Normandy shore was a favorite refuge of English exiles who crossed the channel to avoid scandal, following a path beaten long before in the Georgian era by "Beau" Brummell, whose legendary status became even greater in France than in England. Algernon Swinburne, who had lived near Fécamp for some years, remained the model of notoriety so far as Lorrain's home town was concerned; the lurid decor of Swinburne's house, and the scandalous things that were rumored to have gone on there, remained common knowledge long after his return to England. Although Paul Duval never met Swinburne, he did become acquainted with the similarly-scandalous Lord Arthur Somerset, who seems to have had a considerable influence over his tastes and attitudes.

Somerset's influence was, however, probably outweighed by Judith Gautier, whom Paul Duval met while she was holidaying in Fécamp in 1873 and by whom he was fascinated. Judith, who was ten years older than him, was by then separated from her husband, Catulle Mendès, who was later to become one of the pillars of the Decadent Movement, producing large quantities of short fiction with narrative strategies and themes analogous to those produced by Jean Lorrain. Judith Gautier does not appear to have attached any importance to Paul Duval's brief infatuation—she made no mention of it in her autobiography—but he was later to wax so lyrical about the change it had wrought in his life that his firmest friend, Edmond de Goncourt, became convinced that it had been the ruination of him. Goncourt came to believe—falsely, one presumes—that Lorrain's homosexuality was some kind of traumatic response to his doomed infatuation with Judith, and that everything he did thereafter was little more than a painfully-protracted moral and physical suicide. Whether the misogynistic Goncourt was homosexual himself or not remains a matter of speculation—he certainly never came out—but if he was, he would probably have been so disapproving as never to admit it even to himself.

When he had completed his military service, Paul was sent to study law, but had no interest in that career, and, when he announced his determination to follow a literary vocation instead, his father agreed to provide a modest allowance, on condition that the family name was veiled by a pseudonym. In 1880, therefore, Paul Duval became Jean Lorrain, found lodgings in Montmartre, and launched himself into the stereotyped lifestyle of a literary Bohemian, hanging out in Le Chat Noir with the members of Émile Goudeau's literary club, the Hydropathes, and the most colorful members of the Decadent Movement. His first collection of poetry, published under those influences, *Sang des dieux* (1882), had a frontispiece by Gustave Moreau, and Moreau's art became a very considerable influence on Lorrain's literary imagery. In 1883, however, Lorrain became a regular participant in Charles Buet's salon, where he made his most significant literary acquaintances: Jules Amédée Barbey d'Aurevilly, Joris-Karl Huysmans and "Rachilde" (Marguerite Eymery, who subsequently married Alfred Vallette, the editor of the Symbolist periodical the *Mercure de France*).

Barbey d'Aurevilly was one of the leading exponents of the philosophy of "dandyism," whose manifesto he had provided in *Du dandyisme et de G. Brummell* (1845), and although Lorrain had neither the means nor the breeding to compete with such notorious homosexual dandies as

Robert de Montesquiou and Pierre Loti, he did what he could to keep up appearances, to the extent that Remy de Gourmont described him as "the sole disciple of Barbey d'Aurevilly." When Lorrain met him, Huysmans was working on his classic handbook of dandyism, *À rebours* (1884; tr. as *Against the Grain* and *Against Nature*), the book that became the prose Bible of the Decadent Movement. Lorrain's fourth collection of poetry, *Les Griseries* (1887), consists of material explicitly inspired by *À rebours*, and much of his fiction echoes it. Rachilde's literary career was yet to begin in earnest in 1883, although she had already started to cultivate a reputation as an *enfant terrible*. She shared Lorrain's passionate fascination for masked balls, which were then in their last period of great fashionability, and he became her regular escort, enthusiastically competing with her in the outrageousness of his costumes.

While he cultivated these acquaintances, Lorrain was making a name for himself with the outspoken reviews that he wrote for the *Courrier Français*. His negative reviews were poisonous, and surprisingly indiscriminate, while his favorable ones tended to the opposite extreme. The latter included, unsurprisingly, paeans of praise addressed to both *À rebours* and Rachilde's *Monsieur Vénus* (1884; tr. as *Monsieur Venus*). Lorrain's enthusiastic advertisement of Rachilde—entitled "Madame Salamandre"—became her launching-pad, cementing a scandalous reputation that she carefully cultivated in appearance, and scrupulously belied in private.

In 1885 Lorrain met Edmond de Goncourt, who was thirty-three years older than he was, but who swiftly became eager to take the younger writer under his wing, perhaps seeing him as a kind of replacement for his younger brother, who had died in 1870. Lorrain thus became a regular at Goncourt's salon, the "Grenier," which was the effective heart of the Naturalist Movement, because Zola had moved out of Paris. Lorrain thus had one foot firmly planted in each of the supposedly rival camps. Goncourt's tutelage had its limits, however, and one can only imagine how distraught and disappointed Lorrain must have been in 1896, when he found out that Goncourt had left him out of the list of writers mentioned in his will as the recipients of the bequest that permitted the foundation of the "Goncourt Academy." It must have hurt him almost as much as the discovery he had made ten years earlier, when Amable Duval died in 1886, leaving nothing to his children but debts.

Lorrain's mother had kept control of her own money, and was not reduced to absolute penury by her husband's hidden profligacy, but she could not maintain her son's allowance. His career as a journalist suddenly became a matter of extreme urgency, but if he began to regret the many enemies he had made with his vicious reviews, it was too late for him to change course; his reputation was already formed, and could only be cultivated—which he did with great success, probably becoming the highest-paid journalist in Paris by the mid-1890s, but not without personal cost. In order to maintain his ferocious rate of production, he had to have recourse to artificial stimulants, and began taking ether for that purpose. The ether kept him awake, and provided him with hallucinations that he eventually mined extensively in his short fiction, to great effect, but its long-term effects on his health were catastrophic.

When he left Montmartre in 1887 Lorrain installed himself in an apartment in the Rue de Courty, which he furnished in a calculatedly bizarre fashion that took aboard the lessons he had learned from Lord Arthur Somerset, Barbey d'Aurevilly and *À rebours*, reflected in the descriptions of more than one of the rooms featured in the stories translated herein. Under the hallucinogenic influence of ether, however, the apartment came to seem direly discomfiting, and he began to refer to it as his "haunted house." He moved to Auteuil in 1890, telling his friends that he was doing so in the hope of recovering his health and composure. He had probably given up ether-drinking by then, but if not, he certainly discontinued the habit when his mother moved in with him in 1893, although it was only then that he began producing the definitive series of *contes d'un buveur d'éther* that were reprinted under that subtitle in the collection *Sensations et Souvenirs* (1895).

The *fin de siècle* was winding down, a prisoner of the calendar, and Lorrain, as the most outspokenly fascinated celebrant and most enthusiastic scourge of the mores of the yellow nineties, would doubtless have been keenly aware of the countdown even if his health had not been suffering badly enough to motivate a removal to Nice before the century's end. Once settled there, he set out to write two novels that would provide a kind of retrospective summary of the Decadent Movement and the world that had given birth to it: *Monsieur de Phocas. Astarté* (1901; tr. as *Monsieur de Phocas*) and *Le Vice errant* (1902). They were not greeted with any considerable critical or popular acclaim when they were published, however, and Lorrain's fortunes went into a steep decline when his former friend and protégée, the artist Jeanne Jacquemin, recognized herself as one of the characters in "Les Pelléastres," a story

xvii

serialized in *Le Journal* in 1902, and sued him for defamation of character.

The court—presumably more desirous of expressing disapproval of the defendant than in assessing the justice of the claim—awarded Jacquemin astonishingly high damages of eighty thousand francs, the settlement of which left Lorrain financially ruined and conspicuously vulnerable to further attacks of the same kind. He was soon called to answer a formal charge of corrupting public morals by literary means, brought against *Monsieur de Phocas. Astarté.* A similar charge leveled against *Les Fleurs du mal* (1857) half a century before had been the making of Baudelaire's reputation and fortune, but in Lorrain's case the response to the accusation only served to illustrate how dramatically the tide had turned, and how ardently twentieth century Paris wanted to believe and prove that the nineteenth century decadence was a thing of the past. Lorrain was disappointed that hardly anyone came forward to speak in his defense—the most notable exception was Colette—and deeply hurt by the fact that Huysmans, whose *À rebours* had provided the model for his own enterprise, remained silent.

Lorrain began once again to write at a furious pace in order to pay his debts, but much of what he produced was pure hackwork, lacking the distinction of his earlier material. His health continued to deteriorate steeply, and he began signing his articles in *Le Journal* and *La Vie parisienne* "Le Cadavre." In June 1906 he returned to Paris to help organize an art exhibition and to assist in an adaptation for an opera based on the most famous of his *contes*, "La Princess sous verre" (1896; translated herein as "The Princess Under Glass"), and it was there that he died of peritonitis when one of the ulcers in his colon perforated explosively. His reputation took some time to recover, but his best works continued to be reprinted, and by the time the next *fin-de-siècle* period arrived, historical distance permitted his crucial contribution to one of the most fertile and most remarkable periods in French literature to be accurately assessed and properly appreciated. The present collection will hopefully help to demonstrate to readers in the English language what a uniquely brilliant writer he was, in his own intensely peculiar but uniquely insightful vein.

Brian Stableford

THE SOUL-DRINKER

AND OTHER DECADENT FANTASIES

Sonyeuse

To my friend Gérard

To Antonio de Gandara,
These pages of a story of distant childhood
remembered before two of his portraits.
in fervor and in melancholy,

His friend,
Jean Lorrain

TEN years ago at the Champ de Mars, in the same room where the folly of the movement of Dannat's *Spaniards* swayed and twisted, demonically and frenetically, to the great exasperation of the bourgeoisie,[1] almost opposite that painting exacerbated and brutally pushed into the blue, on the same molding where Boutet de Monvel exposed the porcelain nullity of his vaselined *Dianes* and his socialites with enameled eyes,[2] but side by side with the deliberate boldness and savant play of light of a true painter, Monsieur Alexander,[3] three large portraits of

---

1 The *Quator Espagno* [Spanish Quartet] by the American artist William Turner Dannat was one of the sensations of the Salon of 1884.
2 Louis-Maurice Boutet de Monvel, best known as an illustrator of children's books.
3 John White Alexander (1856-1915).

equal size attracted me particularly by virtue of the agate hue and the preciosity of their atmosphere.

Before even having made out the individuals standing in the middle of their frames, a hallucinating expression of dream and reality had gripped me by virtue of those three forms, no longer fixed on the canvas by more or less ingenious methods, but seemingly alive, living a life of mystery in the austerity of vast unfurnished rooms, the neglected drawing-rooms of patrician dwellings appropriate to evocations; and within those large frames, open like portals to the emptiness of I know not what sumptuous interiors, the indefinable atmosphere reigned of fluid amber and milky gray, a strange atmosphere in which flesh became nacreous and blues iridescent, as in moonlight, and which I only knew in three painters in the world: Reynolds, Burne-Jones and Whistler.

They represented three females, those portraits, and were signed "A. de la Gandara":[1] three female figures, all standing; an old woman in black, a young woman in green, a child in yellow, the child in the middle; the same gray wood paneling with thin gold inlay ran behind them, and made all three of them inhabitants of some equivocal Empire drawing-room, or perhaps—who knows?—wanderers astray in the long corridors of a House of Usher. A similar phantasmal life animated them all, and their projected shadows loomed up behind them, sufficiently disquieting for one to believe the room haunted; but the young woman and the child, especially, were obsessive.

---

1 Antonio de La Gandara (1861-1917) was relatively unknown in 1884, having only exhibited for the first time the year before; he went on to become one of the leading portrait painters in Paris—Lorrain, who befriended him when he was just setting out, commissioned him, once he could afford it, to paint a portrait of his mother.

Oh, the lady in green! In what tale by Edgar Poe had I already encountered that pretty expressive face, so pale beneath the silky gold of her hair? And those beautiful eyes of a transparent and humid blue, those liquid eyes, those two large irises, distraught, as if plaintive, in the supplication of an eternal adieu? Where had I already seen, loved, loved passionately, adored and mourned, in dream or in life, that fine pallor and that delicate profile, and all the suffering of that aristocracy, itself afflicted in its touching grace by some unknown stupor?

Dona Ligeia, Morella, Berenice, or perhaps the so melancholy and so delightful lady whose life, gaze and smile vanished one evening, when her friend had fixed them on an imperishable canvas, and who died, drawn out of herself by the adoring ardor of her painter, enclosed with him in private . . . and the names of morbid and fugitive heroines, of hallucinated beauties even more hallucinating pressed upon my lips, but without any suitability and applicability to that dolorous and charming head, to the satin sheen of that snowy neck, to the profound blue of her two burning eyes, eyes of tears and flame, such as only exist in the amorous agony of a soul, the soul of a mother or a lover.

Tightly clad in a gray-green dress, with a slightly stiff corsage that made her timeless, she was gliding rather than walking at a quasi-phantasmal pace over the parquet of a high-ceilinged empty room; the bouffant of her sleeves further exaggerated the slenderness of her neck, and one sensed that the heavy train of her dress must have slid soundlessly, as in dreams. Slow and supple, but with a stiffness nevertheless, perhaps a trifle spectral, in the very upright stature, she was moving, seen from behind, toward the back of the room, already almost plunged into the vagueness of the wood paneling.

The apparitions of fantastic stories have those gliding exits. Oh, she was not emerging from her canvas, that one; she was not making for the window to the public, but, already surrounded by mystery, was slipping away with her fragile and doomed beauty, like a cherished shadow who would never return; and it is the poignancy of that adieu that squeezes your heart, an adieu of the entire body, half-turned toward you and darting at you, already in the unknown, the "forget me not" of her resigned and soft eyes.

In the frame immediately neighboring hers, against the same background of cold and sumptuous paneling, a strange little girl, very tall for her six years, opened in a child's sad and fearful face the same large irises, transparent and blue, the same haggard and suppliant liquid eyes.

That became hallucinatory. I knew those eyes too, and I had seen that child somewhere; there, the costume disturbed and deflected my memories somewhat: the sheath of yellow silk in which she had been dressed, a luminous golden dress, very straight, which made her a royal child, and the aureole of brown curls around her young forehead, put me less at ease than I had been before the portrait of the mother—for the frail lady in green was surely the mother of that pretty child. Their gazes were too alive with the same suffering, the same expression of anxiety and ardent tenderness, in the same shade of blue; and what struck me above all about that child was that manner, already observed elsewhere in another little girl—where and when encountered?—of holding the head inclined over the shoulder, that timidity of attitude, that slightly fearful alarm of a little precocious soul in arrest before life, in shivery retreat; the impression that I had once baptized, in another, of "a little bird fallen from the nest."

And then, comparing the portrait of the child more closely with that of the mother, there was a flash of light in my memory, a memory of childhood became precise—and what a memory!

Sonyeuse!

And all the melancholy of that mysterious adventure, which impassioned the little provincial village in which I had been brought up for ten years, suddenly revived before me: all that dolorous and tragic amorous adventure, whose heroes had disappeared from the region without having allowed their story to be penetrated, and of which thirty years passed over a tomb, today undiscoverable, had not yet untangled the enigma.

Sonyeuse!

In the little village in the Ouest, where I love to go every year to spend the last fortnight of October and live there, in the gray mist of memories, the torpid and almost extinct life of small provincial villages; among so may ancient dwellings, as if defunct forever and immured in silence with their shutters closed, one in particular attracts me and retains me with the obsession of a regret; and yet it is not the familial house with the good yesteryears of childhood and the soul still new, and the pleasant evenings in the soft warmth of the lamp and the log fires; neither the familial house nor the old patrician house of the Neymonts, outlined against the pale water of the quays with blacks and etched streaks; the Neymont house, already a dismal tomb of antique splendors in my vanished times, where,

7

in the long sadness of Sundays, a piano moaned, lightly tapped by the fingers of a dowry-less virgin, Mademoiselle de Neymont, entered since into the Ursulines of Caen. Oh, the sadness of provincial Sundays, the shutters closed and the tools at rest, the rare passers-by in the lethargic isolation of the streets, and so many bells in the air! It is necessary to have lived their bleak somnolence, like me, as a young child, those sad Sundays, as sad as All Saints' Day, to understand the vagueness and the torpor and the charm, simultaneously muffled and monotonous, ultimately soporific for the nerves and the heart.

The crowds heaped up in the churches, where the dull chant of vespers drags on, and, on the quay, the solitary promenade of customs officers before the restless sea, and the eternal retreat of the horizon; it is there that my reverie returns in tranquil memories toward a Louis XIII detached house surrounded by high walls, already deep in the valley, sheltered from the westerly winds and the rumors of the port, in the devotee quarter of convents and churches, deafened by carillons.

Built on the site of a former cloister of the Sisters of the Annunciation, in the depths of one of those large gardens of bowling-greens and quincunxes, which are only seen in the provinces, even in the sullen weather of the coastal region, where the sky is always full of clouds and squalls, it was as radiant as a fairground at the end of its great avenue of chestnut-trees, that Sonyeuse house, named for its owner, the Marquis de Sonyeuse, although he did not live there: the Marquis de Sonyeuse, one of the greatest landed fortunes of the province, *noblesse d'épée* become *noblesse de robe*, and President of the Tribunal of Rouen, where the Sonyeuses had lived, father and son, for two centuries.

What caprice, or what prescription of the Faculty, recommending the revivifying sea air to one of the frail young women of the family, had cast that elegant Louis XIII architecture, red brick with heavy stone entablatures, into that corner of a coastal valley, into the very heart of that old dead town, into that cold quarter whose slow church carillons, sounding every quarter of an hour, are the only movement: heavy flowers of iron shedding petals of ennui?

No one knew. From father to son, the Marquis de Sonyeuse, the head of the family in person, had the custom of coming twice a year, at Easter and Michaelmas; they descended upon the detached house and spent two days there, time enough to receive his farmers, who came to pay their rent. The Sonyeuses were the owners of most of the land in the vicinity. During those two days of the year alone, the ground-floor shutters, always hermetically sealed, were seen agape; then, the Marquis having departed, the uninhabited house fell back into its slumber—but it kept nevertheless, in spite of its abandonment, the gaiety of its walls, white stone and pink bricks, dazzling in the midst of the dormant shadows of its profound garden: a garden that terminated on the side of the valley with an immense meadow planted with poplars, bordered by the river, with the distant hills of the peninsula of Cotentin for a horizon, fleecy with brambles and gorse.

The Sonyeuse house! The long walks and pleasant alarms of my childhood through the shaded pathways and the silence of its quincunxes, and my childish games on the sunlit lawns, its great lawns of wild grasses in seed, where the caretaker's three cows grazed in winter and summer alike; that great garden, half-forest and half-meadow, so calm and solitary with the silhouette of the dormant house in the background, but a calm and a solitude so particular that my overexcited infantile nerves ended up vibrating there like the strings of a harp, and I sometimes stopped in the midst of playing with a hoop or a top, shivering with an unspeakable fear.

And yet, entry to that enchanted garden of sorts was a privilege envied by all the other children of my age. Only I, and my maid, had the right to go into it, and there was, in the brief but suffocating heat-waves of July, a repose and wellbeing in the hours of siesta spent in the green shade of tall lindens, in the calm and the silence of that profound and cool garden, all abuzz with swarms of insects. The gardener, a former imperial grenadier cast adrift after Waterloo in that hole of a small town, who consoled himself for lost glories by cultivating flowers, had been kind enough to confide one of the keys to the old estate to my father.

"The kid will be more at ease there than under the chestnuts of the avenue," he had muttered brusquely, one day, in a fit of tender enthusiasm before a collection of double tulips; mutual exchanges of seeds and cuttings had created a kind of botanical amity between the old curmudgeon and my father, a passion for horticulture that it is not rare to see at the approach of fifty in the calm life of belatedly married provincial bourgeois. It had begun with hyacinths bulbs; grafts of Souvenir de la Malmaison roses had tightened a relationship that was already excellent; they had been impassioned by chrysanthemums, and a bed of tulips had cemented the liaison.

That old Père Bricard—the physiognomy of an old polar bear with his white hair shaven, giving his pink cranium a light sprinkling of snow, and his moustache yellowed by tobacco, the color of sable with two drooping ends—lodged in the depths of his quasi-park with the right to sell vegetables for his only salary; he had vowed to the Marquises de Sonyeuse a worship all the more extraordinary, in such a man, because no Marquise of that name had set foot in the house for more than a hundred years.

To be sure, Marquises de Sonyeuse existed; one of them had been the Duchesse d'Angoulême's maid of honor and had officiated at the Tuileries; that must have been the dowager Marquise, still alive, resident at the Hôtel de Soissons in the Rue des Carmes in Rouen. The young Marquise, the daughter-in-law, one of the Boisgelon-d'Esprises, of whose marriage a few families in the town had received the announcement a month after the ceremony, lived in the familial house with her husband, the only Marquis de Sonyeuse presently alive.

Was it for the dowager Marquise or her daughter-in-law that Père Bricard raked the principal pathway—the one that led from the gate to the main door of the house—so indefatigably? Was it for the old woman or the young wife that he groomed the first lawns surrounding the great perron so conscientiously? That always remained between him and his old military conscience.

"I'd like Madame la Marquise to have no complaint to make, that's my idea," he repeated obstinately to my maid and me in the course of our walks in the great house in the Rue Viorne.

"But since she's never come, your Madame la Marquise, and won't be coming," my good Héloïse strove to prove to him.

"But what if she did? Does one ever know . . . with women?"

11

And he would pick up his fork or his rake; it was his obsession: to content Madame la Marquise; he awaited her arrival like his colonel's order to advance; the devotion of an old soldier turning to mania in what was almost a second childhood, all the more touching because no slipper worn by a Marquise de Sonyeuse had ever trod the sand of that unique driveway, well-maintained by him, any more than the rye-grass of the little lawn, the object of his amours.

It is also necessary to add to his praise that, outside the area encompassed between the gate and the dormant house, Bricard was leaving the entire property to return apace to wilderness: no more shrubs, but brushwood; long meadow-grass in the middle of the pathways; saplings in the quincunxes and virgin vines in garlands around the chestnut-trees of the bowling-green.

As for the kitchen garden, it was a marvel: frames, seedbeds, vegetable-patches, greenhouses and melons under glass; Père Bricard harvested *petit pois* in December and asparagus in January. In our day, the worthy man could have earned a good income on the *carreau* of Les Halles. In winter, he contented himself with selling his produce at high prices to the gourmets of the town, and in summer market traders bought his crops of beans and onions wholesale. Here and there, between a patch of cauliflowers and a plantation of courgettes, there was a bed of flowers for picking: carnations, chrysanthemums, roses, irises or tulips, the most beautiful flowers of each season. The wherewithal to make a royal bouquet for Madame la Marquise! One of the old pedant's hobby-horses.

Although the Marquise did not come to that beautiful slumbering garden of Sonyeuse, of which she bore the name, one day, another woman came, and it is for her sake that, gripped involuntarily by the charm of memory, I have attempted with my pen to breathe a little life into that old dwelling, where the story to be told here unfolded so tragically.

Young as I was, I shall never forget the impression of my first encounter with Lady Mordaunt. Was Lady Mordaunt her real name? What highly-placed individual of the English aristocracy had to bury herself and veil herself from all curiosity? Many contradictory rumors ran around on the subject of that Lady Mordaunt, whose strange adventure was the great event of my early youth, and for ten years the conversation of that somnolent little town; but the woman who was to preoccupy passionately the imagination, normally so calm, of an entire provincial society lived mysteriously, and even the epitaph on her tomb, the tomb that has replaced, for so many of the disappeared, the ancient legendary well from which Truth emerged nakedly, has not betrayed her secret.

It was one of those bright gray days in October, of which it is commonly said in Normandy that it is weather for retaining swallows. I was wandering with my maid over the lawns of Sonyeuse, not far from a clump of double dahlias, with enormous fluted flowers, still pearled with raindrops from a morning shower, and my childish play consisted of shaking all those huge ruffs one after the other over an old watering-can; my maid was walking behind or in front of me, I no longer remember exactly, when the sound of a soft voice caused us to raise our heads simultaneously.

On the other side of the double dahlias, her feet on the moist grass of the lawn, a lady was standing a few paces away from me.

Tall, slim and with a singularly supple figure, in a carrick with little shoulder-flaps in *"ventre de biche"*—a hue extremely gentle on the eye, the name of which I only learned long afterwards—she appeared to me, in her garment and her gait, in her grace itself, to be a person of another race, of a nature other than my mother and the women of the town that I saw every day.

Her costume was, however, very simple; I have understood since that she was in her traveling clothes that day; but it was the first time I had seen a carrick with little shoulder-capes, and the woman who was wearing that carrick had a beauty so delicate and so pale; her neck stood out so slenderly and with such elegance, not seen before, above the fabric of that mantle; her oval face, perhaps a little too elongated but exquisite in its delicacy, astonished the gaze with the milkiness and satin texture of her skin. It was snow in all its dazzling transparency, and never since have I encountered a woman whose flesh was so luminously white; one might have thought that the aurora was infused beneath her temples; enveloped as she was in veils of yellow gauze, seething above a huge straw hat of the kind then in fashion, through that gilded mist, her blonde complexion was dazzling; but what completed the disconcerting effect of that radiant visage, and simultaneously pricked your heart, were the eyes, the eyes with dark blue irises, two sapphires, almost black, wide open beneath the bruised eyelids; two dolorous gazes, as if bathed in tears, and yet afflicted by I know not what stupor.

Oh, the alarm of those distraught and charming eyes, in their mute supplication! I have often thought of it since, and I have always retained the conviction that the woman who bore such eyes had to be under the influence of a narcotic, or some mysterious power.

Those reflections, of course, I only made many years later, many years after the death of Lady Mordaunt, when the events . . .

That day, I contented myself with remaining silent, my eyes gaping, before the beautiful foreigner. Père Bricard was accompanying her, head bare and back bent, kneading an old straw hat between his dirty fingers. Very humbly, he seemed to be doing the honors of Sonyeuse. The lady, having stopped a few paces away from us, had not seen us; she was probably looking in front of her, without an objective for her gaze; she had resumed her visitor's stroll and was now going across the lawn, her stride sinuous and soft, lifting up her dress with one hand.

Then my maid and I saw that the lady was not alone; a man, of whom we only saw the back that day, elegant and well-dressed in an olive-green frock-coat, with a youthful demeanor and a muscular stride, was accompanying the foreigner in the yellow veil—doubtless her husband, for an adorable little girl, who might have been about my age, nine or ten years old, was skipping along, suspended from his coat-tails, each bound putting the pink of her bare legs into the green of the long grass, and sending the tresses of her blonde hair flying into the air.

"They're English," summarized Héloïse, with her peasant wisdom: an opinion based on the bare legs and the free tresses hanging loosely over the child's shoulders.

That was all, that day.

In the evening, at table—in provincial life there are no trivial facts and everything that is not ordinary and anticipated takes on the proportions of an event—I did not fail to mention my encounter.

15

"Foreigners at Sonyeuse," my father thought aloud. "Bricard's palm must have been greased; that would astonish me slightly, and will spoil my old Bricard." Then, struck by a thought, he turned to my mother, who was busy serving the soup. "Might they be the English people from the Grand Cerf?"

There were English people staying at the Grand Cerf, then? The Grand Cerf was then the best hotel in the town. Who were these English people about whom I knew nothing? My childish curiosity could not have been more excited. My father and mother exchanged a few words in whispers. Héloïse, who was serving at the table, was interrogated.

"And the child was bare-legged and had disorderly hair down her back?" asked my mother.

"Yes, Madame, beautiful blonde hair."

"They're English," my father concluded.

That day, I did not discover any more.

But what I discovered, and could not doubt, the following day, was that Sonyeuse and its magnificent garden of the Sisters of the Annuniciation was henceforth a closed door to me. My maid and I ran into an inexorable order; old Bricard came during the day to reclaim the key to the little door from my father; the foreigners encountered the day before at the turning of a path were henceforth the tenants of the house and the garden; Monsieur le Marquis had rented Sonyeuse to the English couple and a whole army of laborers, carpenters and house-painters was already overturning the commons and the bowling-greens.

Sonyeuse: Monsieur le Marquis had leased Sonyeuse. He was not coming back to the locality. Sonyeuse, which, for three hundred years, had not left the family . . . it must surely be to some associate or relative! And what about the farmers? Where would Monsieur the Marquis collect his rents henceforth?

Who were the English people? Where had they come from? What motive brought them to S——? Would they be received? Were they married? (The first question that the malicious gossip of suspicious small towns asks of any young man and young woman recently installed within their walls.) Would they make visits? Would they be returned? Did anyone know them? And the usual sequence of a thousand and one malevolent question marks that a provincial society raises around any unknown couple.

As to what it was appropriate to call the worthy company of S——, a few arrogant and stuck-up families of the petty *noblesse de robe* did not have to take the trouble to make impertinent enquiries. Lord and Lady Mordaunt did not visit anyone; in retreat behind the high walls of Sonyeuse, they lived there in absolute solitude, without even appearing to suspect the extent to which they were preoccupying opinion.

Except for the nine o'clock low mass at the Abbey, to which a hired berlin took them every Sunday, one did not encounter Lady Mordaunt anywhere. Lord Mordaunt, a dark-haired man with an impassioned face and olive skin, with the profile of a bird of prey, who appeared to be much younger than his wife, rode through the town almost every morning on a superb horse that was worth a good three hundred louis; another horse waited in the stable, apparently, for milady's orders and caprice, but it was a caprice that she did not have, for, on the rare occasions that I crossed her path outside the church, where her presence gave me culpable distractions during the offices, she was on foot, and always accompanied by her husband and the child that I had seen with her on the first day.

Her husband! It was necessary to hear the inflexion of those two words—"Her husband"—by Madame de Saint-Énoch, among others, the most stiff-necked woman in the little town of S——, where her judgments regulated opinion. "Her husband" and "her daughter"—"for that man is far too young to be the father of that child; he's twenty-three years old, that so-called Mordaunt; for me that has nothing Catholic about it, and conceals some mystery!"

And that was also the opinion shared by my parents, by my mother especially, who nourished a suspicious aversion for the foreigners of the Rue de Viorne.

Did there enter into that sentiment a little jealousy for the exquisite loveliness and innate elegance of the foreign woman? Had my mother drawn that kind of hateful malevolence from her pride as an honest woman, wounded by the irregular happiness triumphantly installed before her eyes? But I twice had the opportunity to take account for myself, child as I was, of that unjust hostility.

The first time was at church, at the Abbey of S——, where hazard had given us the Englishwoman and her daughter as neighbors in the stalls, and where, for six months, every Sunday, my mother and I heard the nine o'clock low mass, only separated from the two strangers by the thickness of a wooden pillar.

Needless to say, I did not share the maternal sentiment with regard to the pretty foreigner; the first impression made on my child's senses in the abandoned park of Sonyeuse had only increased and grown; during the offices I could not weary of admiring the delicacy of that profile and the slenderness of the neck that had struck me so forcefully on that first day: the transparency of that complexion and that dazzling pallor, which, in the half-light of the church, was further refined and paled, as if idealized by the mystical light falling from the stained-glass windows; that elegance and that pallor hypnotized me—and if I employ that very modern word, which jars, by virtue of its impression of technical terminology, with the grayness and effacement of this melancholy story, it is because I can find no other to characterize the species of obsession that the pallor and the flesh in question already exercised upon me.

Since then, I have often told myself that Lady Mordaunt must have been my first love, that of an imaginative and precious small boy, and I find the confirmation of that opinion in the memory of the many small details still alive in my mind, very minute details inherent in the woman, which generally do not overly preoccupy the imagination of a child: the memory of her perfume, for instance; a sweet and penetrating perfume, in which there was iris and jasmine, and which rose from her as soon as one came close, as when one passed her in June along the hedge of a flower-garden: that heady and suave perfume, with which all her garments were impregnated, and a long time after she had left the church, the lower part of the nave, where she heard mass alongside us, retained the embalmed wake she left behind persistently.

That perfume, a tenacious obsession, I breathed in all day long on Sunday in my room, in the drawing-room, or at table, where the subtle effluvia still spoke to me of her, and, my nostrils voluptuously open, I only had to close my eyes in order to see her delicate aristocratic profile and that fine pallor shaded by blonde tresses under her hood of velvet plush.

The little girl with the long hair the color of ripe rye, who was capering on the day of our first encounter suspended from Lord Mordaunt's hand, accompanied her to church every time: a poor fearful child, out of her element in that little unknown town, whose habits were no longer her own.

She too was very pale of skin and very frail in her structure and joints; she already had in her big blue eyes her mother's dolorous and surprised gaze. There was alarm in the timid glances that she sometimes darted at us at the beginning of the mass, as if covertly, before kneeling down—but what an adoring and fervent tenderness there was in that sweet face when her lovely frightened eyes met those of her mother! It was touching to see them together; the mother and the daughter idolized one another.

Poor little thing; I can still see her, giving the impression "of a bird fallen from its nest," as our old family doctor, Dr. Lambrunet, said when talking about her. He was the only man in the town admitted to Sonyeuse, and who went there often, to the house forbidden to everyone else, summoned to the child of the English couple, whose health was delicate, like the fragility of a luxury flower.

It was for the sake of the little girl's health that Lord and Lady Mordaunt had come to live in S——; the physicians in London had prescribed the saline and yet temperate air of a valley on the coast of Normandy for the child's slightly frail lungs. At least, that was the reason for their sojourn here given by Dr. Lambrunet, besieged from dawn to midnight with all the town's questions, because he was the only man received at Sonyeuse. The mysterious English couple had only come to bury themselves in S—— for the sake of the child.

The society of S—— did not want to believe it; there must certainly have been something else, but what was that other thing? The old physician did not say a word about it.

At any rate, he cared for the child—or "the two of them," La Saint-Énoch added. I have never known why, but public opinion wanted Lady Mordaunt to be even more afflicted and suffering than her daughter by the mysterious malady that had assigned S—— to them as a place of healing. She was so frail and so pale, that Lady Mordaunt; so strange, especially, in the expression in her broad irises, her large eyes, drowned and seemingly haggard.

It had also been remarked that she never went in the direction of the sea; all their walks as a threesome—the father, the mother and the child—were directed inland, outside the town, and when they were encountered during the long warm evenings of August, and sometimes late in the autumn, under those clear and melancholy October skies that are the charm of Normandy, it was always in the valleys, and the entrance to some woodland path, on the edge of some remote and solitary forest.

The little girl was also encountered walking along the quays and along the harbor wall, hand in hand with her father; but Lady Mordaunt never went past the site of the Abbey, whose foundations were set in the very heart of the town; one might have thought that she was afraid of the sea and everything that might come from the sea.

"She's a woman with something to hide." Again, naturally, the words were La Saint-Énoch's.

It was with regard to "the woman with something to hide" that I twice caught my mother—who was, however, a good woman—*in flagrante delicto* in the kind of hostile and suspicious arrogance that was the mentality of the women of the town.

The first time was in church, at the Abbey, where my mother and I were accustomed to hear the same low mass as the two Englishwomen from Sonyeuse, only separated from them by a distance of a few feet.

For the entire duration of the offices, Miss Mordaunt, the "poor little bird fallen from the nest," who could not amuse herself every day, being brought up separately and alone as she was, without ever playing with other children of her age, poor little Miss Mordaunt never ceased to turn in my direction the alarm of her great questioning eyes; she would have liked nothing better than to make my acquaintance, the poor little solitary, but she dared not, watched as she was between long lowered lashes by her mother's gaze, and not much encouraged by my mother's stony physiognomy, and mine, but manifestly excited by my surreptitious glances and the faces I pulled on the sly.

In the course of one of those mute comedies, her missal, a jewel of binding, sheathed in mauve velvet, whose clasps in the form of enamel trefoils I had noticed long before, slipped from her fingers.

The book slid along the floor noisily, and came to rest at my feet in the middle of the dusty flagstones; blushing crimson, she did not move, and I was already bending down to pick the book up and return it to her when my mother, who had seen the movement, seized me abruptly by the arm; I was paralyzed by surprise, and rightly so.

Lady Mordaunt then bent down, as naturally as could be, and, with an inclination of her entire beautiful supple body, picked the book up from the floor and placed it, open, in the child's hands—but she had not missed anything of the scene and my mother's action, for her beautiful hands were trembling slightly as she riffled through her own missal to find her place, and in the surprised glance that she darted at me there was a kind of *thank you*—but why was that glance so astonished? What had I done that was so heroic as to occasion surprise?

Did my mother, who was profoundly virtuous, regret the gratuitous impertinence directed at Lady Mordaunt and her child? At any rate, after the *Ite missa est*, she got up, hastened her prayers, and found herself at the font at the same time as the English duo. Lady Mordant, who had risen to her feet first, had already dipped her gray-gloved hand; my mother then, as if nothing had happened, moistened her own fingers in the marble bowl, and, turning toward the little Mordaunt, held her hand out, moist with holy water, to the fearful child.

Lady Modraunt gave her an imperceptible nod of the head, and passed on.

Which did not prevent my mother, that same day, at lunch, having this revelatory conversation with my father: "It would be very kind of you, at the first opportunity, to ask the beadle to change my two places and to place me further forward toward the choir; the Englishwomen from Sonyeuse are distracting your son during the offices."

I lowered my head and did not say a word.

The following Sunday, my mother and I took our seats directly under the pulpit, mid-nave by the choir; as I went into the church I darted a rapid glance at my former place. Lady Mordant and her daughter were no longer there; they too had abandoned an importunate proximity and had moved toward the choir, but in the direction directly opposite to ours. The main aisle now separated us.

Lady Mordaunt and my mother met once again that Sunday at the font, but that day no holy water was offered, nor any inclination of the head.

The second time was in the course of one of the long walks in the environs of S———, on which my father, an enthusiast for nature brought up in the school of Jean-Jacques, had the custom of taking my mother and me every Sunday for six months of the year, from Easter Sunday in April until All Saints Day in the autumn.

Among the admirable landscapes of that region of the Ouest, all the woods and meadows have little valleys and nearby cliffs; my family had adopted a few sites, and among those favorite places was a narrow valley profoundly encased in the fold of a hill, heavily wooded, trees mingled with thickets, creating a kind of centuries-old forest invaded by brambles and creepers; a corner of enchanted nature, of unknown origin, mysterious and wild, in the midst of the restful intimacies, sometimes a trifle commonplace, of fertile Normandy: the Normandy of ever-new verdure, washed by the rain, that one of our enamored story-tellers, Barbey d'Aurevilly, has compared to a little girl with pink cheeks moist with tears.

I was only twelve but, an avid reader of romances of chivalry, my brain already larded with epic narratives and fabulous stories, I had, in my childish imagination, baptized that leafy and solitary corner with the charming name of Broceliande.

Broceliande: the forest of apple-trees in the land of Bretagne, where the shrewd and svelte enchantress Viviane had caught the old mage Myrdhinn in her trap; Broceliande, where the old forgotten bard had been sleeping his sorcerous slumber for hundreds of years, buried in the greenery, exiled from death and removed from life.

> *The broom was golden, and in Broceliande*
> *The blue iris, jewel of springs, lavender*
> *Embalmed the air. It was the blessed month*
> *When thickets awake to the infancy of nests,*
> *Apple-blossom snows in the cool, calm wood*
> *At the feet of enormous oaks, between the leaves*
> *Of April ferns and clumps of lilies*
> *Viviane and Myrdhinn were sitting in the shade.*

I have always thought that those lines, which I composed much later, in my twentieth year, had been inspired by a tenacious and delirious impression of childhood, and if I have celebrated so extensively in prose and verse the Gallic Viviane and the enchanter Myrdhinn, the image of Lady Mordaunt has certainly not been unconnected with that obsession with a legend that is, after all, more English than French, and the species of posthumous amour avowed by me, beyond space and time, to Merlin's blonde enemy.

Broceliande! That corner of the forested park , which was, in reality, called Franqueville, really was Broceliande, in fact, when I was walking with my parents that day, on a bright and warm Sunday in June: Broceliande, with the flowery snow of wild apple-trees, clenching their rugose trunks in the shade of firs, and that grave silence in which the flutter of wings in the foliage and the sound of foot-falls on the moss were like palpitating voices and in the air that intoxicating odor of bitter almonds emitted by flowering hawthorn.

As the three of us—my father, my mother and I—were climbing along a narrow path through a ravine, plunging steeply under the trees, obstructed by branches and enormous roots trailing serpentine knots over the clay of the banks—I shall always remember the intense and raw blue of the sky shining over our heads that day—we found ourselves face to face with the English threesome from Sonyeuse, father, mother and child.

We were going up the path; they were coming down.

Had Lady Mordaunt recognized my mother?

The path was, as I believe I have said, very narrow; with an exquisite politeness, the guests of Sonyeuse all arranged themselves against the bank and stood back to let us pass. But in that movement, Lady Mordaunt's large straw hat was caught on a branch and, suddenly deprived of her hat in passing, the Englishwoman stopped abruptly, her waist and shoulders as if inundated, submerged by an aurora, suddenly draped in a mantle of blonde gold.

Her magnificent hair had been unbound as she passed, and, its weight drawing it down, had unfurled like a wave from her nape to her heels.

It was dazzling.

That Sunday, Lady Mordaunt was wearing a spencer, with green silk trimmings over a white muslin dress with frills. A final magic; a ray of sunlight was caught in that molten metal.

My father and I had stopped involuntarily, amazed, admiring that adorable and frail white vision, coiffed with a golden stream, standing out in steaks of light against the green and mobile darkness of a wood. I was walking, personally, in mid-reverie; that Franqueville really was

Broceliande; Viviane had surged forth there in the hollow of the valley.

With what a passionate expression in his eyes Lord Mordaunt looked at his wife then! The anxious adoration of his gesture as he came to her aid, trying to repair the disorder of her hair! No, it would be necessary to have seen it to comprehend the quasi-savage folly that doubtless inflamed their liaison.

Everything was pleading and imploring in the proud profile of a bird of prey—a hawk suddenly tamed—and the fervor of that gaze, ordinarily of onyx, mistrustful and hard! That man with a nose like an eagle's break, and a torrid, grilled complexion, also had, beneath his meeting eyebrows, as sharp as if traced in Indian ink, two very curious eyes, true eyes of stone, gleaming and cold; but that day, I can assure you, those eyes had all the humidity of passion.

I was still very young to be able to analyze all that, but, in surprising the Englishman's gaze as he looked at his wife, and the glance that she returned, her lips parted in the moue of a half-smile, I had the sensation that my heart had been gripped, and I knew, for the first time, or at least believed that I knew, the bite of jealousy.

But that incident scarcely lasted a minute, and I am taking an hour to recount it.

Lady Mordaunt went into action now, very confused, trying to repair the disorder of her hair, and, with hairpins between her teeth, and her arms raised in a movement that gave full value to her breasts and her hips, she had twisted her hair into a thick cable, and was trying to secure that cable with the teeth of a pink coral comb, which had the pink of a rose-blossom in all that golden froth.

But the rose-blossom was Lady Mordaunt herself. Ashamed, as if of an immodesty, of that displayed hair, a rush of blood turned her neck, lips and cheeks scarlet; and, crimson all the way to the neckline of her silk spencer, she hastily recoiffed herself, feverishly, and her embarrassed smile degenerated into a pout, and her beautiful alarmed and fearful eyes seemed to be begging for mercy. They were requesting forgiveness, those eyes.

She finally succeeded in remaking her coiffure, and, advancing a slender foot, she passed by, lightly and furtively. Her husband raised his hat and followed; then we, still standing open-mouthed in the same place—my father and I, at least—returned the salute and were continuing on our way when my mother, who had remained slightly behind, mute and cold, on the very spot of the encounter, looked us up and down, and, adjusting her silken mantlet on her back with a shrug of the shoulders, said: "Those creatures!" loudly enough for the Englishwoman to have heard it.

Those creatures! And throughout the entire walk, she did not breathe another word.

Those creatures! My childish imagination labored long and hard over that gibe. "Those creatures." Was Lady Mordaunt, then, not like my mother and the other women I saw at the house? *Those creatures?* The haughty phrase of a respectable bourgeois, which kills like a bullet and lowers social status with a word.

It was in the same year as that encounter that the tragic adventure burst forth which was to break those two lives and reduce the appearance of their happiness to dust, and it was precisely with regard to that anxious and fearful little girl, whom they were always dragging in their wake, she with adoring eyes and enveloping gestures of solicitude, he with the attentive complaisance of a cicisbeo, more gallant than paternal, evidently preoccupied with the child because of the mother.

That poor little Miss Mordaunt, so pretty, and above all so pitiable, with her frail and delicate visage, eternally tilted over her left shoulder, giving the impression of a little bird fallen from the nest, as the doctor put it, and the awkwardness of her little idle hands, the weak hands of a lonely, bored child.

We encountered her often in the town in her father's hand, trotting with all the might of her little bare legs to regulate her pace with the firm and seemingly determined tread of the Englishman; since the places had been changed in the church she no longer dared to raise the mute supplication of her blue eyes toward us; she preoccupied us nevertheless, my maid and I, and more than we admitted, that melancholy and solitary child of rich parents, a poor little pariah who never spoke to anyone and to whom no one ever spoke.

Her name was Hélène, and that was all we knew about her; but not a day went by when my maid and I, either going for our walk, or on the way back, did not pass her on the way to the fields, as if indifferently, on the cold and calm Rue Viorne, at the very gate of Sonyeuse, where we never failed to pause.

The silhouette of the detached house still loomed up at the far end of the broad drive lined with chestnut trees, with its high roofs, guilloched with skylights; the heavy stone entablatures stood out even more palely than before against the rust of the bricks, now carefully washed, but Sonyeuse maintained nevertheless its aspect of a house asleep in the midst of its lawns and its great motionless shadows, as if they too were slumbering in a centuries-old forgetfulness; and in the distance, the fugitive valley; and it seemed all the more somnolent, that melancholy domain of Sonyeuse, the name of which returns to my pen repeatedly with the knell of a obsession, occupied as it now was by those indecipherable English people, its shutters hermetically closed, on the side facing the street, at least.

The Mordaunts lived in the apartments overlooking the valley; there was among those English people such a need to retrench themselves, alive, from the world and to live hidden from all eyes, that they had refurbished the ancient wooden shutters of the gate, and on some days, my maid and I ran into a barrier of screens painted the rawest red, like a butcher's stall.

On those days, no more Sonyeuse: a caprice of Lord or Lady Mordaunt had robbed us of the view of the melancholy old domain, the domain from which their presence had already exiled us. But in turning away, slight crestfallen, our curiosity disappointed, what my maid and I regretted was not having been deprived on the sight of the tall three-hundred-year-old chestnut-trees, or the mown and raked grass of he lawns, but the little English girl, often glimpsed through the bars of the gate, sitting on a bench, with the head of a big dog on her knees, or standing, hoop in hand, in the middle of a path.

Poor little bird, her expression always so distraught and sad, and yet so prettily and simply decked out, so neatly dressed! Almost naked, in winter as in summer, in delightful little white dresses, or others in exquisite pastel shades.

That little forsaken girl had the wardrobe of a princess; the Mordaunts had to be immensely rich to dress a child scarcely eleven years old with a luxury that would have been difficult for the greatest millionaire lords of London or Paris.

She did not seem any more cheerful for that, poor thing. She might well have had a hoop or a ball in her hand, but I cannot remember ever having seen her play; she was always standing still, planted on the smooth sand of a pathway, or walking, very gravely, with measured steps.

Before the adventure of the book in the Abbey, under the persistence of my glances, she had ended up looking too, and recognizing me as her neighbor in the stalls, had addressed a vague smile to me, but she had never approached, had never even made a movement toward us.

She must have had a very timid and very proud nature. Since the unfortunate affair of the missal, when she perceived me at the end of her driveway, she turned her head and went away slowly.

A dolorous childhood veiled in mystery.

But I'm forgetting to stir the extinct ashes of yore, the dust of childhood memories, and my story is lingering and dragging. I shall get to the point.

During the winter that followed our encounter with the tenants of Sonyeuse in the Franqueville wood, the rumor went around in society that Lady Mordaunt was pregnant.

That rumor, born no one knew where and founded on the increasingly rare appearances of the young woman, Doctor Lambrunet, when interrogated, did not even take the trouble to deny. If Lady Mordaunt had not come to church for two months, if one never encountered her, even in the berlin, in the grassy and solitary streets of the town, it was because her health, already so delicate, had deteriorated further; Lady Mordaunt was having a most difficult pregnancy.

Condemned to an almost absolute immobility, she now lived nailed to a chaise longue in the adoring and continuous company of Lord Mordaunt, who no longer left her; cloistered in the kind of idolatry that he seemed to have avowed to his wife, the restless and passionate Englishman had become invisible from day to day; no one any longer encountered him in the town; amour had made him a recluse. On the other hand, we all crossed paths with little Hélène Mordaunt every day, much less severely dressed than before, and now accompanied by a governess, a tall English chambermaid with the appearance of a lady, and I know not what false impression of Lady Mordaunt distributed throughout her person.

Was the servant applying herself to copying her mistress, or did she owe to Lady Mordaunt's wardrobe, which she ended up wearing manifestly, that distant resemblance to the most ideally distinguished woman I have ever known?

At any rate, all S—— was preoccupied all week long with that aristocratic chambermaid.

It was perfectly natural, in sum; would Lord and Lady Mordaunt have confided the custody of their Hélène, that quasi-royal child, to just anyone?

In addition, the society of S—— began to relent somewhat in its hostility to Lord and Lady Mordaunt; the dolorous pregnancy of the mother had softened the good souls of the place, and a current of sympathy was established around that perilous maternity; human egotism, before evil, when it senses itself exposed, has sudden fissures of pity.

Even my mother now seemed to be taking an interest in the beautiful tenant of Sonyeuse, and not a day passed when she did not ask Dr. Lambrunet for news of that disquieting pregnancy and that frail health. Her curiosity could not have been better served, moreover, than by a slight mucous fever that kept me in bed for a fortnight and brought the doctor to us regularly, once a day.

The good old doctor had the custom of arriving at our house at about half past six in the evening, when his daily visits were concluded, and would linger in the good lamplight to satisfy my mother's curious ear with the news brought from one house or another. A genuine ambulant gazette, was our old friend Lambrunet, but with a discretion proof against anything when it was necessary to be discreet; nevertheless, I always figured that my mother and he did not dislike that daily visit, in which the entire cargo of anecdotes and trivial incidents of the town was unloaded in less than half an hour; it was, I'm convinced, the best hour, the blank hour, the *alba hora* of their day. They found one another there in a pleasant and mild intimacy, in the heart-to-heart of two existences lived side by side for years, united in the same path of honesty and duty, happy to rest in the wellbeing of that bright closed room from the fastidious chores and obligations of everyday life.

When the doctor rang the doorbell, merely by the manner in which my mother, always bending over some work of sewing, pricked up her ear in the direction of the staircase, without interrupting the back-and-forth movement of her needle, I recognized the doctor's ring myself.

Behind the curtains of my bed, carefully drawn and only allowing a little of the shaded lamplight to filter into the obscure warmth of the alcove, my respiration regular and my eyelids closed, I too was all ears; my mischievous childhood experience had already taught me that, in the presence of adults talking about serious matters, scamps of my age should always be asleep. So, as soon as the doctor rang the doorbell, I fell into a profound sleep; the door opened, and a confused whispering immediately commenced between the visitor and my mother. I distinguished a few words in passing and at hazard.

"How goes it with our invalid?"

"Better."

"Has he eaten . . . ?

"The fever . . ."

"He's asleep. . . ."

He's asleep. With that, the doctor advanced on tiptoe to the alcove, and, parting the curtains with infinite precaution, delicately took my hand, dangling outside the bed, between his thumb and forefinger, took my pulse, and then, gently replacing my hand under the sheets, drew the bedclothes up over my youthful torso, closed the curtains again and went to install himself by the fireside, next to my mother.

At first, they spoke about me, then about Sonyeuse and the people of Sonyeuse, the health of Lady Mordaunt and her incurable melancholy.

At that point, my father came in, and after the customary politenesses and questions, the conversation became general, taking on the tone of a discussion, and, in the midst of outbursts of voices and the enthusiasm of hypotheses, I grasped, child though I was, that Lord and Lady Mordaunt merited pity more than respect; that they had buried in Sonyeuse an adulterous and culpable liaison—

and the word *adultery* made me pensive, thinking that little Hélène was not the daughter of Lord Mordaunt and that her beautiful and melancholy mother was dying slowly in that isolated villa, because of her own fault and that of her amour: revelations that were interrupted by the regular "Madame is served" of Héloïse announcing dinner, and the irruption into my alcove of that old chatterbox Dr. Lambrunet, finally deciding to give his consultation.

My mother was standing beside him, projecting upon me all the light of the lamp, the shade of which my father had removed; this time, they had no fear of waking me up. Lambrunet palpated me, kneading the moist flesh of my thin adolescent arms between his fingers, slowly examining my eyelids, the pinkness of my gums and my tongue.

"Anemia, still the anemia," he concluded, tapping me on the cheek. "Quinine and iron, but not too much iron. How agitated he is! What ideas have you got in your head, child?"

And after having poured a little water on his fingers and dried himself on my napkins, he went downstairs to write the prescription, escorted by my parents and the lamplight, whose sudden disappearance left me in obscurity.

Three times a week, my parents retained Dr. Lambrunet to dinner.

My dear little convalescent's alcove, with its neat linen and a new basin of water every evening—it was in its warm shadow, as if refreshed by the kindly presence of my mother, that I was to learn, shred by shred, the atrocious adventure of Lady Mordaunt.

My fever approaching its end, a few days before entering convalescence, at about six o'clock on a cold blue winter evening, as I was sleeping in the dampness of my little alcove, my mother, ordinarily so calm, started with her entire person when the doctor rang the bell. I was not mistaken; all day she had been agitated and nervous; I had already noticed the curtness of her voice in the orders she gave and sometimes, in the glances darted toward my bed, an alarmed and fearful affection that I did not recognize.

At the footfalls of the physician, that day, she stood up very straight and went to open the door herself. I confess that I thought my illness was worse, and the idea that I was in danger crossed my mind for the first time. I propped myself up on my elbow, my throat suddenly choked by emotion.

"Well, have they found her?"

Such were my mother's first words to the physician, and, in response to an interrogative glance by Lambrunet in my direction, she replied: "He's fine; he's asleep." And, taking the doctor's hand, she forced him to sit down beside her, and with a passion of which I had not thought her capable, said: "Have you seen them today? Is anything known about the poor child?"

Lambrunet, with a heart-rending distress in his old face, and trembling hands, replied: "Yes, I've seen them. I've just left the house. The child is well and truly lost. Abducted!"

"Abducted!"

"Yes, abducted, stolen! And the man who struck the blow knew full well where it would fall, the wretch. The child won't be found, and the mother will die of it."

The mother, the child . . . has malady the gift of second sight? I had immediately understood that it was a matter of Sonyeuse, of Hélène and Lady Mordaunt; the impression had been so strong that I bit my sheets in order not to cry out; my mother had drawn her chair closer to the doctor's; now they were conversing in whispers, but in the contained ardor of that feverish, as if transported, whispering, my overexcited hearing divined rather than overheard entire passages of the tragic history.

It was already two days since the child had disappeared; she had not come back from one of her daily walks with her English maid, that was all; the chambermaid had not reappeared either; on the first evening it was thought that they had got lost, having taken refuge in some farm in the vicinity and spent the night there, but in those two days the country had been searched for ten leagues around, and all the police in Rouen were on foot; no trace had been found, no clue, and today was the fourth evening, the evening of the third day.

The northern jetty and the quays of the new town were the last place where the passing of the child and the governess had been observed on the Friday, the day of their disappearance; and in the sea nearby, a pleasure-boat had been remarked upon in the harbor.

There had certainly been an abduction, a kidnapping: Lord Mordaunt did not seem to have any residual doubt about that, and the chambermaid was an accomplice; she was the one who must have taken Hélène to the place agreed on with the abductor; the wretched creature had allowed herself to be bought; she had committed treason for money—doubtless a great deal of money. How much had she received for committing that infamy? She would only have had to talk and she would have been given twice or three times as much not to do it!

And the voice of the doctor, almost solemn, rose up in the silence of the closed room.

"The unfortunate fellow was painful to behold; he was accusing himself and getting carried away. 'The coward, the coward!' he fulminated, his lips taut and utterly white. 'Have I ever refused him a reparation, an encounter? He could have killed me, if necessary. . . . I would have understood that . . . but to kill the woman in her child . . . for she adores that child; it's a folly, her passion for that child, I know her; Lady Mordant will die of it; just look at her—is she not already dead?'

"And the fact is," the doctor added, "that the poor woman has received the *coup de grace*." And in response to an urgent interrogation by my mother: "She, Lady Mordaunt, the unfortunate creature, did not say anything; she didn't even complain. She's overwhelmed, crushed, mute. It's necessary to have seen her, as I have, collapsed on her chaise longue, her face as white as a sheet, her eyes staring, haggard, lying there for hours on end, her mouth twisted and her hands inert.

"And not a single tear, not one sob. No, but something more frightening than tears: a flame, a frightful gleam in the gaze within the red, dry eyelids, the eyes of a dead woman, with a dolorous and stupid expression, whose mucus membranes are bleeding, and can no longer weep."

"And you dread . . . ?"

"A premature birth first . . . and madness thereafter. Since yesterday, she has had an unusual manner of caressing her forehead with her hand, as if she wanted to move a curl of hair away from her temples . . . those gestures don't deceive us, we physicians . . . the fixity of the stare, the gleam of the dry eyes and that heart-rending, pitiful gesture . . . if we can't bring her to a crisis of tears between now and tomorrow . . ."

My father came in at that point.

"Well, doctor, the Mordaunt child—what an atrocious adventure!"

But he did not know any more than Lambrunet.

He was, however, arriving from his club, where there was talk of nothing but the English people of Sonyeuse and the mysterious disappearance; the event had revolutionized S——; the entire town now had compassion for the unfortunate lady.

The doctor confirmed for my father the rumors already going round regarding the poor woman's afflicted health; in return, my father brought one last detail: a stranger, well-dressed but equivocal in appearance who had stayed at the Grand Cerf for some weeks before the abduction had been seen prowling around Sonyeuse and, an aggravating indication, talking to Bellah, the chambermaid who had disappeared with little Hélène.

"And that he would be . . . ?" interrogated the doctor,

"The Other . . . the father . . . come to take back his child. . . ."

"And, by the same blow, to kill the wife and mother! Yes, that does, in fact, concur with the reticences that escaped Lord Mordaunt. But will we ever know the last word of this whole enigma, with people as chained and barred with silence as the English of Sonyeuse? In the meantime, Lady Mordaunt is well and truly on the way to going mad. A strange story, all this. But let's see how the boy is doing."

Lambrunet had risen to his feet, my mother behind him holding the heavy lamp in both hands; I lay back, all moist, between my sheets, abandoning my pulse to the doctor's groping fingers. Had my disturbance enlightened Lambrunet? Had he divined the extent to which that atrocious adventure had upset my frail convalescent organism? The fact is that he found me that evening more agitated, with a recrudescence of the fever; he tapped my cheeks with his caressant hand nonetheless, but he exchanged a significant glance with my mother, the significance of which I only understood the following evening.

In fact, the following evening, after a whole day spent devoured by my impatience, without having addressed a single question to my mother, for fear of awakening her perspicacity, when Dr. Lambrunet, already announced by his trepidant ringing of the doorbell, came into my room, he went straight to my bed without any fear of waking me this time, and, having taken my pulse and examined my tongue, he sat down with my mother and chatted with her indifferently about various things. Of Sonyeuse and Lady Mordaunt there was no more mention. Then my father arrived, took up the conversation where he found it, and when Héloïse came in to announce dinner, all three of them withdrew, taking away the lamp and leaving me distraught with curiosity and indignation.

It was the same in the days that followed; an order had been given, and everyone around me obeyed that order, and yet, I sensed that the drama of Sonyeuse was not yet concluded. On the contrary, its course must have been impassioning the entire town, as if falling asleep in the somnolence of those short, sad winter days.

I evoked Sonyeuse in my mind, white with snow, quilted with frost, with the dead silence of its pathways and the little stars of the feet of blackbirds still imprinted in the white velvet of the lawns, the bleak lawns between the gleaming foliage of the holly and arbutus. It was before that desolate landscape that Lady Mordant was doubtless agonizing, impenetrable and mute as the frozen horizons of that nature in mourning.

By my mother's pallor, by the urgency of her hugs as she kissed me on the forehead in the evenings, I also divined that "the little bird fallen from the nest" had not returned. . . .

I was patient for five days, always attentive for a word slipping from the doctor's mouth or my mother's lips, but on the fifth day, maddened by the deliberate mutism, once Lambrunet and my parents had gone down to the dining room, I waited feverishly for them to sit down, and, taking my courage in both hands, I slipped on a vest and trousers and, barefoot, at the risk of catching malady and death on the cold tiles, I went down the stairs on tiptoe, my fingers clamped on the iron of the railings, my hair stuck to my temples by sweat, posted myself in the vestibule, and there, my teeth chattering with cold in the cavernous air of the corridor, I listened. . . .

I listened. . . .

My anticipations were not mistaken; my parents had retained the doctor to dinner, and it was about Sonyeuse, and nothing but Sonyeuse, that they were talking at the table.

"Well, my God, yes, it's over," murmured the doctor's voice. "It's just a matter of time now; the malady is irremediable. Lady Mordaunt can no longer recover her reason."

"And the child?" interrupted the slightly shrill voice of my mother. "Is she demanding her daughter? Is she talking about her child?"

"Not even that," the doctor replied. "Her memory has fled, like water from a cracked jug. She doesn't remember anything; she no longer even knows her child's name. You can pronounce the name before her a hundred times, the charming name of Hélène, without even seeing her eyelids flutter, without a muscle in her face quivering. Her poor empty head has become burning and dolorous; she's still caressing her forehead, but even more frequently now, in the gesture I told you about the other day. 'Oh, it hurts, oh, it hurts so much, so very much,' she moans, continually touching her temples. Those are the only words that Mordaunt and I can any longer obtain from her. Since yesterday, however, that doleful statue has had a caprice and a strange mania: that of combing, slowly and gently, in all its length, her magnificent blonde hair."

Her blonde hair! In the blackness of that cold vestibule, scarcely lit by the fanlight of the door and the reflection of the snow outside, I still had present before my eyes the dazzling vision of her auroral tresses, illuminating the green depths of the forest of Franqueville.

"Yes, it's her final folly, a caprice of the dying that can no longer be resisted. Lying on a gilded rattan chaise longue in her bedroom, her face buried in the shaven velvet of cushions or the batiste of pillows, she holds out to Lord Mordaunt the heavy and fluid silk of her beautiful hair. 'Comb it for me, comb it for me, my head is hurting so much. . . . ' And her voice is like an imploring sigh, coaxing and caressing. 'Comb it for me.'

"And, with absent eyes and his mouth twisted in a heart-rending smile, Lord Mordaunt obeys.

"Slowly, gently, with infinite precaution, he passes the teeth of the comb through the bright moving amber of her hair, and does it for hours on end, for a whole monotonous and dying day, without a gesture of fatigue, without a movement of lassitude or ennui; with savant expertise, he sometimes leans on the teeth of the comb, sometimes scarcely making contact, a caress; and she, the frail and sensual creature, under the combing hand, relaxes and abandons herself with an ecstatic smile and the fixed gaze of a torture victim who seems still to be taking pleasure in dying.

"Strangely enough, those sessions, which extenuate her and exhaust her, are the only relief I know of for that bizarre and disturbing illness. After five or six strokes of the comb, given in a certain manner and expertly prolonged, sleep arrives—but a profound sleep, with clenched features, eyes wide open and staring, as if under magnetic passes; somnambulists have such fits of alarming sleep.

"So long as Lord Mordant keeps her hand in his or strokes her hair and the nape of her neck with his fingertips, she sleeps; but if Mordaunt ceases to make contact, and anyone else but him—me, for example—tries to prolong her slumber by continuing the friction, she immediately wakes up with the violence of an electric shock, and, prey to her illness, her sorrowful voice resumes: 'Comb it for me, comb it for me,' with the tenacity of an obsession."

"And the touch of Lord Mordaunt is the only thing that calms her?"

"And Lord Mordaunt alone; one could believe that that man has already magnetized and hypnotized that poor woman; there's magic and bewitchment in it. At any rate, dormant and unconscious as she has become today, that man still possesses a terrible power over that frail female organism; it resembles the attraction of iron for a magnet. If he has the determination, he alone can perhaps prolong for a few months the sensual existence of the damned soul, he alone might perhaps be able to order her to live . . . a mysterious example of the empire exercised by one soul over another, or—who knows?—the simple and omnipotent force of an ardent amour."

"Don't tell me that," interrupted my mother's quavering voice. "Lord Mordaunt has never said anything worthwhile to me. Oh, that lynx-like face with that hooked nose and those eyes like ardent coals! I've always held him in dread and horror myself. Who can tell whether he might not have made that unfortunate creature drink some drug, in order to convince her to leave her homeland, husband and family, and bring her where there would be just the two of them, to woe and punishment?"

I almost uttered a scream. In the depths of that corridor where I was shivering, my ear glued to the keyhole, two brilliant eyes were fixed upon me in the milky light of the panes of the fanlight: two dark blue irises, the dolorous and wide-eyed gaze of the pale Lady Mordaunt; the two mad eyes of the lady of Sonyeuse.

I went back upstairs precipitately, bumping my bare feet on the edges of the steps, and, more dead than alive, groped my way back to the warmth of my sheets.

All night long an atrocious nightmare caused me to raise my head, the nape of my neck damp and my pulse beating like a drum. A frightful vision of the head of Lady Mordaunt, seemingly decapitated, exsanguinated and pale, with dead eyes and drowned in stupor, was dangled at the level of my lips by the hand of a man with bony fingers clenched like a claw in the golden blonde of her hair: the willful hand, the possessive hand of Lord Mordaunt, become the brutal hand of an executioner.

For three nights running I had that vision, distinct and present; my fever must certainly have got worse as well, for I lost all notion of people and things for several days; there was a continual buzzing in my temples, and vague shadows—my mother and Héloïse, moving silently and gravely around me; then the slight sound of a little spoon in the depths of a cup of heavily sugared tisane, which a hand made me drink in little sips, while another hand behind the nape of my neck supported me—that was my life for three days . . . a week . . . what do I know?

How long that lasted! I had fallen into such a condition of weakness and torpor that I had completely forgotten Sonyeuse and its tragic inhabitants; I must have caught a chill in the cold draught of that black corridor, my feet bare on the cold floor-tiles; hence the recrudescence of the fever, with delirium, hallucinations and a relapse—a fairly serious relapse, to judge by my mother's first words, on the ninth or tenth day, as she sat by my bedside, her eyes looking into mine, welcoming my entry into convalescence.

"Naughty child, you won't be listening at doors again, will you?"

And, throwing her arms around my meager little torso, she pressed her cheek to my cheek, where I felt the warm flow of large tears.

Poor mother! Her eyes swollen, her expression distraught and the first white hairs cruelly apparent on her temples, she must have spent the night with me. *Naughty child, you won't be listening at doors again, will you?* My fever had betrayed me, then. I must have talked about Sonyeuse and Lady Mordaunt in my delirium or in my sleep.

I threw my lips on to my poor mother's hands, sticky with syrup and tisane, and huddled in her bosom, shivering.

"How is she? Is she cured?" I ventured, with a supplication on my lips and in my gaze.

My mother's silence was reproachful, but then she passed her hand through my hair.

"Lady Mordaunt? Oh, Lady Mordaunt is cured and little Hélène found."

"Found! Hélène!"

"Yes." And she hastened, feverishly, as if in a hurry to finish. "Lord and Lady Mordaunt have gone back to London. Sonyeuse has been sold. You'll never see them again—never."

"Is it really true, all that, Mother?" A doubt still remained.

"Really true. And what a question! Go on, enough for today; go to sleep, naughty child."

And, patting my pillows and plumping them up with her hands, she kissed me on the forehead and pulled the bedclothes up over my shoulders.

I entered into convalescence: convalescence and its doleful tenderness, the mind more subtle in a delightfully exhausted body, and, in the appeasement of dusks as mild as a good death, the warmth of the bedroom devoid of a lamp, the obscure bedroom with the mat whiteness of embroidered curtains over the windows, like a white spring putting healing flowers over the closed windows.

Then old Dr. Lambrunet's visits became more spaced out. Two or three times he talked to me about my friend Hélène, now in England with her mother and Lord

Archibald Mordaunt, but without insistence—and my satisfied curiosity ended up sinking into an egotistical numbness.

How did I not have any suspicion before the decision evidently taken only to talk about Sonyeuse in my presence as a last resort, and the observed precaution never to leave me alone? My maid Héloïse now came up to my bedroom and stayed there during my parents' evening meal. How did the suspicion of a conspiracy woven around me never become clear, especially before the embarrassment and unease of that girl, as soon as she found herself alone with me, before the comic alarm of the maid's entire physiognomy when I occasionally pronounced the name of Sonyeuse or Lady Mordaunt?

It's true that since then . . .

But memory has these holes, intelligence these lacunae.

One day, however—can one give the vague presentiment I experienced the name of intuition or suspicion?—in the course of that long and coddled convalescence, I had the intuition, the bizarre and indefinable consciousness of something that was being hidden from me. That intuition I have since had more than once in my life, the effect of a nervous and almost unhealthy sensibility, from which I have already had my full share of suffering, and from which I am, I'm very much afraid, still called upon to suffer as long as I live.

It was one morning in April, in the final week of the convalescence that had dragged on for two long months; the fine weather had returned; my mother had opened my casement slightly to let in the warm air and renew the atmosphere of the bedroom.

Still very weak, my arms limp, but voluptuously weary, I was gazing from my bed out of the open window, at everything one can see of a provincial town through a window: trees, steeples, hills, roofs, and large sunlit clouds sailing through a morning sky, deafened by bells ringing since nine o'clock in the morning.

They were ringing for a burial, those bells, and slowly seemed to be lamenting between themselves, incessantly and mercilessly, the heartbreak of a death; but the sky was so blue that morning, and such a breeze of flowering spring was blowing from the valley, where the hasty apple-trees were beginning to powder themselves with white, that the knell seemed almost cheerful to me, in life and in the sunlight.

Suddenly, my father came into my room. He was in ceremonial dress, in full mourning. "Do you have my black gloves?" he asked my mother. "The cortege is already at . . ."

A glare from my mother, who had stood up very straight, stopped him abruptly.

"I'll be late," he concluded, searching his pockets feverishly.

"Have you looked in the chest of drawers?" my mother replied, tranquilly—and she stood up, and went into the room next door, sure of finding the gloves.

Outside, the bells were still sounding their melancholy knell.

"You're going to the burial, Papa?" I ventured, my fingers caressing the lustrous cloth of his sleeve. "Who has died? Tell me."

"Père Asthier, the registrar."

"Ah!"

My mother came back with the pair of gloves, and my father left.

At the Abbey, the knell was still tolling.

Never since, I believe, have I listened so attentively to bells. At one moment, their ringing increased.

"They're coming out of the church," my mother thought aloud. And twenty minutes later: "They're going into the cemetery."

And the bells fell silent. That was all.

Why, on the evening of the same day, in the silence of the somnolent bedroom, overtaken by darkness, in the hour when the sinking soul seems to be entering into darkness, and feels darkness entering into itself, did that question come to my lips?

"Lady Mordant is in England—is that really true, Maman?"

Oh, the shudder that ran through my mother's entire being, as she suddenly ran to my iron-framed bed and covered me with I don't know what avaricious affection with her whole womanly body, and then embraced me and forced me to lie down among my pillows with kisses, to go to sleep.

"Still in London, my darling—but why are you asking me that?"

"No reason. To know."

Without thinking about it any longer, I was already drowsy.

Still in London.

Why had my mother lied? On the doctor's orders, or for fear of disturbing my sensibility, sharpened by illness?

Lady Mordaunt was really dead, having died of chagrin and languor, died from being driven mad by the loss of her daughter, of whom no search had been able to find any trace, died in that mysterious house of Sonyeuse, where little Hélène had never reappeared.

The bells, whose distant ringing had occupied an entire morning of my convalescence, really had been weeping over her funeral; it really was her burial that had sent my father in quest of his black gloves.

Scarcely was I reestablished than my mother admitted of her own accord to the pious lie erected to spare my precocious childish nervousness and excessively heated imagination.

When, on my first excursion outside I stammered the name of Sonyeuse, my mother, adjusting her shawl over her shoulders and the strings of her hat under her chin, took my little arm for the first time, and, proud of that honor, which gave me a new importance, she took me without saying a word in the direction of the Abbey and the quarter of Vieux-Hôtels and convents. But at the beginning of the Rue Viorne she turned abruptly to the left, took the Rue des Capucins and the Rue de Saulnes, which terminates at the wrought-iron gate of the cemetery of S——, so delicately apertured between its ivy-clad pillars.

"But we're going to the cemetery."

My mother contented herself with leaning silently on my arm; we were walking among the graves now.

Almost cheerful, that little cemetery of S——, between its four bare walls, descending a gentle slope above the town, on the side of a cultivated hill; yes, almost cheerful, with the white patches of its sunlit tombstones, its paths starred with periwinkles, and, in the blue air striped with the still leafless rods of poplars and willows, the almond odor of flowering hawthorn: to the left, the bell-towers and roofs of S——, framed in a fold in the hill; on the right, the rip of cliffs and the lightly rippled silk of the sea.

My mother was still drawing me through the calm cemetery; that day, apart from two laborers occupied in digging a grave, there was no one in the necropolis that was warmed by a beautiful one o'clock sun; after a pause before my grandparents' grille, we went up the main path toward the top, into the part affected to the graves of paupers and foreigners—every family in S——, as in all provincial towns, has its crypt and its concession—and we stopped in front of a large tombstone, still new, as if placed the day before in freshly-moved earth.

A gilded grille ran around the grave, with lightly-wrought ornamentations; hung on the railings, enormous wreaths of verdure and moss were rotting. Those wreaths could not be more than a month old, for the mold, which must have been that of natural flowers, was crushed between large knots of mauve silk and crepe; one of the disemboweled wreaths had let a trickle of detritus run down on to the stone, of camellias and bouquets of withered violets.

With the tip of her umbrella, my mother parted those old shreds of offerings, and the epitaph appeared.

HERE LIES HÉLÈNE
BORN IN JANUARY 1812
IN EDINBURGH, SCOTLAND
DIED IN APRIL 1840
IN S——, FRANCE

And that was all.

"Lady Mordaunt," my mother said, slowly, the tip of her umbrella still resting on the *Here lies Hélène*, "or rather, the person who was known here as Lady Mordaunt. She wasn't yet thirty!"

I stood there stupefied, with the mounting humidity of large tears in the corners of my eyes. My presentiments hadn't deceived me then—the presentiments that other people had wanted to deflect; that tomb and the detritus of those flowers were all that remained down here of that exquisite and delightful foreigner, the adorable and sad tenant of Sonyeuse, the beautiful Lady Mordant.

Then my mother took me away, hurriedly, as if she were in haste to snatch me away from those memories, to take me back.

"We had to hide the truth from you, my child," she recited into my ear like a lesson learned. "The doctor prescribed it. That frightful adventure overexcited your nerves, had already made you ill; it was a subject of continuous anxiety to us, and a real danger for you. Now that you're better, I owe you the truth.

"Lady Mordaunt died a month ago, of a disturbance of the brain, her reason completely gone, driven mad by the grief of losing her child. Little Hélène has never been seen again.

"The Marquis de Sonyeuse came from Rouen to lead the mourning of Lady Mordaunt. Like all the men in the society of the town, your father thought he ought to follow the unfortunate young woman's procession. Lord Mordaunt, or, at least, the man who called himself by that name, left the town within a week, and"—after a long pause—"Sonyeuse is for sale. There isn't anything more."

"And what do people think, Maman?"

"Lord and Lady Mordaunt weren't husband and wife; they were hiding a culpable liaison here; the Englishman of Sonyeuse had abducted that woman from her husband. The husband took his revenge by taking the child, and the mother, Lady Mordaunt, died of it. God punishes adultery; he puts a curse on unions that religion hasn't blessed."

My mother owed my fifteen years the moral of the story. Sonyeuse was for sale. There wasn't anything more.

Yes, there was something more, but I only discovered it much later, thirty years to the day after the tragic denouement of the story, when, while work was being done on the embankment of the cemetery during the exhumation and the translocation of the dead, it was necessary to violate and open Lady Mordaunt's coffin.

A frightful thing: there really was a woman's skeleton in the coffin, but a decapitated skeleton; a framework of white bones devoid of a head, which had scarcely been exposed to the air than it turned to dust and fell into ashes.

What sacrilegious hand had dared to mutilate that cadaver and remove from the tomb that beautiful expressive head, so pale in the fluid heavy gold of its hair?

While those beautiful dolorous eyes of dark and limpid blue were alive, those two large, distraught, seemingly haggard irises, were they already fixing a visionary gaze upon the horrible mutilation that the adorable head was to suffer after death?

In the locality, all those who remembered having seen Lord and Lady Mordaunt, did not doubt for a single minute that the body had been put into the coffin decapitated. The sinister and impassioned visage, the onyx stare, sharp and cold, that Lord Archibald Mordaunt had, authorized all hypotheses.

"That man frightened me," my mother often said.

I understood now the mystery deliberately thickened around that story, and I shared her fearful aversion. The author of such a crime could not be anyone other than that impassioned and somber figure, whose silhouette alone justified all suspicions. But what could he have done with the miserable severed head of the martyr? In a madness of exasperated amour, surviving beyond the grave, had he ripped it from that poor cadaver in order to have it embalmed, to fix forever, in balms and unguents, the charming visage of an idolized being?

In the depths of what country of the Three Kingdoms, in what isolated house in an old seigneurial park, was he still spending mournful days combing the hair of a mummy? In what dark room, with closed shutters, furnished with a bizarre and suggestive taste, already old and worn out, was he still kissing the annealed eyelids and the hardened lips of the face of a dead woman plastered in greasepaint?

That horrible vision has often woken me up with a start at night—and that of the other, the svelte, blonde, charming young woman, so melancholy and so tender, the anonymous Lady Mordaunt whose beauty had revolutionized my childhood and the opinion of an entire small town, a tomb without even a name. . . . Hélène, nothing but *Here lies Hélène*, a coffin rotting in a foreign land, devoid of friends, devoid of relatives, among strangers, and in that coffin, not even an intact cadaver, a dishonored skeleton, decapitated, and her head elsewhere, no one knows where, perhaps traveling the world in the valise of a monomaniac tourist.

Now that I have stirred with a weary and even more sorrowful hand the dust still moist with the blood of that melancholy history, perhaps you will understand why Sonyeuse is still for sale, still for sale after the thirty years that have elapsed since that drama, and why I have never wanted to go through the gate of that great park, dormant beneath its dark foliage.

I'm afraid of hearing footsteps resonating there to the summons of my footsteps, afraid of awakening the echo and the voices of the past.

The Unknown Woman

AT the last Opéra Ball, at about one o'clock in the morning, already wearied by four tours of the hall and I don't know how many comings and goings in the corridors and the boxes, the impressionist painter Inotey and I were near the main staircase in one of the loggias of the perimeter, and there, half-sitting on the marble banisters, in one of the gaps between the columns whose double friezes were staged above our heads, we were chatting, our backs almost turned to the public, teasing the exaggerated points of our varnished shoes with the tips of our evening canes—yes, indifferent, in sum, to the incessant promenade, almost brushing us, of women in mantillas with ebony whistles, in quest of Francillons,[1] we were talking about the beauty that is increasingly difficult to find nowadays among women of so-called pleasure, and especially the absolute lack of the unexpected and the new in modern gallantry: gallantry with regulated tariffs, debated in advance, like a supplier's accounts.

---

1 *Francillon* (1887) is a play by Alexandre Dumas fils, in which Francine, Comtesse de Francillon, retained at home nursing her baby herself (rare in those days among Parisian aristocrats) suspects her husband of having a mistress, having previously sworn that if she ever found out that he had one, she would take a lover in revenge. Moved by her suspicion, she follows him one night to a masked ball at the Opéra, where she does indeed find him in the company of a mistress. . . .

"Personally, I'm content with my models; that's what I've come to," concluded Inotey, between two measures of the waltz that was reaching us in gusts from the foyer, where a gaggle of fops were dancing to the sound of Broustet's orchestra.[1] "When the sitting's over, if I get the itch, I push the girl down on a divan in the corner of the studio . . . then I pay her double for posing. At least they're well-made, and almost healthy. I know what I'm getting . . . yes, lovely bodies, the bitches, but sometimes filthy mouths . . . oh well!"

And that "oh well" summarized my own impression so well, the obligatory and bleak resignation of the artist of the year 1890, in the approximation of life, the approximation of beauty and the approximation of amour, that I didn't say another word. A great silence fell between the two of us, a silence cut by dance music and the resounding sonorities of brass, and, our foreheads lowered beneath our tilted-back top hats, we had resumed teasing the exaggerated points of our evening shoes with the tips of our canes, offering people the joyful sight of two individuals "bored to death," when Inotey leapt to his feet, abruptly dived into the corridor of the boxes to the right and disappeared into the crowd.

I stood up too, and, adjusting my hat on my head, started to follow him.

Suddenly, an arm slid under mine and: "Here I am. Come this way. Follow me," murmured Inotey's voice— Inotey himself, who, having suddenly surged forth beside me, come back I don't know how from I don't know

---

1 Édouard Boustet (1836-1901) was a composer particularly well-known for his dance-tunes—including polkas, mazurkas, waltzes, etc.—which provided the accompaniment to many an Opéra Ball.

where, led me in the direction of the right-hand boxes, into the corridor into which I had seen him disappear a minute before, drawing me into it in his turn.

"What's got into you? Are you going to explain?"

"Soon."

"A woman?"

"A woman, yes: a woman I thought I recognized, who went in here, I don't know exactly where—there or there."

He waved at a series of boxes, 30, 32, 34 and 36, that we were alongside; his features were distraught, his eyes shining, luminous and feverish in his ordinarily phlegmatic, youthful and rosy Anglo-Saxon face. And, very pale, with his whole mouth twisted, he nervously kneaded the arm inside the sleeve of my jacket, violently enough to hurt me.

I had never seen him like that before.

"A woman . . . an adventure, then? A mistress who . . . ?"

"That's what it's about!"

"What?"

"It's a proof, I tell you. I'll explain later. Let's stay here, eh, walking back and forth—help me to keep watch on these doors, for she's going to come out . . . she'll come out. . . ."

"Did she see you?"

"She . . . I hope not. I won't know anything then. We had our backs turned to the stairway, didn't we? The people coming up couldn't see us, recognize us, could they? Answer me, then . . . in any case, is it her? I don't know anything yet . . . perhaps that step, that attitude . . . oh, I have to make sure. . . ."

He was speaking as if in a dream, for himself alone: a veritable talent for monologue that I didn't know he had.

"Is she alone, this woman?"

"Alone, yes . . . which is to say, with a chambermaid."

"A woman in society, then: Francillon!"

Inotey made a vague gesture; he didn't know. I couldn't get anything out of his strange preoccupation. Suddenly, his arm stiffened under mine; the door of one of the lodges we were watching had just opened by a crack. While observing from the corner of his eye, Inotey had abruptly turned his back, and I saw him take a false nose out of his pocket, with a feverish hand, and fit it on his face—a frightful bulbous nose with a moustache, one of those monstrous caricatures that render a man unrecognizable by disfiguring him.

"Have you gone mad?"

He had already turned to face the lodge, and, crushing me silently with his hand, watched the woman in number 34 peep out of the crack in the door, as if hesitant to emerge.

Buried, or rather immured, in a long and ample black silk domino, with the hood of the cape pulled down over her forehead, with thick Chantilly lace covering her nose, mouth and chin, she leaned out, looked to the left and the right as if to make sure of the security of the corridor, and then suddenly, lifting up the train of her skirt with one hand and using the other to hold a broadly-deployed black silk fan at eye level, she moved into the crowd and, svelte and undulating in the stiff fabric in spite of the inhibition of her black disguise, fled with rapid steps, fraying a path through all the masks and that mass of black suits, impenetrable, almost invisible so extensively was she

59

veiled, and yet making all heads turn, all gazes sparkle and all nostrils flare at the passage of her little feet, sheathed in black satin, and the amorous promise of the sinuosities of her narrow waist and smooth stride.

Inotey had waited until a distance of at least a hundred paces separated her from her box; then, having abruptly caught up with her, passed his arm under hers in a familiar fashion and whispered into her ear, strutting and disguising his voice.

The domino that he had accosted so boldly had neither recoiled not manifested any alarm, and if her attitude with regard to Inotey's false nose lacked—oh yes, absolutely lacked—enthusiasm, the words that he spoke to her did not seem to have displeased her overmuch, when she suddenly extracted herself from Inotey's grip and started running, fleeing straight ahead, as if prey to a veritable terror—and my friend Inotey, holding his false cardboard nose on with one hand, and trying with the other to seize the fugitive's hood, started giving veritable chase to her, while groups were beginning to form.

I thought I ought to intervene.

A circle had formed around them; a few black suits had already interposed themselves.

"But Madame knows me," my painter friend replied, with perfect composure. "We're in number 34, we've taken the box together." And tranquil and mocking, his hands in his pockets, he followed on the heels of the domino, who, now caught between two rows of gawkers, could no longer advance, hampered by her train; and, confused and ill-at-ease under all those gazes seeking to get a glimpse of her, not breathing a word and bowing her head, lower and lower, while the insupportable Inotey, still with his hands in his pockets, played her escort, prancing à la Paulus and singing into her neck to the tune of a well-known ditty a frightful variation of his own:

> *Mademoiselle, listen to me then!*
> *Is it bad when your head is cut off?*
> *Mademoiselle, listen to me then!*
> *Is it bad when you have no more body?*

The gawkers, thinking that it was a joke, had drifted away. "Drunk," opined one mask, and the crowd had dispersed, some shrugging their shoulders, others declaring that all was well—and the comedy was still continuing between the domino and the black suit, an atrocious comedy that was turning to drama—that I couldn't doubt, now that I had drawn closer to the two actors in the scene; I saw the woman hastening her steps, her back turned to her box, trying to flee, no matter where, straight ahead, and, losing her head, staggering and stumbling in her dress, with such a pallor spreading over what one could make out of her face through her lace, that with every forward step the unfortunate woman took, I expected her to fall in a faint.

"Inotey! Inotey!" I tried in vain to intervene, but he, still phlegmatic and mocking beneath his grotesque false nose, continued to prance on the woman's heels, still singing to the same tune:

> *Mademoiselle, listen to me then!*
> *Was the weather good in the Place de La Roquette*
> *When that baker's boy Monsieur Deibler*
> *Chipped our little darling?*

If the poor lad no longer has a body,
That's no reason to pull faces at me!
Others than him have a body and head
And only want to show you a good time!
Mademoiselle, listen to me then!
Was the weather good in the Place de La Roquette?
Mademoiselle, listen to me then!
Is it bad when you have no more body?

He had driven her into a corner, and the poor woman, half-suffocated, a supreme aguish in her eyes, still bowing her head and hunching her shoulders, was trying in vain to get away, when with a loud stifled cry she suddenly collapsed on her persecutor's breast.

Inotey finally took off his cardboard nose.

"You . . . you . . . so it's you!" she stammered, without drawing breath, and I divined that she must be smiling beneath her mask of lace: the simultaneously grateful and wry smile of a woman who has just escaped a frightful peril.

"Who did you expect it to be?" murmured Inotey.

"Yes, I was foolish. Oh, it's good to have been afraid . . . once the fear has passed—but you, here, to find you here?"

"Aren't you here?"

"Oh, me!"

"Come on, take my arm and collect yourself."

With a glance, Inotey had nailed me to my spot. She had taken his arm, and, chatting, whispering like two old friends, I saw them plunge into the crowd and go into the buffet hall.

It was evidently an unexpected encounter after a long absence, one of those encounters fecund in reciprocal confessions and interminable stories, for I had been walking back and forth in the corridor for a full hour, my patience running out, when Inotey touched me on the shoulder and smiled delightedly.

"You're growing old, poor fellow. Here I am."

"The fact is that you've taken your time. Not expeditious, the lady?"

"Shh!"

"Oh, you know, personally I think it's bad. . . ."

"Oh, but when you know, when you know . . ."

"Yes, but I don't know anything. . . ."

"Shh, not tonight . . . the night isn't over, we're still floating in mid-adventure."

"What—your domino?"

"Oh, I've taken her back to her box; I handed her over to the chambermaid personally."

"And you're having supper with her?"

"Me, no—you, perhaps."

"Me?"

"Or someone else."

"She's a whore?"

"I don't think so."

"A woman of status?"

"I have every reason to think so."

"Married?"

"That wouldn't astonish me."

"A young woman?"

"Fairly."

"And a virgin?"

"Yes, if Messalina can be a virgin."

"Oh, you're mocking me, Inotey,"

"Me? Not in the least. But let's not stay here. If we want to see her again, let's go down to the ballroom."

"The ballroom?"

"Yes, from strength to strength, as at Nicollet's—and you, to govern yourself, take for tonight's rule of conduct the *nihil mirari* of the ancient philosopher: whatever happens, let nothing astonish you."

"Is she at least pretty, your mid-Lent swallow?"

"Pretty? Ravishing my dear. Pretty? As an amour. Otherwise, where would be the monstrosity of the thing? Anyway, what's that to you?"

It was written that I should know nothing more that night, and yet, the enigmatic black domino and I were to find ourselves, a few minutes later, face to face. It was in the ballroom, in the midst of a crowd of dancers and masks; in one of the corners the crowd had made a circle around a clowns' quadrille, executed by four disguised individuals, two of whom were men dressed as women. We had taken our place in the circle, simultaneously sickened and amused by the honking and the entrechats of a gross hairy-chested milkmaid jiggling and giggling with a superb guardsman who had a punch-flame moustache, a pot-belly and legs molded in barely-adequate deerskin: the salaried rabble of public balls, more-or-less inscribed in the records of the moral police, but sometimes diverting in the cynicism of their antics. At the flick of a fan on his shoulder Inotey turned round; the black satin domino, still impenetrable, was standing behind us. Another domino was accompanying her, similarly black, but less nimble and less aristocratic in her bearing—the chambermaid.

This time the domino was no longer afraid; her eyes were even laughing in her lace, provocative and impudent; with the tip of her fan she pointed at the guardsman, and her gaze, meeting Inotey's, posed a mute question, Inotey smiled and whispered the truth to her . . . undoubtedly, since the domino formed a mocking "Oh!" behind her suddenly-deployed fan. It nevertheless returned to the charge, and, this time looking me straight in the eye, consulted the impassive Inotey in the expectation of an immediate approval.

"A journalist—I already told you," Inotey replied.

"Ah!" riposted the domino. "Too dangerous, but then . . . it's simply dead here." And with a dry click, the fan closed again.

"So why come here looking?" sniggered Inotey. "Much too *proper*, the Opéra—snobs and simpletons, nothing to do here for you, my dear. Would you like my arm? It's only three; I'll take you to the Élysée Montmartre."

"Seriously?"

"I'm always serious."

"What about him?" And her gaze, which had not quit me, indicated me once again.

"Not your business, and then, I've already told you, he's a journalist."

That Inotey—I could have strangled him. I divined a moue under the lace of the mantilla. A nervous handshake from Inotey intimated an order not to follow them, however much I might want to do so.

Curiosity, and the hope of learning everything the following day caused me to enter into the skin of the new role. I remained where I was; the strange domino took Inotey's arm, favored me with a brief nod of the head in passing, and then, followed by her chambermaid, plunged into the crowd with her cavalier.

The quadrille had just finished; there was a dust of masks in the hall; I lost sight of them almost immediately; on the platform, the orchestra launched into a mazurka. Seized by I know not what whimsy, perhaps to escape the obsession of that adventure, as striking as a nightmare, I spotted a woman and started dancing the mazurka to a waltz rhythm; I ought not to say anything more about that night.

The next day, at about noon, Inotey came into my apartment. "Finally!" I exclaimed, folding my arms. "Am I going to have the key to that intrigue? Confess that you were mocking me excessively." I took him over to the window. "Well, you're not too worn out, for a man who's spent the night with Messalina. My compliments, old fellow."

"I believe you; I've just come from the Turkish bath, where I slept for four hours and breakfasted on a bottle of port and three dozen oysters."

"Oysters and port—a strange mix!"

"Excellent for the marrow, my dear."

"I don't doubt it. For a man loved not ten hours ago by a Roman empress. . . ."

"Me—what an error! Look at me, my dear; I'm neither a street-porter nor a gladiator, to inspire the whim of Messalina." He let himself fall into an armchair. "What if I told you that at six o'clock in the morning I left her supping at the main counter of Les Halles with a superb pimp, picked up an hour before in the rabble of the Bal Kolkus?"

"No!"

"As I tell you. Pass me the cigarettes. A strange young woman, phosphor and cantharides, burned by all covetousness and burning with all the vices!"

"And last night you snuffed me out . . . well, you're a fine friend; the moment I saw her clearly, she had a yen for me. . . ."

"Of course—you have a butcher's moustache and a dirty shirt . . . oh, pardon me, plastron . . . an Opera Ball plastron, three hours after midnight. . . ."

"And you prevented her—for it was you that prevented her!"

"As I shall prevent it again . . . one can take Pasiphae to the bull, but one doesn't deliver a poet to Messalina and her friend Cleopatra with a blithe heart."

"Pasiphae, Messalina and Cleopatra . . . and Marguerite de Bourgogne, no doubt."

"Exactly."

"She's an Encyclopedia, that woman."

"Of all the vices, ancient and modern, and very interesting to riffle through." He started stoking up the fire. "There's everything in that woman, of the ghoul, the lamia, the Greek courtesan, the Barbarian queen, the low prostitute, the great lady of Rome, with something very particular, very gripping, very corruption of the *fin-de-siècle*, very Baudelairean, if I might put it like that: a slightly funereal seasoning of lust and quasi-Christian resignation; she's a subject, a case-study. . . ."

"For the Salpêtrière, eh—let's say the word. Another neurotic."

"Undoubtedly the woman is sick, obsessed, a hysteric . . . but her case has the particularity that she's conscious of her shame and her malady. Passion, however . . . and what passion . . . has become in her such a physical need—and a real physical need, accompanied by appetites and spasms, like thirst and hunger—that . . ."

"Yes—a nymphomaniac!"

"But a nymphomaniac with a cerebral lesion, with complicated and bizarre appetites that can only be satisfied in certain milieux, for, strangely enough, that lubricious individual is chaste; after a crapulous night like the one she's sleeping off at this moment in I know not what horrible hovel in the vicinity of Les Halles, on the breast of that ignoble pimp, she's gripped by singular modesties. Disgusted, frightened by herself, she falls into continence for three or four months. Her past horrifies her, and then, one fine morning, the frightful need suddenly flares up in her, and, like a hunted beast, suddenly she sets off on the prowl, roaming and sniffing through suspect adventures; her vice has her in its grip again, but she defends herself until the moment when, bitten by some hideous caprice, she comes back to run aground, a dismal wreck of lust, in her banal and ugly vomit."

"A fine piece of literature! And the name of this interesting neurotic?"

"Oh, that I'd be very embarrassed to tell you, and for the best of reasons. What if I confessed to you that I saw her last night for the third time in my life, and that I talked to her yesterday for the second time? Is she a woman of high status, as I believe? I don't know myself. In any case, she has nothing of the whore about her, and besides, if she belonged distantly or in close proximity to the society in which we amuse ourselves, I'd have some information about her; in that world, a beauty like hers—for she's delectable—couldn't pass unnoticed. She must be rich; she pays generously for her fantasies of an hour . . . or a night . . . but what she is above all, and that blindly, is passionate and bold; for it's more than her reputation, but her life that she's risking, and putting at stake routinely in these sinister adventures. The danger attracts her; worse, it intoxicates and excites her; she loves it, that peril, with the same savage and furious amour with which she seems to love and pursue Death. There's something of the heroine and something of the ghoul in her . . . poor woman! For me, she's bound to end up some day bathed in blood, the blood that swells and floods with an eternal moist redness the tender pleated skin of her lips."

He interrupted himself in confrontation with my smile. "Anyway, if I discoursed for hours on the enigma of that temperament, I wouldn't convince you any more. The facts have had a very different eloquence, and when I've told you in what circumstances I made the acquaintance of that lady for the first time, perhaps you'll finally grant me mercy from your skeptical grimaces and your knowing expression."

"All right, I'm listening," I replied, sinking into my armchair. "But permit me to light a cigar. There—it's done."

Then Inotey went on: "You remember Lebarroil . . . the wrestler, the one who posed for me as the athlete in the foreground three years ago? My *Marseille's Tent at the Fête du Trone*—a fellow of medium height, thickset, a trifle short in the leg, but with superb pectorals and arms, a fleshy mouth, a squashed nose: you can see it from here, the head of a white negro, the ugliness of a sensual and expressive brute. And with that jest of the possible, all the spirit of the Parisian mud enameled with argot—and what an argot!

"My painting was finished, exhibited and long sold, but he'd got into the habit of coming to the studio from time to time to hang out when he had nothing else to do—to clear his phlegm, as he put it, while rolling cigarettes. He lifted weights in a corner, fenced with my foils against the wall. I let him do it—the fellow amused me; in between, he told me unspeakable stories. His first mistress had left him, the second was in Saint-Lazare, a third was making eyes at him; simultaneously the best fellow in the world and the worst rabble on Earth, part-fairground performer part-pimp, thief when necessary, changing his domicile like his mistresses; sometimes in Grenelle, sometimes La Villette, following the itinerary of the Parisian fairs and the caprice of his amours.

"I knew him—he didn't hide any of it; but I never had any reason to complain about him; I never found anything missing, even a cigar, after one of his frequent visits to the Rue Notre-Dame-des-Champs. So I received him, and hardly a week passed without seeing my fellow 'drop in,' his heels in clogs and a big butcher's blouse passed over his striped leotard; standing on the threshold, kneading his silk cap in one hand and scratching the top of his head with the other, he'd throw me, almost timidly, an 'Auguste isn't disturbing anyone? Can one have a smoke and kick one's heels in Monsieur's studio?' I'd shrug my shoulders and he'd come in. It's my vice, if you like.

"So, last winter, I was only slightly surprised, but very disagreeably impressed, on receiving from the said Auguste a letter sent from the Mazas. My Lebarroil had got himself pinched. I'll spare you the style and spelling of the note; the gist of it was that he'd been arrested, locked up—unjustly, it goes without saying—and he was asking of me and our good friendship—*sic*—to go there, at all costs, immediately, to find him in his cell and help him establish his innocence; I alone could save him, or it was the Nouvelle for him, if not the Abbaye—which is to say, the *Abbaye de Monte à Regret*: the scaffold, the guillotine. "That annoyed me somewhat. Given my name and my demi-notoriety as an artist; that intimacy with a thief, perhaps a murderer, seemed to me to be a bit stiff to go and confess in the middle of a police station. Fortunately, I had some connections in the place. Oscar Méténier—I can name him, Oscar Méténier, the private secretary of Monsieur Taylor and one of the glories of the Théâtre-Libre, author of *La Chair*, *En Famille* and the *Puissance des Ténèbres*, such a curious interpretation of Tolstoy.[1] I went to find him at the Prefecture and, thanks to his well-known kindness, two hours later, I was introduced into cell 103 of the detention section at the Mazas.

It was thorny, the case of my friend Auguste: quite simply, he was accused of complicity in the murder of an old woman, an unfortunate vegetable-seller, found stabbed on the night of the fourth of February in a rooming-house in the Rue Croix-Nivert. The poor woman, transported in a dire state to the Hôpital Necker, didn't survive her wounds.

---

1 Oscar Méténier (1859-1913), who had followed his father into the police service before making his name as a prolific playwright and novelist, was still at the beginning of his literary career when this story was written, far from the fame he eventually achieved. He subsequently helped adapt one of Jean Lorrain's novels, *Très russe*, for the stage in 1893. *La Chair* (1885) is a novel; *En Famille* (1887) was a one-act comedy. The Tolstoy adaptation cited, made in collaboration with Isaac Pavlovsky, was staged in 1888. In 1897 Méténier founded the famous Théâtre de Grand Guignol.

71

"The murderers still escaped the research of the Sûreté, except for my Lebarroil, arrested two days later in a cheap hotel in the Rue de Vertbois near Les Halles and found, damning evidence, in possession of two hundred-franc banknotes and fifty francs in gold—and three hundred francs was the sum stolen from the victim, all she possessed. True, no trace of blood had been found on his clothes or underclothes, but when interrogated, he couldn't provide an account either of his whereabouts on the night of the crime, or the provenance of the money—the proceeds of his savings as a wrestler, he claimed—and, on the day before the murder, he had been refused credit at a restaurant in the Rue Cambronne for arrears of fifty francs, which he settled the next day. Finally, his mistress, a prostitute in the Rue d'Aboukir, far from excusing him, had accused him with an extreme violence, alleging that not only had she not seen him that night but that he had not slept there for a month and that he had to be doing some villainous work because, for a month, she hadn't given him a sou. He could deny it all he liked; for everyone—me as well as the prefecture—my Lebarroil was guilty.

"You should have heard the cry with which he greeted me. 'It's you, Monsieur Inotey, there's a good God after all! Oh, I knew that you wouldn't abandon me!'

"He had tried to seize my hands, but seeing that I stepped back and was obstinate in withholding my hands from his, he went on: 'Oh, you too! You think I'm guilty of that—of killing a poor old woman! Me, who has my own old lady! My arm would have withered rather than do such a thing! Oh, Monsieur Inotey, you're breaking my heart!'

"He had fallen back on the bench of the cell, and, with his face hidden in his huge knotty hands, he was choking, as if shaken by genuine grief.

"I sat down beside him—Méténier had arranged for us to be left alone. Putting my hand on his shoulder, I articulated, in a firm voice: 'Lebarroil, tell me, what were you doing on the night of the fourth?'

"No response, except for muffled sobs. I repeated my question twice, leaving him time to regain possession of himself; then, confronted by an obstinate mutism, I got up to leave.

"'If I tell you,' he cried, in a heart-rending tone, 'you won't believe me any more than the others.'

"'Speak anyway, Lerbarroil. Look, I'm waiting.'

"'Well, on the night of the fourth, damn it, I was having it off with a chick.'

"'Your mistress, Irma Frodin?' I was curious to see if he was going to lie.

"'Irma? It's a long time since I've screwed her, the tart, although she must have told a pack of lies about me, a whore like her. No, someone else."

"'Someone else—where?"

"'Where? At the Plat d'Étain, Rue de Commerce, a filthy dump where one can lodge for the night—but the manager knew nothing about it; there's a door downstairs with a corridor letting out to the street; she had the key in her pocket; we went in at ten o'clock, and left at midday. If I only have the testimony of the master of the hovel, my goose is cooked.'

"So many precautions in advance to recuse a testimony was a bad sign. 'What about the two hundred and fifty francs found on you, Lebarroil?'

"'She's the one who forked them out, of course!'

"'Two hundred and fifty francs for one night—you did well, Auguste.'

"'Three big ones—yes, thee hundred francs that she laid out, the Mi-Mi.'

"'The exact sum stolen from the street-merchant of the Rue Croix-Nivert; you don't have any luck, Lebarroil.'

"'It's true though, honest!'

"'And the name of this woman—the chick, as you put it?'

"'Her name! That's a good one! If I knew it, would I be here?'

"'You don't know the woman's name?'

"'Nor her estate, nor her address.'

"'And you want me to believe that a whore in the Rue du Commerce . . . you're making fun of me, Lebarroil.'

"'I told you that you wouldn't believe me! Oh, I'm doomed. Doomed, poor sap, and the poor old woman out here!' With the back of his hand he wiped away a tear.

"*It won't be said*, I said to myself, *that I've come into this fellow's cell for nothing.* 'That's right, Lebarroil,' I said, aloud, 'think about your mother, who'll be desolated by your condemnation, dishonored—she might even kill herself. A mistress, especially a mistress in a cheap rooming-house, might well compromise herself. The name—the woman's name?'

"'If only I knew! But since I don't . . .'

"'It's not the first time you've seen her, though?'

"'No, we've been together for a month.'

"'A month—you've seen her every day, then?'

"'No, twice a week, sometimes in one hotel, sometimes in another, never in the same place; oh, she's careful, she's suspicious. More often and she would have given it to me, her name and address.'

"'She's not a prostitute, then,' I exclaimed, caught in spite of myself by the strangeness of the adventure.

"'Oh, if she is one, she's a high-class one, for she was dolled up, with nice perfumed underwear—oh, like I've seen before,' he said, with a boastful wink. 'These adventures happen to us more often than you might think . . . wrestlers and acrobats . . . and generous—two or three louis every time.'

"'And you don't even know where she lives—you've never tried to follow her, to find out?'

"'Not likely—she wouldn't have come back! Me, I don't do blackmail. I don't crush chickens in the egg. In the trade, we know them, those sorts of women—the passionate, as we call them—oh, it happens! That type only like the rough, the leotard, the biceps . . . us, the rabble . . . and the posher they are, the more dolled up, proud of their appearance and their clothes, the hotter and sweeter they are in the sack—real tarts! Oh, we don't have any trouble recognizing them; they stand in front of the wrestler's booth at the fair, they make a circle in the crowd around the open-air work, on the streets, they go, they come, they prowl, and they don't seem to be doing anything, but a wink from the corner of the eye, that's bait, and there it is . . . a flutter of the eyelid, a smile . . . understood. You draw away from the crowd a little, meet on a corner, in a wine-shop or behind a booth, you arrange a rendezvous—and that's that. It's a hundred sou windfall for us, ten francs, a louis, or four louis, that depends on the fancies and the purses—the little perks of the trade. Oh, it's not the first time.'

"'And this woman, the one of the night of the fourth, the last?' I interrupted, interested.

"'Oh, that one, she picked me up like that a month ago, near the Arc de Triomphe, one day last month when I was shamming in a leotard with Robine and the Lyonnais at the entrance to the Avenue de la Grande-Armée, in the Place de l'Étoile. It was very quick—rendezvous the same evening, Place de la Bastille. That night, we bedded down in a garno in the Faubourg Antoine—and a sweet chick, Monsieur Inotey, such as you rarely see, even in carriages: skin like satin and two satanic eyes that warmed me to my marrows. And passionate, I could have eaten her! What sacred nights we spent there, Monsieur Inotey—true, it'd be worth the stroke of the guillotine if I wasn't basically an honest man and if I didn't have an old mother out there in Menilmontant, Rue du Chemin-Vert.'

"'And generous?'

"'Generous! I told you . . . two, three, four louis every session.'

"'And three hundred francs the last time,' I couldn't repress a smile.

'Word of honor, as I told you. She told me she was leaving Paris . . . she lives in the provinces . . . because, you see, in bed, by certain mannerisms, I could see that she didn't have trained habits, that she couldn't be a Parisienne. *Here,* she said to me, *here's three hundred francs; when I come back, be a little better-dressed, and we can go to dinner somewhere and spend the evening together; that's a hundred francs for your week, two hundred francs for your clothes—and above all,* she added, which is sad when I think about it, *don't murder anyone, Auguste.* And that's the truth, Monsieur Inotey, as I'm telling you.'

"'And left without leaving an address. No luck, decidedly, my poor Lebarroil.'

"And I stood up. I judged that I had heard enough. The wrestler was under no illusion as to the meaning of my departure. 'You don't believe me? You don't believe me either?' He had taken a handful of his bushy hair and was shaking his head convulsively.

"'Give me a means of finding her, your woman. Then I'll believe you, Lebarroil.' And I headed for the door.

"'Where to find her? Where to find her! Wait . . . there is a means—but would you want to do that for me? Only you can do it, because, that . . . oh, not for anything, not even for three thousand bullets, would I want to put the cops on to her. I don't want you to think that I'm a killer, though, a murderer of old women. Here, listen carefully . . .

"'The chick . . . I have a rendezvous with her tomorrow, that's when she's returning to Paris. Would you go in my place? I'll give you her description, but keep it to yourself, eh? Not a word to the cops. You go in my place, you go up to her squarely and tell her that—and it's the truth—only she can get me out of it. She only has to come and give her statement to the magistrate or the commissaire. But will she do it, careful as she is? In any case, Monsieur Inotey, don't force her. Explain the thing carefully, but don't put any pressure on her . . . if she doesn't want to . . . well, Auguste will do without; her secret is her own, that woman, and I wouldn't want any harm to come to her because of me.'

"I had seized Lebarroil's hand. 'And where's the rendezvous?'

"'Tomorrow evening between seven and eight we're to dine together at the corner of the Avenue Bosquet, near the Pont de l'Alma: the Pont de l'Alma Bastille omnibus station. Oh, you'll recognize her easily, always in black, very simple, but chic, slim, with the cleavage and waist of an actress in the great theater, a pretty face, all pale, with big peepers—two soft bright eyes that eat her face . . . and then, you'll recognize her by her attitude of a woman who's waiting, by her mouth'—he suddenly slapped himself on the forehead—'she has a mouth like no one else, red lips, red as blood.'"

"And that was the woman of last night?" I put in.

"Yes, the domino of last night, my unknown woman." Inotey looked at his watch. "But time's passing—let's cut it short.

"The next day, at about half past seven, I had my cab stop a little way short of the Pont de l'Alma station, and there, I had no need of a long examination to recognize, standing on the threshold of the omnibus office, ready to open her umbrella against the pouring rain, the woman described the day before.

"Even without her strange dark eyes and the bloody patch of her mouth, her preoccupied air brought her to my attention readily enough. I went into the office, stood directly behind her and murmured very softly, but distinctly, in her ear: 'Madame, Auguste Lebarroil, the wrestler from the Place de l'Étoile, can't come this evening to the rendezvous you've given him here.'

"She turned round, with an indescribable terror written all over her face. 'Monsieur, I don't understand . . . I don't . . .' she tried to stammer—and, feebly, her eyes desperately fixed on my eyes, she took a step to leave. It was her.

"I pushed her outside, gently. 'Madame,' I continued, this time walking beside her, 'Auguste Lebarroil has been in a cell at the Mazas for a week. He's accused of the robbery and murder of an old woman found stabbed on the morning of February fifth, in a rooming-house in the Rue Croix-Nivet; the crime was committed on the night of the fourth. That night, Auguste Lebarroil spent at the Hôtel de Plat-d'Étain in the Rue du Commerce with a person you know, Madame; the most serious evidence against Lebarroil is the sum of two hundred and fifty francs found on him on the day of his arrest, two days after the crime. You know, Madame, who gave him that sum. Only your declaration can save that man; he'll go to prison for it, if not to the guillotine; it's up to you to decide; I'm at your orders.'

"'But Monsieur, I don't know . . . I can't . . .'

"'Please take note, Madame, that I don't know who you are, that I'm not trying to find out. As for me, here's my card. Lebarroil has posed for me as a model; when he was arrested there was no one but me to whom he could turn. I responded immediately to his appeal. If I've come to find you this evening, if I've been able to find you here, it's on his indications and on his behalf. You alone can establish an alibi, explain the provenance of the money found on him. Without your declaration—Lebarroil and I don't know who you are—no commissaire or tribunal will believe the truth; for all the world, Lebarroil is guilty; he'll be convicted. A prostitute would save her lover; decide, Madame, what you have to do.'

"'Then he told you . . . ?'

"'Everything.'

"'The wretch!'

"'Don't get carried away, Madame. We don't know who you are, and I give you my word as a man of honor that I won't try to find out; I'm fulfilling a duty, that's all.'

79

"'You must be very scornful of me, Monsieur.'

"'Thus far, Madame, I feel sorry for you.'

"'Ah!' All her pallor became pink. 'And what would it be necessary to do to save this fellow?'

"'Climb into this fiacre, which will take us to the Prefecture; go with me to the commissaire's office, and make your deposition there.'

"'And give my name and my address there?'

"'Oh, that's more than probable, I can't hide it from you.'

"'Ah! that, no. Never. It's impossible, impossible, impossible.'

"She was walking in the rain, biting her handkerchief convulsively, her eyes staring through her tears. I had taken the handle of the umbrella, and it was me who sheltered her.

"Oh, that long walk through the darkness of that deserted quay, under the glacial February downpour—that walk, which might have been thought gallant, if not amorous, and on which a man's life might depend. . . .

"'But it's my destruction' she said, stopping. 'You're destroying me, Monsieur, destroying me!'

"'Well then, let's not talk about it any more, Madame. It's that man who'll be destroyed.'

"She shuddered, shot me a black look, and then said in a hoarse voice: 'Let's go, Monsieur—where's your fiacre? Let's go, but please go quickly. I'll go with you.'

"I installed myself beside her and closed the door behind us. Not a word during the journey. At the Prefecture, Méténier, alerted by me during the day, had us admitted to his office immediately. My companion warmed her feet there without unclenching her teeth. Ten minutes later she was invited to go upstairs and make her declaration to the central commissaire. Since we came in she had lowered her veil; before going out she lifted it, and as she passed me, with a brief nod, she said: 'You're a man of honor, you told me, Monsieur. Will you promise never to look for me or recognize me?'

"I bowed. That was all. The train of her dress, which she now let fall in long folds, undulated with serpentine sinuosity in the doorway; I didn't see her again.

"Two days later, Lenarrroil was released and ran hotfoot to my studio; as soon as he crossed the threshold I declared coldly that I was breaking all contact with a man as dearly loved by women. I gave an order to the concierge not to let him come up again, and I ended up getting rid of that nightmare."

"A slightly tardy measure. And the woman? Thus far I see a hysteric—a sufficiently conscientious hysteric, prudent and controlled in her imprudence . . . but nothing more."

"The woman . . . Méténier, encountered a few days later, met me with a singular smile. 'Forcing her to get her lover released, you must have annoyed her greatly, the woman with the red lips.' And as I protested: 'Yes, the woman with the red lips—she's inscribed under that name in our police records; very well known to our agents and . . . she often gives us leads to follow, because we protect her. She has a singular instinct, that woman. What a policeman she would have made—she has a flair for sniffing out crime. . . .'

"'Inscribed in your records—but in that case she's an . . .'

"'Haven't you given her your word as a man of honor, in my presence, never to seek to know her or to recognize her? Above all, she's a curious pathological case-study. *Bonsoir.*' And Méténier quit me, with his habitual irritating smile of a man in the know who doesn't want to say any more."

"A joke!"

"Wait. A month later, on the night on mid-Lent, the drama of the Rue Montaigne burst forth—the triple murder of Marie Regnault and the two Gremeret women.[1] I won't go over the crime; our ears have been battered sufficiently by it. Paris lived for six months on Pranzini's performances and the letters from his mistresses. That display of horrors so obligingly detailed in all the newspapers left me rather cold; I didn't even go to see the wretch judged at the famous assizes, and his execution, continually adjourned, didn't attract me any more. I was, however, in Paris at the time—a Paris that migrated for a week to the Place de La Roquette, and was disappointed in its expectation every morning for a week. The boulevard was beginning to get very impatient with that eternal postponement until the next day. It was then that I met Méténier outside the Tortoni and made myself the echo of public opinion.

"'Well then, so you're never going to be finished with that wretch—the press has had enough, you know, of dancing for a week before Pranzini's head. Monsieur Deibler can't make up his mind! One doesn't disturb people for nothing for an entire holy week! They'll hiss at your première!'

---

1 The sensational triple murder in question took place on 17 March, 1887; Marie Regnault, alias Régine de Montille, was a courtesan; the other two victims were her chambermaid and the chambermaid's daughter. Henri Pranzini was denounced to the police as the perpetrator of the crime, and was found in possession of some of the jewelry stolen by the murderer, but his mistress, Antoine Sabatier, provided him with an alibi. However, a measurement of his hand taken by the anthropometric service fit a print found at the scene (fingerprints had not yet been introduced as a method of identification) and Pranzini was convicted on that evidence.

"Méténier had stopped, smiling. 'Are you perhaps going on a little voyage? Desolate, my friend—all my regrets. That dear Inotey, who's spent the night for nothing!'

"'Me! Don't believe it, my dear. I don't go to watch these macabre little fêtes; ordinary burials are sufficient for me.'

"'That's a mistake,' said Méténier, smiling his most amiable smile, curiously. 'You'd find yourself quite at home there. Number four, Rue de la Folie-Régnault, among others. One can see very well from there—restaurant on the ground floor, drawing-rooms on the first. One can have supper; it's very nice, very nice. Go—and bring me back your news.'

"'Are you serious?'

"'As serious as can be. Go—I can assure you that it'll be tonight.'

"And that, my friend, is how it came about that I went on August twenty-third to see Pranzini executed in the Place de la Petite-Roquette, an execution at which I encountered you . . . well, no need to insist. As for number four, Rue de la Folie-Régnault, a *barrière* drinking-den packed out with reporters and petty journalists, and the cream of the girls from Peters and Sylvian's come in a gang from the boulevard, cramming themselves into the embrasures of the windows: champagne, charcuterie, cries and laughter, 'Hey Inotey!' here and 'Hey, Inotey!' there—everything there is of the most banal and least meditative before the great tragedy of death. Sickened, I had gone outside on to the sidewalk, renouncing even catching a glimpse of anything between the crenellations of heads and shoulders, when a movement in the crowd jostled me on to the road; I got angry and raised my voice and my cane at the same time.

Two women who were trying to squeeze into the wine-shop were causing all the emotion, they were shoving and elbowing people who wouldn't let them through.

"'That's the condemned man's mistress,' someone nearby whispered.

"'Madame Sabatier?'

"'No, the other one—the society woman.'

"Intrigued, I advanced in my turn. Too late. The woman had finally reached the door. I arrived just in time to see the black undulation of her dress snake through and disappear.

"'Who is that woman?' I asked, spotting Adnie, the journalist.

"'Oh yes—the woman in black, the woman who rents the window for five louis—a real income it makes for the innkeeper. A woman who's come every morning for nine days to see the little machine function. Her casement is booked in a first-floor room, for her and her companion, doubtless her chambermaid: a hundred francs a day. A prime spot that's been rented today for a thousand—very nice. She must be a Russian princess, the last of Monsieur Cherbuliez's Russian princesses.'[1]

"'And opinion says . . . ?'

"'Stupid things. For some she's the mistress of the con-demned man, for others an excessively intimate friend of Madame de Montille; for me she's just a curiosity-seeker, some bored aristocrat in search of a new frisson, an un-familiar sensation, lecherous of the guillotine out of idle-ness, depravity—how should I know? Would you like to

---

1 The reference is to the prolific novelist Victor Cherbuliez (1829-1899), several of whose novels of the 1860s, serialized in the *Revue des Deux Mondes*, had Russian settings.

see her? I have my opera-glasses. If we step back a little . . .
I know the window.'

"But try to move in such a crowd! We made space
for ourselves. jostled and cursed at every effort, but not
enough to be able to see the window, and when I tried to
retrace my steps, curious to catch a glimpse of the 'curiosity-seeker' when she made her exit, it was impossible
to move, boxed in as we were by the crowd, and when,
three-quarters of an hour later, the shaven head of the
condemned man having fallen into the basket, I got back
to the wine-shop in the Rue de la Folie, the lady of the
fifty louis was no longer there—gone, vanished . . . and
to think, my dear, that not for a second, then, did I think
about Lerbarroil's woman, the lady with the red lips, but it
only required the strange coincidence—that and the anal-
ogy with our ideas—at the Opéra, last night, of a train of
black satin undulating in a certain way on the steps of as
staircase suddenly to evoke in my mind a certain exit of
a woman from an office in the prefecture and a certain
entrance of a woman into a sleazy wine-shop in the wan
dawn of the morning of an execution!

"Yes, my dear, I was there, leaning on the banister, chatting with you about indifferent things . . . a domino passes
by, her skirt undulates, and rustles in a certain fashion under her silk hood, and abruptly I see my unknown woman
exit, undulating and furtive, from Monsieur Taylor's secretary's office in order to make her deposition to the central
commissaire; suddenly Pranzini's pseudo-mistress appears,
slipping, shivering and fearful, into the ground floor of
number four, Rue de la Folie . . . and it was her, my dear,
and the same woman both times.

"My unknown had been, I was sure of it, Pranzini's mistress. Why not? She had certainly been Lebarroil's. The two men were much alike—same mores, same milieu.

"Besides which, you witnessed, as I did, her disturbance when I mentioned La Roquette, and then, afterwards, she almost admitted it. Without betraying herself, she gave me a long confession, that night at the Élysée Montmartre, the lady with the red lips; she talked in full confidence, quite reassured now. Oh, she edified me, and the most frightful of all her confidences wasn't what she meant to say, but what I thought I divined and understood.

"Yes, that well-born woman—the horrible already commences there—that woman who has, I'm sure, an honorable family behind her, and perhaps—who can tell?—a husband and children, yes, that woman is not only the equivocal prowler that one encounters by night at the corner of equivocal streets in the distant parts of Grenelle, around the Abattoirs, in the lowest quarters of murderous Paris, thieving Paris, Lost Paris; that woman is not only the petty virgin profile that one is sometimes amazed to see emerging from the trellised corridor of a suburban house, the ashamed, exhausted but unsated Messalina avid for crapulous sprees and chance amours, the ferocious and delicate aristocrat who needs the brutal caresses, booted kicks and foul talk of ruffians; she's worse, she's the woman who goes to the assizes to see her lover condemned to death, curious for the impression that she will feel in her being, and who then, her sensuality excited, goes to see him executed in the Place de la Petite-Roquette: the impression of the blade after that of the verdict.

"She's the ghoul who, devouring the kisses of the head of the man who swoons and gasps in her arms, is intoxicated by the thought that, one day or another, the steel of the guillotine will cut off that head; she's the woman who, is order to be sure of loving a future murderer, a future client of Monsieur Deibler, goes to seek her lovers in the dives of Saint-Ouen, in wrestlers' booths, low taverns and hovels, the woman who depraves her temporary studs with banknotes and says to them at dawn when she leaves them: '*Above all, don't murder anyone, Auguste,*' with the intimate hope in her heart that they'll cut someone's throat in a matter of days. She knows where to see them again, in the Place de La Roquette, opposite the famous window; she's the Little Sister of the Poor of the final hour, the one who greets from afar the last gaze of those condemned to death, and consoles them from afar with her red smile: her kisses have a taste of blood, whence the scarlet of her lips.

"The heads of her lovers, if she could, as a Princesse de Valois once did for a Seigneur de La Môle,[1] she would go to take from their basket, already exsanguinated and rigid, and kiss them long and hard on the lips, their tortured lips, already cold and blue.

"The Marquis de Sade refined the sensuality of Suffering; the lady of the red lips exalts the sensuality of Death. She's the lady with the sure intentions, who seasons amour with the horrors of peril, that enraged spice, and the anguishes of the guillotine, that bitter aphrodisiac; she's the drinker of agonies, who depraves, corrupts and morally

---

1 Joseph Boniface de La Môle, the lover of Marguerite de Valois, the wife of Henry de Navarre, the future King of France, was implicated in a conspiracy against the reigning king, Charles IX and was beheaded in 1574. He is garishly fictionalized in Alexandre Dumas' melodramatic novel *La Reine Margot* (1845).

assassinates, and will end up murdered herself one day . . . the poor creature.

"And to think that there is, I'd swear to it, a small town somewhere in the Centre or the Ouest, where that woman is an honest provincial wife, living in a family and going to church!"

The Lover of Consumptives

"LOOK, another new one!" said an elegant black suit sitting in front of me in the orchestra stalls, at the second performance of Legendre's play,[1] and, smiling into his moustache, he aimed his opera-glasses at the first of the lateral boxes, which a tall, slim young woman had just entered. She was very pale, in an exquisite pale blue tulle costume, which made her even paler.

It was the middle of the second act, the scene in the chapel when Lord Claudio, his brows furrowed and his hand on the hilt of his sword, fulminates at Leonato and the candid Hero with the famous Shakespearean insult: "Keep your daughter—she's too dear!"

Gripped as the audience was by the drama of the scene and the brilliance of Roybet's costumes, sparkling in the astonishing Ziem water-color that Porel has put into the setting, all eyes and all lorgnettes had followed the direction of the opera-glasses, and it was as if the fragile creature, now leaning her elbows on the red velvet of her box, in her disquieting and spectral pallor, were dazzling all the gazes of the men and the women suddenly attached to her.

---

1 Louis Legendre adapted Shakespeare's *Much Ado About Nothing* for the Paris Odéon in 1888. I have translated the cited line from the French; it is not in the original, nor is there any obvious equivalent.

The face a slender oval, with a languorous and suffering expression: the eyes seemingly enlarged, ultramarine tending toward black, disquieting, ardent and dolorous in their blue, bruised circles, flecked with nacre; the nose delicate, with mobile and vibrant nostrils, breathless, as if in an atmosphere too rarefied and insufficient to sustain life; and, her great fan of plumes held against her flat bosom, she was biting the hot crimson flesh of her lips from time to time with the tips of her teeth, bright enamel in the red of her mouth, and causing blood to erupt therefrom.

Beside her, a man had taken his place, tall, robust and healthy, in the full force of age, and very correctly dressed, the long black silk cord of a lorgnon traversing his white silk waistcoat, like a clubman haunted by the princely elegance of a Sagan.[1] He leaned toward the pale woman, whispering in her ear and offering her crystallized Parma violets on a silken bag, which she nibbled, half-smiling and choking.

"She won't last long, the new one," sniggered the man in the black suit in front of me. "She's only good for two months; that little woman is at the suffocating stage; she must be spitting blood from her lungs, but must have a fine temperament from midnight to two o'clock, when the fits of fever rise. Very pretty too—a bit thin, though."

He had taken the lorgnette from his friend's hand, and, the two lenses riveted to the box, was detailing every spasm of the pale blue dress and every urgency of the broad white waistcoat.

---

1 This term is enigmatic; although capitalized, it does not appear to be a proper name; it might be a alternative spelling of *segan*, the Aramaic term for a priest of the Temple.

"Bad taste, all the same," the gawker continued, "to love skeletal woman and subscribe to the funeral pomp of amour. That dear Fauras, I only ever see him with Venuses of the cemetery, and always new ones. How many mistresses has he already expedited?"

"Three or four in two years. It's a monomania; one might think he goes fishing for them at the hospital; disease, especially consumption—that's the charm. We've had the executioner's mistress, he's the lover of the condemned; infatuated with elegies and tears, the worthy Fauras; healthy as he keeps himself, he only loves women who are going to die; the fragility of their existence renders them more precious and dearer to him; he suffocates with their oppressions, shivers with their fevers, and, attentive to their slightest sigh, leans over their suffocations, watches, voluptuous and heart-broken, the progress of their illness, agonized by their spasms, living their death-throes—a sybarite, what?"

"Yes, I know: a ferocious individual, something akin to a sadist tormented by macabre ideas, almost a necrophile, demanding a residue of warmth in the cadaver and seeking in death the ultimate savor of amour: the crimes of Saint-Ouen renewed every evening in the security of the alcove, and the curiosity of the senses guaranteed against judiciary pursuit by the victim's semblance of life."

"Oh, what an error, my dear, you're way off target! Fauras is a tender individual, an elegiac, obsessed with exquisite impressions of sorrow, infatuated with mourning; he wears crepe in his thoughts and has a funereal urn in the place of his heart. Delectably heart-broken, the most angelic of beings, he defoliates the evergreen cypresses of regret eternally, over new amours, a phoenix incessantly reborn!"

"I confess that I no longer understand you."

"Coarse fellow that you are! To love a woman who is going to die, to know that the time of her kisses and caresses is counted, to sense in her gasps the irrevocably fleeting moment, forever lost; despairing in advance and yet intoxicated, to have the consciousness that every sensuality experienced is one step nearer toward the tomb, and, hands quivering with horror and desire, to hollow out in the alcove the grave in which one's amour will lie—that's the savor of the thing! And it's necessary never to have known the bitter attraction of hasty rendezvous without return not be able to understand that melancholy and painful intoxication, the intoxication of liaisons irremediable marked by Death and Pleasure!"

"Monstrous!"

"Absolutely true. Fragility is the great charm of beings and things; the flower pleases less if it is never to wither; the quicker it does, the more embalmed it is; it's life itself that it exhales with its perfume! Similarly, the condemned woman, dying: it's frenziedly that she abandons herself to the voluptuousness that causes her to live more intensely in making her die; her moments are counted; the thirst still animates her; the need to suffer burns and blazes in her; she clings to amour with the supreme convulsions of a drowning victim, and, desirous, multiples her strength tenfold in one final embrace, already contorted under the hand of Death, she would kill for the sake of voluptuousness, if she were not expiring herself, the desperately adored man whose long, heavy and enraged grip is causing her to swoon and die."

"Delightful!"

"Yes, delightful, the amour of consumptives! And there's another advantage too. Fauras thus avoids the ennui of the leave-takings sometimes brutally signified even by a gallant man at the obligatory conclusions of relationships, the scenes of rupture that are often more than painful, always disagreeable, the financial settlements and sometimes the vitriol—all the repulsive dung-heap of terminations.

"Practical and delicate, he does not know the anticipated nausea of amours that cannot last, the sickening and dismal satiation of chronic idylls and rancid liaisons; his adventures reach their denouement over the white sheet, tear-stained with bright silver, of a young woman's coffin, in the midst of bunches of violets and roses, by the light of candles, to the song of organs and epithalamia; and the bride is dead, like Ophelia; a modern Hamlet, he follows the funeral procession of his love, and if his heart suffers a few lacerations, at least his suffering has a beautiful frame, flowers and incense, music and priestly psalms, in a troubling décor of apotheosis: an artistic dolor, in sum, but that of a practical and businesslike artist, for he has death for a notary and counsel, and he has charged the warden of Montmartre cemetery with the liquidation of his sentiments.

"Better than that, he mourns his mistress with genuine tears; he carries the flowers that she loved to her tomb, arranges them piously around little railings, exciting the affection of the relatives of the deceased alongside him, and his life is embellished by the adored images and light phantoms that stream, melancholy and sweet, between yesterday's dear friend and tomorrow's, embalmed with regrets, quivering with echoes, palpitating with hope, nuanced with memories!"

"A monster, a wretch, a . . ."

"A great sensualist and a great savant, my dear, for he has been able to open a joint account with Death in the amorous operations of his life, to give substance to dreams by idealizing that vexatious thing, Memory.

"He's the master of us all, my dear, whatever anyone says, for he's the only man who still mourns his mistresses sincerely, and the only one who is still able to savor regret, the philter and the poison of which the lovers of legend once died, and with which the last wayward lovers of the present century live—this century of incredulity and lucre, in which only phthisis and tuberculosis still cause death."

The Soul-Drinker

To Monsieur Alphonse Daudet

"YES, that's the way he is, poor fellow. If he picks up a fragile object, he's sure to drop it; it's more powerful than he is; his nerves no longer obey his will . . . and in the street, it's something else! He daren't go out alone; the pavement gives way under his feet; he has the sensation of walking on cotton wool, and, another phenomenon, the sidewalks seem to him to draw in against the houses, or suddenly broaden, invading the middle of the road. Sometimes there are upper floors that overhang, and, hallucinated and terrorized, he hastens his faltering steps under an imminent collapse of maidservants' mansards or fifth-floor balconies. Oh, what if it were us!"

To which my friend Serge, with his elbows on the table in the soft luminous circle of the lamp, a tall standard lamp clouded with supple bright fabric and placed with a slightly over-feminine elegance in that severe and sumptuous bachelor apartment, replied in a doleful voice:

"Yes, I know that; I've gone through that, the slow and dolorous clutches of the heart, in thinking that a hand has slid under your left side and is squeezing you gradually, little by little, but with a sure, atrocious, tortuous pressure, and that one is going to die; the anguish of insomnia in the great solitary bed, with the fear of a return of the crisis hammering the temples, the determination to resist the little pinches in the heart that announce it to you; ether drunk in full draughts and the whole night spent shivering, obsessed, almost hallucinated, forehead burning, skin moist and extremities frozen, with the simultaneous terror of staying there and the vague desire to get it over with once and for all.

"Yes, I've known all that. And the troubled hearing, and the troubled sight; the footsteps that you hear moving in the wall, those that you hear pausing under the window, with the conviction that someone who means you no good is there; and the curtains of the casements that open abruptly to let the horrible light of the moon into the room, the curtains that you never see stirring, but whose silk you hear tearing and trembling in the hands of the invisible—in sum, the room that I was obliged to leave because I could no longer live there, because I was suffocating there under a ceiling that was too low and walls that were haunted; the room where, after midnight, I could no longer remain alone, even with the lamps lit, because the light was playing bizarre tricks and the shadows were accumulating, truly too strange and full of menaces, in the creases of the draperies and the obscurity of the corners.

"And all that in order to be enervated for two months in the imbecilic wait for a woman who didn't come back! Look, do you see over there, in the corner of the little square, the street-lamp whose light is trembling, and pooling on the damp bitumen of the sidewalk? I had the same effect of light, the same gas-jet, in my apartment in the Rue Guillaume; I could believe that it had followed me here! Well, when I see the sad light burning like a captive soul, in that solitary street, in the November rain, the conviction grips me that the terrible neurosis afflicted me by virtue of gazing, during autumn nights, as others weep, at that forlorn and bleak flame, then so similar to me; for I was waiting for her and I was stupid—but that's life!

"Oh, if anyone had told me, this time last year, that a time would come when I could spend a day, or a week, without intoxicating myself with the poison of her smile and her eyes, so profoundly blue, which lie so well . . . ! Oh, if anyone had told me that, how I would have leapt at the throat of that imprudent person! And now it's more than two months that I haven't seen her, and I'm not dead. . . . I sleep well, I eat well, I . . ."

"And you have no mistress." And, as Serge started abruptly, I repeated: "And you have no mistress?" I looked him full in the face. "You don't have one of those with whom one has a good time—don't boast, you're not as completely cured as all that."

"Me! If you knew how little I cared about that! I only retain a frightful memory of her, and it defends me against her peers. I'm armored now."

"Hmm!" I ventured. "Ealsie was charming, and if you adored her, she loved you very deeply."

"Loved? Me?"

"Yes, since, in sum, she gave up a position for you, sacrificed a serious maintainer who would have assured her great advantages. I was often envious of the two of you, in spite of your quarrels and all your treasons—for you deceived her too, in spite of your great lyrical and romantic love, in full eruption like Vesuvius and Etna."

"An extinct volcano; the eruption devastated my landscape too much, and a scalded cat fears cold water!"

Upon which, parodying the beautiful sonnet by Henri Becque,[1] I ventured, in slight mockery:

You were brutal and languorous.
She was lascivious and cruel,
You both detested one another.

"Moreover, you still detest her, so you still love her."

"Yes, certainly I detest her, but as an invalid who has undergone an operation detests the surgeon who has just hurt him terribly in order to cure him. I would be horrified to see her again, but I'm grateful to her for having weeded my field of illusions; she was a good collector of nasty plants and wild oats. Oh, you think I want to see her again! Yes, as much as the sheep who has escaped the abattoir desires to see the butcher again!"

I was wasting my time. I picked up my top hat, which I had set down at random on a sideboard.

"Well, I've obviously come at a bad time."

"Why do you say that?"

"After all, let's put our cards on the table. It's just that Ealsie returned to Paris yesterday."

Serge had risen to his feet abruptly, with a great pallor suddenly spread over his face. "Ealsie . . . here . . . in Paris since yesterday. . . ." His hoarse voice caught in his

---

1 The lines parodied actually read, in translation: "I was brutal and languorous,/She was ardent and cruel;/The love of an unfortunate man/For an unfaithful mistress." The poem appears in *Sonnets mélancoliques* (1887). Henry Becque (1837-1899), as he usually signed himself, was best known as a dramatist.

throat, while his eyes rounded in alarm. "She's no longer in Rouen, then—she's left the captain?"

"Apparently. Arrived yesterday; her first visit was for me. Do you want to know what she came to ask me?"

"No. Where is she staying?"

"At the Grand—but if you have the slightest desire to see her again, there's no need to disturb yourself, for"— and in truth, I was risking everything—"I prefer to tell you what the situation is. It's for you that she left Rouen; she still loves you; she loves no one but you." And I continued, without paying any heed to his disdainful shrug of the shoulders: "She came to ask me to bring her here to you, because she wants to talk to you, to explain, and I came up as a scout. She's in my carriage downstairs."

"Downstairs, in the street, under the street-light. Ha ha ha! It's too much." And, with an abrupt burst of laughter, he strode back and forth across the apartment with crazed gestures, his eyes shining, bulging out of his head—and yet the savage burst of laughter broke like a glass in the hoarse strangulation of his voice.

Finally, he said: "Well, let her wait!"

And as I intervened, Serge went on: "You're having me on—and what about all the times that I waited? Oh, she still loves me, she's never loved anyone but me! Her captain has dropped her and she needs money."

"Why are you insulting her? You know full well that Ealise isn't a mercenary woman. A mercenary woman wouldn't have been your mistress; she only wants to talk to you for an hour—you can't refuse her that."

"She has no need of money! I regret it; I still have twenty-five louis at her disposal, and I've been lucky at cards for three days running at the Club. It wouldn't have inconvenienced me in the least, at present."

I broke in at that point. "Come on, my friend, what reply should I give Ealsie? Shall I tell her to come up?"

"To my apartment, here . . . never. I intend to keep the tranquility of my nights; it's enough to have had to move because of her. Ealsie here, so that she can import into the walls and draperies the trouble of the Rue Saint-Guillaume and her frightful bewitchment—no, no, not that; I don't want it; I no longer want it; no more madness, no more neurosis."

With a convulsive agitation of the hands, he had approached the window, had opened the curtain, and, with his forehead applied to the coolness of the windows, he was now looking out into the street where a fiacre with green lanterns was stationed at the coaching entrance, directly underneath his balcony.

"She's there," he murmured to himself, "a victim of the dupery of living, believing that she loves me as I believed that I loved her ten months ago." And he stifled between his teeth an "*Oh, the whore,*" that reached me nevertheless.

"And what shall I say to the person you're treating so kindly?" I persisted, one last time. "Ealsie's still waiting for your response down there."

"You can tell her . . ." And he stammered, fallen once again into his disturbance—he was addressing me as *vous* now. "She's staying at the Grand , you say, well . . . tomorrow, at the Grand. Let's see, three o'clock, that's too early . . . let's say half past four. But not today, that would be impossible for me; not this evening, but tomorrow, at the Grand, half past four—but promise me you'll be there, Jean."

"And will you be there?"

"Unfailingly—don't you have my word?" And he extinguished between his lashes an equivocal flash of joy, which alarmed my suspicion; so I judged it appropriate, in taking my leave, to put a ceremonious emphasis into my farewell remark.

"You'll take account of the fact, Serge, that I'm absolutely responsible with regard to Ealsie for the dignity of this meeting. Assure me that you don't hold it against me."

"How could I, my friend? You can't refuse that to any woman."

And with a cordial handshake, we parted on the threshold of the room. Outside, the rain was getting heavier, causing the hinges of the closed shutters to rattle, and the lantern in the street to vacillate.

The next day, Serge did not come.

Accompanied by his former mistress, I went directly to the Rue Saint-Guillaume,[1] and ran into an inflexible order. Three days after that, I learned that Serge had quit Paris; without news of him for eleven months, last autumn, in the last fortnight of October I received a sealed envelope containing this manuscript:

---

1 The author appears to have forgotten that Serge has moved from that street. The confusion presumably arose because this is one of numerous stories Lorrain wrote that cannibalized other works, much of the opening of this one being transplanted from the short story "Le Mauvais gîte" (tr. as "An Undesirable Residence" in *Nightmares of an Ether-Drinker*), presumably written earlier although not collected until later, in *Sensations et Souvenirs* (1895).

Oran, 4 January.

Five o'clock. The Mediterranean gray-blue and veiled, scarcely different from the vaporous blue of the sky, makes a backcloth of extreme softness for the fortifications, embanked and semicircular, crowned with foliage, which runs along the Ravin Vert or the Oued Rehki, Oran's great ravine, today entirely cultivated, with plantations of cactus, eucalyptus and palm trees, high above which I'm writing, perched on my hotel balcony, overlooking both the city and the sea.

Under my windows the garden of the officers' mess extends in a fan, its foliage already crepuscular; above, the high and eccentric silhouette of the citadel rises up, the same color as the mineral of the mountain: an ancient Arab citadel with low rectangular walls, with the frail campanile of Notre-Dame de Santa-Cruz alongside, and behind it, the rest of the chain of the Mers-el-Kebir, dark green at this hour, the green of the fir trees that the Water and Forests Company has just replanted there.

Behind the mountains, the horizon is a straw-yellow of infinite delicacy, striping with fine gold streaks the agonizing mauve blue of the sky. How does that mauve darken to slate-gray in the east? A mystery. The sky, seen as a whole, appears nothing less than a unity of perfect hue, but already the sea and the sky are no more than one, steeped with the same damp shadow, and on the far side of the harbor, the distant clay- and red-tinted mountains are no longer anything more than a violet band, a bar of darkness, a slightly more emphatic streak in all that half-light.

The winding and shadowy paths of the ravine, with their tall eucalyptus and red rose-bushes in flower, have all become suddenly discolored; a street-lamp lights up at the foot of the high ramparts, and on the main road the increasingly rare pedestrians are already no more than distinct gray silhouettes in the brown air; in the distance, far away, heavy carts are trailing along with the sound of little bells tinkling; it's night, its evening.

The hour that, in the Jewish quarter reeking with the infamous odors of musk and frying, the Zouaves and the sailors are beginning to beat the walls, some in quest of absinthe on which to get drunk, others of some tawdry garrison adventure; in the negro village the indigenous debauchery is brazenly under way under the caftan and the haik at the doors of Moorish cafés packed with tall phantoms huddled silently in white burnooses; the sound of darbukas is throbbing over the city, and I know not what exhalations of wool and spices are floating in the air, indefinable, nauseating and yet flavorsome.

How far away France seems here! Nowhere else have I had a more poignant impression in my heart of exile and isolation. Oran is, however, a French city, a city of pleasures and commerce, one of the centers of government; but it's the sea that I've just traversed, the blue profundity that separates us henceforth, and then, the perfume of Algeria has nothing comparable to it: that reek, simultaneously exquisite and barbaric, of carrion and violent flowers, like the putrescence of incense.

And to think that, if I'm here alone, abandoned, so far from France and my own people, it's out of cowardice—yes, cowardice.

It's because I was afraid of that woman and I sensed that she was about to recapture me that I fled, fled like a coward, suddenly experiencing the need, the crazy desire, to put hundreds of leagues of sea, and the unknown, and the never-seen-before, between that woman and me!

Oh, how she holds me still in the palm of her hand, and how she knows it! How certain she is of her power!

How could I have believed that that liaison, broken for six months, was still so vivacious in my heart? I had been able not to reply to her letters, I had been able to elude her rendezvous, I had even had the strength to not receive her on the evening when she sent Jacquels to me as an ambassador, while she was waiting, obligingly, down below, under the windows, in her fiacre. I'd avoided the meeting at the Grand Hôtel . . . and then, because of having crossed her path by hazard on that mild and rainy evening in December, in the bleak Rue Saint-Guillaume, all my rancor and all my energy had suddenly melted, liquefied like wax, and, my throat gripped in a vice, I remained nailed to the sidewalk with the frightful sensation that my heart had been abruptly unsecured, and was floating hither and yon, adrift, beneath my ribs.

She had only had to advance toward me, quite simply, with her pretty gait, undulating and supple, to smile at me, that slightly sad smile that suits her so well, to look at me slightly dolorously with her big blue eyes, the color of night, which enter into you all the way to the soul, and, hypnotized, charmed, ensorcelled, I smiled at her, in my turn, and gave her my hand.

Oh, her hand, long but strong and sinewy, with the attractive palm . . . it seemed to me that in putting it in mine she was offering herself naked and giving herself to me entirely! Whether it was the coincidence of the singular smile, with which her entire mouth then curled up, or the effect of the long-complicit gaze whose blue radiance suddenly enveloped me, I felt all my flesh rise and go toward her. In that simple handclasp, she had retaken complete possession of my being, annihilated my will, stifled my conscience, my hatred, my remorse, as if a purer and keener air were now circulating around me, stimulating the movement of my blood, and the pulse of my arteries. Only sea air, or ether respired in large doses, gives that sensation of *joie de vivre* and intoxicating alacrity.

The vivifying air of the Ocean, yes, that was what her presence brought me; a stanza of Baudelaire sang in my memory, and it was that stanza, which she knew well for having read and reread it so often aloud together, with which I greeted her.

> *To the very dear and very beautiful*
> *Who fills my heart with clarity,*
> *To the angel, the immortal idol,*
> *Greetings in immortality!*
>
> *She expands within my life*
> *Like salt-impregnated air*
> *And into my unslaked soul,*
> *Pours drops of the eternal.*[1]

And, overcome by the emotion of my voice, which I heard trembling, I almost garbled the last lines. She smiled, with the rising humidity of a tear between her lashes.

---

1 The lines are the first two stanzas of "Hymne," in *Les Fleurs du mal.*

"So you're no longer sulking," she was able to say to me. "It's over, then, those nervous fits, the sensations of ether!"

At that word, I shivered. *Ether*—she was talking to me about ether; but if I had drunk so much of it, to intoxicate myself to the point of compromising my poor, irrevocably ailing brain, was it not her fault? Her—the whimsical, forgetful, unfaithful person for whom I had watched, during so many nights, with my forehead glued to the window and my eyes drilling into the rainswept street, for the futile and desired return! If I had saturated myself with poison like that, was it not to put to sleep the frightful anguish of waiting, degenerating at length into poignant clutches at the heart? But the ether, for which she was now reproaching me with that pretty and forgiving smile of an indulgent big sister, it was her that had led me there, gently, tranquilly, coldly.

It had been necessary to counter my insomnias, calm my weaknesses, cure the nocturnal terrors in which I felt myself fading away and dying; and the remedy for those terrors, those troubles, those visionary nights and those hours of distress and agony, where had I found it? In ether.

And she was the one who was talking about it. And the more I looked at her, with her nacreous complexion and her pearly pallor, her eyes of a somber watery blue, like a glacier lake, her anatomy both delicate and wiry, I saw that the ether was her, that the ether was incarnate in her. Ether had her enveloping and intoxicating charm, her artificial intoxication, which seems momentarily to renew you and revive you and console you; it really was an intoxication of ether, immaterial and quasi-divine, that meeting her brought me—but, like ether, she killed while curing!

A chill had descended upon my shoulders, and when with her singing voice the very dear had said to me, slightly astonished by my silence: "So, we'll be able to see one another again?" I replied, in a blank voice: "Yes, whenever you wish."

"Well, let's have dinner together—would you like that, you great lion?" She was addressing me as *tu* now.

Frightened, I stammered, vaguely: "Yes, all right, tomorrow."

"Why not this evening?" she might have responded—but she didn't raise any objection. So we agreed on a rendezvous for the following day; I would pick her up the next day at five o'clock; she had already been alone and free for a month. And from there we would dine at a cabaret, as in the good times, when one had not had that stupid fear of his little Ealsie, and one had loved her!

Hadn't I, great fool?

And the following day, at nine o'clock in the morning, I was at the Gare de Lyon, and twenty-four hours later at Port-Vendres, and now, in the mild and scent-laden night of Africa, I'm smiling slightly at my cowardice, needless cowardice, for in sum . . . what point was there in fleeing so far, in putting the sea and Spain and hundreds of leagues between her and me, since I'll have to go back sooner or later, to noisy and artificial Paris, ardent and bleak, where I'll find her again, her or someone like her, for is she not the one that cannot be avoided?

In the distance, above the city, the sound of darbukas is throbbing, and I know not what exhalations of wool and spices are floating in the nocturnal air, the scents of Algeria, unparalleled, reeking of carrion and flowery with pepper and jasmine in combination, like the putrescence of incense.

(Here a gap, pages lost or destroyed; Serge's journal only resumed with the date of 29 May, then to become sequential; the poor fellow must then have gone through some terrible crisis.)

29 May.

Decidedly, the summer promises to be bad, and this month of June will be harder to pass than I feared. The temperature is getting mixed up in it now, and in this blazing heat, it does no good to isolate myself behind closed shutters in the dim light of these vast cool rooms; it's the dusty and sunlit décor of the banks of the Seine, where I met her two years ago, that imposes itself imperiously on my memory.

Oh, that torrid and sulfurous suburban landscape, with its slender trees and its vertical factory chimneys on the horizon, was it sufficiently in harmony that year with the insipid and sluggish distress of my soul? And if I loved her so suddenly and so involuntarily, if, on the heavy and scorching June evenings, her silhouette, appearing by chance in the suburban milieu, installed itself so imperiously in my being, it was because the hour of irreparable weakness had sounded for me, and, unbalanced by the life of Paris, my nerves jangling and unhealthy, I had exhausted my strength, defenseless, disarmed and ripe for pity.

Pity: the sponge that soaks up the pith of humanity, as some German philosopher I can no longer remember put it; pity, the most pitiless of all the sentiments; it really was out of pity that I loved her.

And in fact, what did she have going for her, apart from her wide eyes with the slightly bruised lids, as if still astonished to have suffered so much? That fearful and yet naïve gaze, the gaze that seemed to be asking the threats

108

of the future and the chagrins of life for mercy, dolorously instructed as it was already by the past, that gaze and the forgiving sweetness of the smile: a slightly weary smile, which had not entirely renounced hope—all of that, I confess, went straight to my soul, and it was by her soul, which was weeping in her blue irises and pleading on her lips, that I was captured, conquered and enchained.

Oh, that first encounter on the towpath between Achères and Poissy, the gleaming of the mirror of the Seine, as if in fusion, under the arches of the old bridge, and the high forests of the hills of Villènes, their dormant foliage standing out clearly against a low and jaundiced sky, where I know not what oppressive malaise, what stormy atmosphere, was floating that evening; and there, amid the tall grass of the bank, the meager meadowsweets and the mulleins, the silhouette of the unknown woman, slightly stiff in her violet-tinted dress, a red umbrella with white spots leaning on her shoulder, and the face invisible, swallowed up in the dark tulle of an English wide-brimmed hat. Two children were playing around her, two little creatures with legs sheathed in suntan, gilded necks and bare arms.

She was their governess, or at least passed for such in the neighborhood. A governess in the home of that well-to-do widower with the sensual manner: bookmaker or horse-dealer? She lived with him in a villa on the water's edge, beside the factory, and commanded as absolute mistress in the stable as well as the servants' parlor; she was in reality the soul and will of the household.

Why, the following Sunday, did I go to mass—me, who scarcely ever entered a church—sensing myself stupidly weak, my heart uncoupled by the insipid odor of candlewax and incense?

I was not to see her again, since all I knew of her was her silhouette, the scarcely glimpsed gait, and I no more knew the color of her eyes than the lines of her profile, and the lines of her profile no more than the sound of her voice.

And yet it really was for her that I went back there, for that Sunday I should have been in Aix.

One cannot avoid one's destiny; it's necessary to believe that everything that happens is written.

3 June.

Listen to the whisper of your soul's blame,
Do not stifle that voice; listen to its ire,
Do not try to quell the redoubtable flame;
Your maladroit hand will stimulate the fire.

You will drown it better in tears,
Mourn in your heart the other woes,
Think of all those the grip your fears
Weep for yourself and weep for those.

And pity, which sickens and consoles,
And faith, which replenishes the store,
Will perhaps give your forsaken soul
Repose in mercy and peace in amour.

The pity that sickens and consoles! Have I been sufficiently duped by the pitiless pity, and, for having wanted to console and heal, wounded, damaged and infected myself?

Oh, the reconstitution of old dreams and the healing of young hearts: the most delicate of tasks, and a perilous task to anyone who undertakes it! How sure of oneself it is necessary to be, to descend into a past of suffering and amour!

Oh, contagious emotion of tears! One never sees with impunity the sadness and regret of a woman of twenty-eight; and, for having leaned with a slightly curious and perverse tenderness over a life that the attempt was made to hide from me, that unknown existence has now entered into mine; its regrets have become mine, its distress has taken on substance in my anguish; and I am forever riveted to the destiny of a stranger, an impostor, about whom I know nothing at all and who knows nothing at all about me, who has stolen my pity, along with my love, my confidence and the security of my life; for she lied and she has always lied, as she is still lying today in her absence . . . her absence, which is simultaneously a cowardice, a lie and a challenge, since she left without leaving me her address, and I don't even know where she is or with whom.

There are times when I would prefer to know that she is dead.

4 June.

Night is falling, underlining with a red streak the distant hills of Triel, and in the fishermen's island where we had just dined intimately, relatively sure of not encountering a living soul all week in their boatmen's restaurant, with vast lawns of wild oats undulating before us, like waves, with silvery frissons of reeds and willows on the edges of the banks.

In the direction of Migneaux, a great curtain of poplars, those Italian poplars with the eternally restless foliage, extended its tall spindles, simultaneously gray and green, against the orange profundity of the sky; in the distance, the water was shining.

It was like an evening in ancient times, an evening of legend or idyll, as is noted in the imperishable rhythms of the inspired amorous poets of old; a freshness rose from the banks at the same time as a light breeze rose in the leaves, and, delightfully moved, I maintained silence, my eyes attached to hers, understanding that the moment we were living was irreparable, unique, and that the flight of the hour would never bring it back again.

That evening, she had a joy spread over her face, something akin to a happy ecstasy on her lips, and with her slightly veiled voice, whose profound fractures I loved—there was a soul in that voice—she, the unknown woman, spoke to me, interrogated me about Tonkin, about the exotic landscapes of waters and rice, its noisy forests of sugar-canes, where the Black Flags lay in ambush, and the coloration that the splendor of sunsets and dawns acquires out there.

And I listened to her without replying, lulled by the caressing and captivating timbre of her voice.

What could I have replied? In the matter of colonies, I only knew Africa; I had never been to Tonkin, and the little I know about it I've extracted from accounts of voyages and the romances of Pierre Loti. In any case, my silence did not worry her, for she continued her questions, as if talking to herself, comparing the lawns of oats with the distant rice-fields and the already-blurred hills of Triel with the eccentric mountains of Lang-Son.

The moon had just appeared in the sky, and its final crescent, like a thin, broken silver bracelet, was shining softly above the high curtain of aspens, and, as if blossoming in the night, the entire face of the adored one had become luminous, emitting a real clarity, at the same time as her voice slowed down, happily, in a soft chant, like the voice of someone reciting; one might have thought that she was telling some tale to herself.

I have discovered since for what voice she was listening, while numbing herself thus with questions in the night. That transfiguration of her entire face was the shine of deception; that night, in the solitude of the islet rippled by the moonlight and the quivering of the willows, it was the other she was thinking about; next to me, in front of me, it was him, the first lover, the only one she had loved, the only one she still loves, in spite of his abandonment and his crapulous vices of an old sailor returned from the colonies; it was that man that she was evoking in that verbiage of a little girl curious about Tonkin, and it was his voice, his medal-laden voice recounting his campaigns to which she was listening, singing in her own, gripped by the certain charm of words like "plantation" and "maize."

7 June.

> *One is not consoled for anything; time passes, and one forgets.*
> (Barbey d'Aurevilly)

I've spent a frightful night; all night my soul floated, adrift, borne away beneath I know not what livid skies, in the dead and stagnant current of I know not what dismal waters!

In the land of miserable and splendid amour . . .

Where have I read that line? I don't know any more, so much does my memory betray me, but that's certainly the land from which I've come, miserable and splendid, sunlit and bleak.

The sadness of life is the depressing certainty that one ought to have of the recommencement of everything, of the absolute lack of the unexpected, the new or any adventure, of the perpetual repetition of the same stupid ennuis. It's the despairing certainty, combined with the acquired experience, that the rare moments of lived passion, dolor or joy will never return, that to attempt to evoke them is folly and that everything is ashes and dust in the mouth, beneath teeth avid for sensations that are gone forever. Living as I have done for three months isn't living but surviving. There are times when I'm weary of watching over a cadaver.

23 June.

I have to get away.

Yesterday morning, I went to see her, as I often do, attracted by the proximity, by idling, and there, in her little garden abandoned to the chickens and the frolics of her two dogs, a garden without flowers, invaded by long grass, with, in one corner, the unexpected flowering of an entire bed of lilies—large white lilies with a heady and sweet odor—casting the slender shadows of their green stems upon the blindingly sunlit wall, I found her sitting, bare-headed, with her boyish brown hair tangled over her rounded forehead, in the process of studying a role for the Théâtre-Libre.

She stood up in order to extend her hand to me with the "How is the heart today?" with which she welcomes my visits, for she's aware of my difficulties, and I saw then that she had bare feet within slippers of finely woven straw, embroidered with blue and green pearls; she was truly charming like that in her casual attitude and the simultaneously compassionate and ironic cordiality of her welcome. A gray crepe dress, a very soft ash-gray, ornamented at the indentation of the neck by mat gold arabesques, molded her entire body, and I divined that she was naked under the fabric, nothing but a harmony of folds.

Her large gray eyes, the gray of the Ocean under the rain, which also seemed to have suffered so much, had a familiar softness, and in her neutral dress, which the nudity of her body divined underneath rendered timeless, she gave the impression, in the middle of that little sunlit suburban garden, of a barbarian princess, one of those mendicant heroines that one encounters the day after a defeat, following the panic of an army, in Merovingian tales, of a princess chased from her palace and fleeing, anguished and barefoot, the enemy hordes that were searching the region; she certainly had hair in revolt, tangled and as if unacquainted with the comb.

That pretty frightened and smiling face must certainly have reposed in the wind, in the dry leaves of forests and hayricks under the light of the stars; even her young body exhaled a kind of savage perfume of grass roasted by the midday sun, the mingled scents of mint and lilies of the valley; but my errant princess had found refuge

115

in a cloister, and the white sunlit wall against which she was profiled, svelte and supple, was that of the monastery where I was coming to visit her, a vanquished Merovingian prince myself, also fleeing the invasion, and the great clump of mystical lilies swooning under the blue sky really was the complementary and pious note of that sweet epic dream, a morning dream of another age enclosed in a garden of a villa in Auteuil.

My neighbor knows why I have come, for, having disappeared momentarily into the obscure ground floor, now she's coming back with a book bound in pale green in her hand; she has sat down in the shadow of the house, continuously diminished by the rising sun, and now I'm installed next to her, elbows on knees and head in hands, entirely given over to the troubling and powerful charm of her voice.

> *I am thinking of the others. . . .*
> *What has become of their evenings, out there, in the*
>   *shadow, out there?*
> *What has become of their footfalls?*
> *Of the haughty face or the noble soul,*
> *The pride of one or the laughter of another*
> *Which have led them to misfortune or sin?*
> *What has become of them, in their evenings, out there.*
> *Of their dolor, of their sadness, of yours,*
> *You, one of them, and you, the other,*
> *What has become of your footfalls?*

I have never lived and felt so acutely the sadness and nostalgia of those melancholy lines by Henri de Régnier;[1]

---

1 These quoted lines are from Régnier's "Tel qu'en songe" (1892).

her fragile and grave voice gradually deteriorates into hoarse intonations that render them even more touching; poor, charming actress, she becomes emotional herself in listening to her voice, and it's that mounting emotion increasing within her that penetrates me with its reaction. Where, then, have I heard that voice before?

Someone is knocking out there at the door.
And I hear a beggar at the corner of the road;
My evening is troubled by your days;
I hear low voices and loud voices,
One that begs and one that reprimands, by turns
As if living, and as if dead,
At the dissolution of days.

That voice with its profound fractures, that soulful voice, I know it; it was hers, that of the other, that of the one who has gone I know not where, very far away, without even leaving me a word of farewell, the one who was my life, my suffering and my joy for two years, the one whose departure emptied my heart of all my blood like the stab of a knife, the one, finally, that I cannot forget, and she is the one to whom I am listening, lending a ear to the beautiful verses recited by my friend the actress, the barbarian princess in the suburban garden, whose soft and rhythmic chant evokes in me the hours of old.

When I close my eyes, it seems that I can see her.

I have seen too much, for my friend has just closed the book; two stupid tears rolling down my cheek have warned her to cease that cruel game. "Enough for today," she says to me. She looks at me herself with large watery eyes,

---

The second set of lines reproduced do not appear to come from the same source.

which she wants to be ironic but are only compassionate. "I won't lend myself to this stratagem any more if you aren't more reasonable. I'm aggravating your condition instead of curing you, and it's going from bad to worse."

From bad to worse, indeed; I emerge from those visits with my heart capsized and my throat dry, my forehead in a vice, ready for any folly. I have to go away; I'll leave this evening; it's time; I must.

28 June. Saint-Phaland-en-Caux.[1]

Under my windows, a large waste ground, sown here and there with flower-beds, a semblance of a garden planted with geraniums where a goat attached to a stake is grazing: sheds and more sheds; further away, old fences; and, suspended from the balcony of a chalet with a hexagonal turret, the placard: *Villa Casino*. Above all that the haze of an intense blue sky, cut beneath by a band on harsh blue, like a lapis paving on the horizon: the sea.

The beach is deserted; in the waste ground, the property of the hotel, two old Englishwomen in Oxford dresses are walking sadly, one with a folding chair under her arm, the other sheltering under a large green umbrella, both accompanied by an imbecile gentleman in a mustard-yellow outfit, from the trousers to the traveling cap; they are, along with me, the only travelers staying at the hotel; the Casino won't open until the fifteenth of July. On the fifteenth of July, not before, the sheds will be transformed

_____
1 There is no such place and no such saint, but Lorrain used the designation repeatedly as a stand-in for Fécamp, so the "S———" of "Son-yeuse" might well stand for "Saint-Phaland," if it stands for anything at all.

into stalls, displaying their shoddy wares, painted pebbles and sea-shells; only on the fifteenth of July will the placard on the rented villa disappear from the balcony, and the local orchestra will inaugurate the season.

For the moment the town is dead, slumbering in its torpor at the foot of its peeled cliffs, under the burning sun that seems to harden the waves of bright blue enamel; and those dusty and bleak provincial streets, the silent quays of the harbor only animated during three months of winter, emanate such an overwhelming sadness, such distress and such an atmosphere of death, that I could believe myself to be in a town in the wake of a plague, a town emptied by panic, from which terror has chased the last surviving inhabitant.

The blue immobility of the Ocean adds to that impression; at the foot of the cliff, the deserted casino has the false appearance of a leper colony, with its two rows of wooden cabins chapped by the heat.

This region is, however, that of my childhood—but a childhood so gray and heavy with ennui, with eyes always directed elsewhere, that I don't even have the courage to relive it. I haven't even been to see the house where I was born. What's the point? Others live there.

Twenty years ago, a kind of pond glistened in the valley, bordered to the west by a great curtain of trees and cut throughout its extent by the mossy piles of an old bridge; on moonlit nights the steeples of the two churches and the enormous mass of the ancient abbey were reflected there in water as if coated in silver; the Bridges and Highways Department has spoiled my landscape. What have I come to do here, in this sleepy little town where, outside of the cemetery, I no longer have anything, nothing that holds my heart?

To forget that I'm alive, since I'm no longer even conscious of my suffering. I feel numb here, as if intoxicated by opium, heavy with torpor.

I have to go away. The atmosphere of this dead town is like a philter; I can't even feel my heart beating.

29 June.

I haven't gone; I've run into Madame B——. She's a widow; I once paid rather urgent court to her, ten years ago, and, with the fine audacity that I had then, in the first months of her marriage. Today she's free, the mistress of a nice fortune, parading through the coastal towns the mature and restful beauty of a woman of thirty and the overflowing health of her son, a little boy that I knew to be frail and delicate. Madame B—— is embellished; I've never seen her so youthful. A very handsome fellow with soft, profoundly blue eyes—eyes that remind me of others—is accompanying her. Her cousin, she says; her lover, people here whisper. What does it matter? They're both young, agreeable to look at, and give an impression of happiness shared and destinies accomplished. Madame B—— recognized me immediately and that was kind of her, for God knows how I've changed! With her woman's instinct she divined my chagrin; the pity that they all have for matters of amour doubtless alerted her; she introduced me to her cousin, had her son embraced, and took me away with them to the country; all four of us piled into an open carriage, and off we went.

Here, it's necessary to admit, the countryside is marvelous, the crops still in progress put a green swell of quivering rye and noisy oats on all the plateaux, from which the tall trees of farms emerge in islets; here the wheat-fields are still green; in the vicinity of Paris they're ripe.

As we went through Mounetôt, a little village with deserted streets, all the inhabitants being in the fields or collecting seaweed at the foot of the cliffs, Madame B——— had a whim to go into the church: a poor little country church devoid of style and ornaments, with a gray stone belfry coiffed with jaundiced slates, almost collapsing due to old age into the fertile ground of its cemetery.

The cousin and I couldn't help exclaiming: "What are you going to do in that ruin?" but Madame B——— had her idea, and it was necessary to stop the carriage; with one bound she was down on the ground, and with another, striding over the shaky crosses and mossy graves, she went into her barn.

Five minutes later she climbed up to rejoin us, and, as I joked about that devotion akin to a crisis, she said: "You don't understand. I had a prayer to say to the good Lord in that church."

"That church and not another?" I couldn't help smiling.

"Certainly," she replied. "You don't know, then? The first time that one goes into a church, into a church one has never entered before, one can ask whatever one wants of God, and God always grants it."

"Truly, I regret the opportunity lost. Is it indiscreet to ask what you requested?"

Then she suddenly became serious. "Oh, something very simple. I made the sign of the cross and said in a whisper: 'Lord, grant me the mercy of always loving those that I love today.'"

And then, without knowing why, I felt moved, moved to tears, and, word of honor, one of them fell on the little hand that I had taken to squeeze; then I saw in her gaze that she felt sorry for me, and that she, today so happy, had certainly once had her share of ordeals to undergo.

18 July. Le Havre.

A swarm of yard-arms and masts, warships and merchant vessels, like a moving forest looming up on the horizon, dirtied by smoke from the transatlantic liners, with the white dots of sunlit sails here and there out at sea: the new basins of the port.

And over all those delicate and distant silhouettes, a luminous and gilded atmosphere, the dust of bales of cotton and sacks of wheat that are being unloaded, a particular halo reeking simultaneously of guano, leather and pepper, and in that amber fluid, the bare chests of porters, hurrying back and forth, bronzed biceps and backs moist with sweat; and then, over that festival activity, that gaiety of movement and labor, a thousand different sounds, the screeching of pulleys and the grinding of cranes, all the noisy, industrious and swarming of quays suddenly traversed by a muffled bellowing of distress—cattle being loaded—or a loud, almost fateful cry: the cry of a siren, the siren of a steamer coming into the harbor.

It's that amusing and bright décor that I have before my eyes, in the little restaurant called the Port de Bahia, above which I've taken a furnished room, preferring this time, to the simulated luxury of modern hotels, the picturesqueness of a quayside inn.

The Port de Bahia, the Départ, the Antilles and the Bateau de Honfleur; I love, with a slightly puerile affection, those little exotic restaurants and their singing signs, their nostalgic names, like an invitation to voyages. There, in those little neat and narrow restaurants with low ceilings and obscure booths, where the burly hands of former mariners who have now settled down serve strange crab salads and candied capsicum, I rediscover the anguished charm and slightly oppressive malaise of the hour of a departure, a departure for a distant destination, beyond the Ocean, for new lands and a new life, far away in the colonies. The colonies! It really is, in fact, their warm shores and profound blue skies that those singing signs and maritime eateries, the Port de Bahia, the Départ and the Antilles, evoke in my mind.

Oh, the scintillation of those white limestone houses on beaches of yellow sand; perhaps there's a cure in exile to those distant lands.

I want to forget the one I love!
Take me far away from here,
To Flanders, Norway or Bohemia
That my cares might get lost on the way,
What will remain of myself,
When I have succeeded in forgetting?

Forget whom? I no longer know. What did I come here for? Is it the sea of my childhood, the Ocean to which I listened so often in hours of vague ennui, and gazed at even more often with covetous eyes in the epoch of puberty and the awakening of my first dreams, or the voice of the race that is speaking authoritatively within me and recapturing me entirely with its charm? But I'm like a drunken man. Is the sense of dolor deadened? I walk, however, simultaneously indifferent and ecstatic, in a visionary retreat such that, on the old Admiralty quay where I'm staying, everything speaks to me of a town of another age; the reality of things escapes me, and before those old houses with facades of slate, narrow windows devoid of shutters, I catch myself thinking about a Le Havre of ancient vintage, the beautiful Le Havre-de-Grâce of the days of the Regency. The epoch of the Angots of Dieppe[1] and the gallant Indies, and names sing in my memory: Pondicherry, Bombay and Lally-Tollendal.

The Hôtel de la Marine, with its dusty three-hundred-year-old stone entablatures, aids in the reconstruction of my dream, and there are women in hooped petticoats and jonquil Tours fabrics, with narrow corseted waists, like wasps, which fix my visionary eyes, instead of the practical excursionists encountered on the quays, as long and narrow as English umbrellas in their rubber-lined traveling coats.

Where are beautiful ladies parading their hips and their pretty ennui over the quays of old Le Havre, while negro boys, holding up their dresses, shelter them with large parasols, and an old matelot with the look of a pirate offers them a parrot from the isles, or some baboon clad in silks and ostrich plumes? Where have I seen the charming print in which beautiful Le Havre was populated and depicted like that?

Out there, against a delicately pink sky, the slender yard-arms, and the roofs of the Saint-François quarter rise

1 This passage is blithely anachronistic; Jehan Ango, the famous Dieppe ship-owner, lived in the early sixteenth century.

up like saw-teeth, silhouetted in gray-blue in the incandescent evening air.

The sky is as sad and beautiful as a vast altar.

But I search within me vainly for the "violin quivering like an afflicted heart" in Baudelaire's beautiful poem.[1] And I don't think about her for a minute; my indifference frightens me; decidedly, I must be drunk.

Oh, that air saturated with pepper and pitch! Oh, the atmosphere of amber and forgetfulness of that crepuscular Le Havre!

20 July.

I've come back to Paris and I'm still astounded by what has happened to me. The entire region between Médan and Maisons-Laffitte, that entire sector of the great suburb where I lived two years ago the first months of that dolorous liaison, and whose evocation I feared even in memory, I've just traversed on the railway, my arm nonchalantly dangling out of the window, a cigarette in my lips; and before those familiar landscapes, so often traveled together and, so to speak, entirely filled by her, I did not experience a pang or a shiver.

Nothing: nothing stirred within me, and those familiar shores, those banks, where the lawns of the great parks faded away among the quivering aspens—the parks so often visited with her during the long days of July—which appeared yesterday with the rapidity of lightning above

1 "Harmonie du soir," again from *Les Fleurs du mal.*

125

the walls set below the track, I watched them file past me and flee, curiously expecting an emotion, which did not come; and I've come back here bleaker and wearier than ever without the cruel and delightful heartbreak whose catastrophe on which I was almost counting, and through which I would have sweated, drop my drop, my inertia and my ennui.

21 July.

This neighborhood of Poissy, sunlit and seemingly drowsy in the heavy heat, on the edge of the slow stream that is only animated on Saturday evening under the comings and goings of Sunday boatmen, and which seems all week to be flowing through the high dormant foliage of some enchanted land, to think that I was able to traverse its enervating melancholy—the melancholy of meadows extending as far as the eye can see alongside highways bordered with poplars, the melancholy of parks forsaken by their tenants and returning to a state of nature in the tangle of foliage and wild flowers of abandoned properties—without a tremor of the heart the day before yesterday.

One among them, however, ought in passing to have made me sit up straight on my banquette and set me quivering, both hands on the window: the old Parc de Villennes, with its immense lawns of green wheat and oats, where the rare clumps of trees seem today like so many islets.

Villennes, the folly and disaster of the fortune of a parvenu, dissolved in the hands of a black band of architects, Villennes and its marvelous greenhouses, the fantasy of a financier obsessed with Ferrières,[1] whose framework alone stands today beside the hideous industrial carcass of a railway station with the fronton garlanded with knots and Louis XVI attributes of a delightful stylish château.

An old seigneurial domain spared by the Revolution, even respected by the horrible bourgeois tastes of 1830, whose high-ceilinged rooms, spoiled by the prodigality of painting and gilded plastering of an Empire banker, now gape, their windowed doors wide open to the sun and the rain, with a futile *For Sale*, already fallen from a balcony two years ago, lying in the middle of a great perron with broken steps, an old perron of honor.

How far away it is, the day when she consented to give herself to me in that park!

It was at the beginning of our liaison, and the first time she found a means of avoiding the functions of mistress of the house and governess—mistress of the father's house and governess of the children. She had twenty-four hours to herself, an entire day and night to give me, and, like a schoolgirl on vacation, all pink in her pale blue organdie dress, she had stood out before the railings of the old park . . . almost supernatural in truth, so luminous did she seem, brighter even than the light of that warm summer's day, with her silky hair forming a nimbus over her forehead, her milky complexion almost too pale and the unaccustomed smile of her mouth.

That smile was belied that day—as always, alas—by the saddened dream of her great profound blue eyes, but how confused and blurred that vision already was! And of that

---

1 The reference is to the Château de Ferrières, built in the 1850s by the Baron de Rothschild, the largest and most luxurious château of the nineteenth century, a model for universal envy.

unforgettable day, followed by an even more unforgettable evening, I could not, no matter how I tried, extract or evoke anything.

My mind is torpid, my memories absent, gone . . . where? I can't say; and of that obstructed and smoky past, of that day all of whose minutes were once lived cadenced by the muffled pulse of my arteries and hammered out by the blood of my heart, I have conserved nothing but an impression of wellbeing overwhelmed by the heat and the long motionless grass beneath an implacably blue sky, in the depths of an abandoned park, as if put to sleep by old age and pleasant fatigue in the midst of the countryside.

Yes, one detail does come back to me: we heard the noise of scythes in the distance, behind the walls, and that was the only noise in the silence, with, from time to time, the soft fall into the grass of an overripe plum, invisibly detached, the warm odor of which evoked in our eyes the amber flesh, split and juicy, of the fruit.

And that was like the taste of her lips. That detail alone remains to me; all the others have fled.

Valmont, 28 August.

Valmont with its wooded hills, its historic château whose high tower and slate roofs today overlook an English park descending in gentle slopes to pastures surrounded by trellises; Valmont and its lively waters murmuring in all the corners of the hedges and setting in movement through two leagues of the valley the mossy wheels of old mills; Valmont and its solitary fish-pond, reflecting the arches and corroded pillars of a ruined abbey; Valmont, whose romantic name and contrived keepsake landscape charmed and whiled away in dreams, for such a long time, the hours of disturbance and vague curiosity of my distant childhood, in the epoch of puberty.

Valmont, whose name I was to rediscover in the most wicked book, the most cruel and the most dangerous of the eighteenth century,[1] and the melancholy and sweet memory of which, made of tall trees, the water of springs, and slow and silent walks along the covered pathways on the edge of a pool where swans were swimming, is always confused in my memory with romantic chromo-lithographs, Scottish lakes surrounded by forests, and castles beyond the Rhine overlooking valleys, and pieces of music played twenty years ago on my mother's piano. How have I run aground here, in this little neglected town in Normandy, so close to a region that I hate, in the company of the madcap and joyful Miss Holly?

She has, however, nothing of the other about her, this one, with her abrupt profile with its snub nose, her blue, slightly bulging eyes through which no shadow of sadness ever passes. Oh, no, she has nothing of the other about her, with her square boyish shoulders, her androgynous silhouette and in insolent brightness of her complexion, blossoming like a bloody flower.

And yet I have just spent two days with her in this poetic and old-fashioned little corner, under the title of romance, and that for having seen her, tall and lithe, like a novice in her blue Mathurin jersey, running along the beach at Trouville with her two Scottish griffons, her serge skirt stuck to her legs, and her yellow brodequins soaked to the ankles, paddling in the waves where her dogs were

1 *Les Liaisons dangereuses* (1782) by Choderlos de Laclos.

bathing? No, but for having exchanged two or three words with her, which almost revealed to me a soul, or rather a woman—for *soul* is a very big word—in that beautiful girl with a tomboy allure.

I had crossed paths with her two or three times in winter, in amateur circles where pantomimes were being performed, supple and nimble in a floating Pierrot blouse, her forehead striped by the black head-dress; I had thought her a very odd figure in her face-powder, made up as a comedy baker's boy. I found her again in Trouville in the middle of race week, in the process of revolutionizing the beach with her costume and her abrupt mannerisms of a jolly sailor—a sailor with ten-thousand-franc pink pearls in her ears, for Miss Holly is very well off, and possesses, in addition to an annual income, a few houses to rent out in the sun. It was nearly midday; recognition was quickly established.

As we both went back to the boardwalk before separating, she to return to her villa in Hennequeville and me to go back to the Roches-Noires, we went to have a vermouth at the little wooden bar opposite the casino. The dogs, streaming with sea-water, shook their tails, and gravely sat down two paces away from the table where Miss Holly avidly consumed five cakes.

The pleading eyes of the two dogs touched me, and I signaled to the stallkeeper. "Two cakes for my dogs?" said the beautiful eater, divining my intention. "Oh, are you mad, cakes for dogs when there are people who have no bread? What are you thinking?" And she got up abruptly, giving the signal to depart.

That remark, in the mouth of a woman, astonished and charmed me. Instead of quitting her, I took a few more steps beside her, seized by a sudden curiosity.

"Oh, it's because I know, myself, what poverty is," Miss Holly went on, and looked me straight in the eyes. "I'm the daughter of a mason, or rather a manual laborer, for he followed all the métiers, my father, and when he was brought back to us at the house, half-dead, we were seven, and dancing on the brink, four boys and three girls, the eldest of whom was sixteen, with no mother. I had killed Maman in being born."

She had said that frankly and simply; perhaps her great limpid eyes shone a little more brightly, with a sudden redness in the cheeks and ears, which made the two ten-thousand-franc pearls in the lobes a little rosier.

"Indeed, the poverty of London . . . ," I said stupidly.

"London? Are you joking?" Miss Holly interrupted. "I'm as English as you are. My name is a *nom de guerre*, a caprice of my second lover, the one who launched me; I have no need to make my brothers blush if I've turned out badly. English! You think I'm English? That's a good one. I'm from this region, on the far side of the Seine, twelve or fifteen leagues from Le Havre, and from a pretty place, in truth: Valmont. Do you know it?"

"Valmont? You're from Valmont?" And as I drank in her eyes, I know not what stupidity softened me.

"Well, that astonishes you! What's got into you, my friend?"

And when I had explained that I too was born in the same valley and the same region, two leagues away, me in the town and she in the village, separated by the twenty water-mills ranged along the stream that takes its source in Valmont to empty into the Channel, before the house where I grew up, an emotion seized us both, and we put our hands together, gazing at one another as if we had never seen one another before—and Miss Holly suddenly appeared charming to me, and it's necessary to believe that at that moment I didn't displease her, since, with the voice of a little girl, she said: "How old are you—about thirty?"

"No, more."

"You aren't forty?"

"No, less than that."

"Bah—that's nothing! Me, I'm twenty-seven, and we surely saw one another as children, but you were already a little rich boy, and a little rich boy from the town. Do you know what we ought to do, when we leave here for the races at Dieppe? Go to spend a couple of days together in the area. It would give me pleasure to see that corner of my childhood again, the cottage where I was born, the road to the school, the church, if it's still standing, and the quarry where Papa was killed. Oh, it hasn't budged, opposite Le Vivier, near the Neuf-Terre. Would you like that?"

When I raised the objection of possible encounters with family that had remained there, and the probably jealousy of the man maintaining her, she said, slowly shaking her head: "My brothers, no danger, I no longer have anyone out there—and then, who would recognize me? It's ten years since I quit Valmont. As for the other . . ." She made a little gesture of carelessness to the intention of her lover. "I'll take care of the other."

Saint-Phaland-en-Caux, 31 August.

And I made the perilous journey, and now I have the curiosity of suffering and tears. It's the other one, the disappeared, who has given me this sad and cruel sensuality.

I wanted to see how the peasant soul of the pretty kept woman that Miss Holly is would engage with memories of childhood and the locale.

Needless to say, Miss Holly has been charming. To deflect all suspicion, I left in advance, bound for Honfleur. She simply embarked at the promenade jetty, and we met up again at Le Havre station, as if by the greatest of hazards.

Miss Holly has done a thousand childish things. As we were climbing into the first-class compartment she spotted a third class carriage in which the extinct lamps made the compartment utterly black. It was absolutely necessary to get into that one. Fortunately, there was no one else there, and we made the journey huddled together in the gloom, our eyes lost in the confused nocturnal landscape of farms and woods fleeing past the window, our fingers interwoven, without saying a word.

At Beuzeville, where we were to spend the night, another fantasy! My companion wanted to push on as far as Saint-Phaland, the dismal and devout little town of my youth, and to sleep there in the quarter of convents and churches, in an inn of curés and peasants, where her relatives had taken their meals when they went to town on market days, doubtless sitting at the end of the kitchen table with the domestics, and where the story of her first visit to the town was set. The two leagues that separated Valmont from Saint-Phaland was devoured in singing by her worthy father, a kind of Norman colossus, carrying three of his children in his arms that day, her and two of her brothers, the older of whom was perched astride the giant's shoulders.

It was the organ of the Abbey that woke us up in the morning. Miss Holly insisted on taking the old rattletrap that carried the mail, and it was perched on the banquette on top, between our luggage and sacks of potatoes, that we saw emerging one by one, from the morning mists trailing along the stream, the pointed roofs, velveted with moss of Saint-Valéry, Saint-Ouen, Colleville and Rouxmenil, all of them clusters of mills . . . and along the route, stories and more stories. . . .

At Valmont, my companion's chirping gaiety of a wet bird shaking its wings hectically in the sun was suddenly appeased, and her babble was extinguished. I counted that to her credit. It was at a slow pace, and in silence, that we visited the Vivier and its surrounding wood. Miss Holly is a meritorious hiker; she made me walk two leagues in the valley, stopping for three minutes in front of a small kitchen garden planted with beans and sunflowers, with a long low cottage at the back, set against a bank—that of her parents, and even appeared to reflect for a moment, leaning her elbows on the fence, suddenly having gone pale, in her pink bastiste. She had a pretty smile on encountering three ragamuffins trotting along the road barefoot, with faggots of dead wood balanced on their backs; pointing at them with her finger, she murmured in my ear: "Me at ten years old; my brothers and I were sent to fetch wood."

She also wanted to take me to the quarry, the one where her father had been killed extracting marl, a quarry now abandoned in the midst of landslides and jets of wild brambles that made thickets of verdure with long grass, with the umbels of hemlock here and there, and large wild mulberries. But she hastened her steps past the cemetery, refusing to go in.

"What's the point? We were poor; I wouldn't be able to find the place."

And throughout that melancholy promenade through the past, I followed her step by step, watching out for a tear in the corner of her blue eye, desiring and summoning an alteration in her voice.

But Miss Holly remained calm. Softened, she was certainly that—but the health and strength of her nature is resistant to nervous starts and sudden weaknesses of the voice and gaze: those abrupt effusions of dizziness made of contractions and tears, through which the dolorous past of the other, the past that she never wanted to talk about, shivered and vibrated so delectably, shaking us both at the same time.

She had, however, pretty stories on the tip of her tongue, Miss Holly, during those two days spent with her at Valmont in the sunlit calm of those pastures and great woods, and there were curious corners in her childhood: the covered pathway between two walls, the walls of two parks, where little girls and boys united in a troop to go past because of a statue of a nymph—the White Lady, visible between the trees of one of those parks, in a lawn that is all rye and oats today—and the irrational panics of all the brats, not daring, on certain evenings, to venture along the Lady's path, and making a long detour to go to school; and the barn where an old shepherd, something of a sorcerer, put on marionette shows for all the wide eyes of little peasants come from three leagues around, each with a candle and their one-sou entry fee, and the girls who were already big being kissed and groped by the boys in the obscurity of the improvised spectacle hall, in the warmth of bales of hay; and the little fir-wood on the hill above the house, where, as a little girl, she liked to go and sit for hours in the high, noisy branches, to listen to the song of the wind.

Lying next to me in a field of heather, under a little wood of ash-trees, she talked as if in a dream, and it really was about dreams that she talked, in fact: of the disconnected and charming memories of childhood, which she recited aloud for herself. At our feet, the valley was hollowed out, with its solitary pond, its pastures surrounded by hedges, where cattle were wandering, its ruined abbey and its enclosure of large woods.

I listened to her and, with my head hidden in my hands, and my hands on the ground, I put on a semblance of being asleep, thought about the other, and wept.

Saint-Phaland, 3 September.

> *They are at rest; life's ardent and sad alarms*
> *And chagrins no longer haunt their peaceful pillow;*
> *Each morning's dawn bathes them with its tears.*
> *Life is a tomb at the turning of a path.*

Leaning on my elbows against the ivied railings of a grave, I reread that epitaph, which I composed seven years ago, on the day after my father's death, and in the utmost depths of my thoughts I arrive at envying the departed, buried there in that little provincial cemetery on the side of a hill; and, abandoning myself to regret, it is me that I regret, in me that I pity the idea of the repose of the heart that I have never possessed, and will never know in this world, I fear, since I carry in myself, alas, the incurable and dolorous cause of my pain.

They are at rest.

The sky is gray, charged with rainclouds, and from the path where I am I can look over the white wall of the cemetery at the little town of Saint-Phaland framed between its high cliffs, with its harbor, absolutely deserted in summer, and its sad houses coiffed in slates, silhouetted in grayish blue against the glaucous extent, monotonous with foam, of the sea. It has rained all morning, around me, the cypresses and the willows are weeping droplets, and the clumps of ivy on which I am leaning have liquid pearls in the corners of their leaves.

Oh, that unquiet sea, perpetually uplifted beneath the low, windswept sky, and the fearful flight of the clouds!

They are at rest.

Why can certain beings only love once, while so many others . . . ?

And, stirred by the idea of that sovereign injustice, now I start talking, involuntarily, about my adieux to Miss Holly, whom I did not want to accompany to Dieppe, and whom I quit two days ago.

I have on my person a letter from her, received this morning, the poor and naïve letter of a little girl. I cannot help smiling as I read it.

My dear friend,

I arrived in Dieppe yesterday, still full of the emotions that I experienced in visiting my homeland. I truly do not know how to thank you for the generosity you have shown me; I shall remember that journey all my life, and especially that admirable wood of Franqueville that we walked through together. It's you who had the idea of taking me there. Do you know that I would have liked very much to stay with you forever in the woods? You're so good, and you're not like anyone else, and you're sad, while I'm cheerful; I adore that. Why are sad people always better than others?

I'm going to have difficulty resuming life in Paris after those two days spent with you; Dieppe is already boring me. Deep down, I detest big cities; I'm a peasant, and I felt better at Valmont with you.

Will you be staying in Saint-Phaland for a few days? I'm here for a week. How kind it would be of you, my friend, to wait for me to come back and spend a few more days together, the two of us, at Franqueville or at Valmont.

I do not kiss you, for I know you are a strange and wild man, but I hold myself very close against you, my dear Serge.

I love you very much.

Poor and charming girl, will she also be caught by the dangerous charm of pity? Has the eternal sympathy that slumbers in the heart of women for misery and woe, the dolorous voluptuousness of suffering that makes saints and sisters of charity, penetrated in my company the frank and vigorous health of body and soul that Miss Holly has?

She must have divined my chagrin, then, and those two days spent together have sufficed to contaminate her! Am I really as contagious as that, and am I not a little culpable? Am I not too often reminiscent of the fine sprig of Normandy in the unforgettable lines of Baudelaire's "Litanies de Satan":

138

You who put into the eyes and heart of young women
The worship of the wound and the love of rags

and have I not taken a malicious pleasure in displaying my wound and my moral rags to the tranquil and hitherto untroubled gaze of my compatriot Miss Holly?

Including that last walk in Franqueville, in that kind of forest of beeches and wild apple-trees growing no one knows how outside the enclosure of an old park, on a hill planted with firs, pouring in a bewildering tangle of verdure into the simultaneously luminous and obscure hollow of two narrow ravines.

Did I not have, for my part in the choice of that décor to frame our adieux, a slightly perverse intention, and was I not obedient to a secret desire to sadden and render melancholy the soul of my friend, by taking her, at the moment of our separation, to a landscape designed to aggravate the irreparable and indescribable impression of distress inherent in any departure?

"Every landscape is a state of mind."[1] A litterateur of the vitiated marrows of literature, I remember my authors too well, and it's certainly in memory of slow and melancholy excursions on horseback at twenty when, as a young man kept on a tight rein by an economical father and forced, for want of money, to live in the provinces, I came to wander there, during interminable and mortal days, in the impatient reveries of a captive, certainly in memory of those bleak rides of my youth, that I took Miss Holly to the high forest of Franqueville two days ago, to those pro-

---

1 Lorrain is quoting from the *Journal intime* of Henri-Frédéric Amiel (1821-1881), fragments of which were first published posthumously in 1884.

found and sonorous beech-woods, where, so many times, my heart in revolt and gripped by sadness, I listened to my mount whinnying loudly in the wind.

The wind, as of old, caused the birches and the beeches to rustle and whisper; a little sharp and cold breeze was blowing from the east, in which one nevertheless sensed the humidity of the sea; and, standing in a broad covered pathway, as if carpeted in green by the velvet of moss, we gazed, Miss Holly and I, at the clusters of rowan berries illuminated redly between the leaves, with a tangle of branches and treetops above us, set against the saddest sky—a sky as surly and gray as today's, a typical sky of the end of October, which left the woods devoid of gaiety, devoid of sunlight.

Behind us, the dormant shadows of tall fir-trees with enormous branches emerged at intervals above the boundary wall of the park, and then the fields, the heaths and the tall, tall ferns. . . .

Suddenly, a gust of wind shook the treetops of the fir-wood more forcefully, a plaint ran along the wall of the park, and Miss Holly had a little coughing fit that forced her to stop; she was truly charming thus, her face suddenly crimsoned by the coughing, with two large tears in her eyes; the palms of the ferns came up to her waist. . . .

I detached from my waist the three meters of black cloth that was serving me as a belt, and I wound it around her neck as a scarf. She thanked me with a glance.

"I'll keep it, you know," she contrived, through a smile. "It's beautiful here—and to think that we might never come back!"

Never!

At the foot of the hill, on the main road, the carriage was waiting for us with the luggage.

I looked at Miss Holly obliquely. What would I not have given, ten years ago, to have encountered her and had her there, all to myself, when I was wandering on horseback, so dismal and depressed in the clarity of those green fir-woods? Before having known the other one, the other whose phantom returned more tenaciously and more implacably, underlining every gesture and accompanying every step of poor Miss Holly.

Why did I not encounter you,
My dear soul, a year ago?
I would doubtless have adored you,
Having known you in my dreams.

Oh, when I wrote those lines eight years ago, before having passed through all my ordeals, I did not suspect that I was prophesying so accurately, a poet of ill-omen, a prophet of woe, and of my own woe—a sad and dolorous prophet.

Paris, 8 September.

I've come back from Sèvres, having just spent the day with my friends the Lostins; I like that little household of artists—the man an engraver and a wife a painter—with an almost grateful affection. Thy live so far from the present century and the preoccupations of the boulevard, on the bank of the Seine, both smitten with the Primitives and impregnated with mystical reading, whose atmosphere has ended up surrounding them both with something akin to a aureole and giving them the ecstatic eyes and luminous faces of Gozzoli archangels.

The wife, especially, is extraordinarily curious, with her gazes into the beyond, drowned therein as if reaching it, in the intense blue of her irises, while her simultaneously sensual and savage mouth forms the smile of a mystical bacchante; and then, I like her art, a visionary and morbid art, and the doleful color and precious and sumptuously rare brushwork of her pastels; I like the distressing severed heads of martyrs that she evokes, inevitably posed on the underside of a platter or bathing, like cut flowers, in the bloody water of a glass bowl in the form of a chalice; finally, I adore the transparent and cold blue eyes of those pitiful heads, those forgiving and weary eyes, in which I rediscover her own irises, like two translucent enamels, as they emit from their interior such a perfume of simplicity and faith.

The man and the wife are certainly two complicated brains, but their souls are fresh; their modest situation is so valiantly accepted by those two beings, such a charity reigns within them, such order, and with that such a love of the beautiful, so well revealed in every corner by some unexpected religious trinket, that I've ended up considering their hospitable little house in Sèvres as a haven, a port, a safe and salutary harbor for my chagrin and my ennui.

I always emerge better, more serene, if not healed, from their little studio decorated with varnished pottery and florid with greens and old grays. Is it the reproductions of Botticellis hanging on the walls, the Donatellos in faience painted in the antechamber, the old chasubles trailing on the divans, or the church lamp and the great altar crosses, whose bright silver blesses their mirror? At any rate, I always come back from Sèvres calmer, less feverish, the wound in my side bandaged and refreshed.

Why did I not have that impression of wellbeing and freshness in my heart on quitting them today?

12 September, evening.

Another letter from Miss Holly. I haven't replied to the first; I found this one at Auteuil on returning to Paris; it's still dated from Dieppe; a few fragments:

> *My dear friend,*
>
> *It will soon be ten days since I wrote to you and you haven't replied; I believed, however, that I was sufficiently your friend to merit a reply; it appears that I was mistaken. Have you found her again, the one for whom I caught you sobbing and weeping beside me like a child at Valmont?—and God knows, that day, that I didn't hold it against you. If it's her, so much the better; I'm not jealous, for you love her too much to be able to forget her; but if it's another one, so much the worse, for I'll be forced to consider you as worth no more than a heap of other men, and that would be a great chagrin for me, for I pleased myself in setting you apart. . . . Like others, you whom I've seen with tears in your eyes at the mere memory of. . . .*
>
> *Do you have troubles? Are you ill? No, you aren't, are you? In any case, reply to me; that would give me pleasure; I shall be able to hold myself together and will do my best to forget you. It will be difficult for me when I remember our beautiful walks in the woods in Franqueville and Valmont.*
>
> *I love you very much even so.*

Poor Miss Holly. I crumple the thin sheet of mauve paper between my fingers and I believe, honestly, that I smile a little as I crumple it; I don't feel the slightest pity for the little cry of dolor that whimpers in that letter. Fundamentally, my experience puts me on guard, and it's my egotism that defends me. What point is there in resuming the eternal adventure of misunderstandings and betrayals? Miss Holly is charming, though, and she gives the impression of having a soul . . . if women have one! But I don't have the courage to attempt the risks of a liaison again. Why try to inscribe eternal thoughts in sand and build duration with the wind? It's our need to think and live that makes us forget.

The game of destinies
And the hazard of years
That want all flowers faded,

as a poet and friend, Henri de Régnier, puts it in such a melancholy fashion—and I no longer have the energy to think otherwise.

What to do, then? Go away . . . always leaving, taking one's incurable misery to new climes, with unexpected horizons of mountains and oceans, through populous and swarming distant cities, at which our curiosity marvels and is astonished; to try in the course of one's voyages to hold a minute of infinity in irreparable and brief adventures, encounters devoid of tomorrows, to scatter oneself to all the winds. . . . That is where harsh experience ends up bringing the faithful and the tender, to the libertinage of the heart, the last resort of sentiment!

Oh, the sad savant that I have become before the art of living . . . which is also the art of suffering—necessarily.

When one knows one is caught, it appears that one finds a sort of sad sensuality therein, of which the psychologists have made the dilettantism, and that's how the comedy ends . . . in little sobs and little songs. . . .

(The journal ended there.)

"Well?" I interrogated, leaning on the back of the armchair into which he had just let himself fall with the exhausted gesture of a supremely weary man.

"Well, the proof has not succeeded, my friend. Certainly, the little one is charming; from the physical point of view, she's surely the prettiest animal one could wish for in an alcove; she's young, she has skill, suppleness, even enthusiasm, and her skin smells good; better than that, I think I'm not indifferent to her, for it's now three nights a fortnight that she gives me, and every time I emerge from her arms as fully satisfied and sated with caresses as a fervent lover can desire; but what do you want? The joy she gives me is entirely physical and goes no further. My heart is emptier and more disjointed than ever when I quit her, and when she gives me her lips, there are times when I want to weep; worse, when she calls me by my first name and lingers seductively over the two syllables of *Serge*, I have to make a great effort not to slap her, for the other sometimes had those intonations, and fundamentally, it's the other that I regret and the other that I love, and that's that!"

And, having got up with a bound from his armchair, he went to stick his forehead to the unsilvered mirror of the high window, and gazed out obstinately at the autumn rain streaming in a downpour over the fiacres at the station, stopped in a file at the corner of the little square.

The poor fellow, it pained me to see him with his brows contracted, his eyes having suddenly hardened, as if recoiling beneath the heavy lids, and the determined mutism of his entire face of stubborn spitefulness and furious obstinacy.

"It's not yet over, then?" I hazarded, in a timid voice, and sat down on the corner of the table, just behind him.

"Over! When I croak! And then, how does one know? Perhaps one suffers in the tomb. There are corpses that have strange grimaces on their faces when they're disinterred, as if they remember down there all the filth of this life. Oh, my friend, my poor friend!"

And with the recklessness of a child, having put his arm around me:

> *The lovers of prostitutes*
> *Are happy, hale and sated.*
> *As for me, my arms are weary*
> *For having embraced clouds.*

And, as if softened by that quotation from Baudelaire,[1] he said: "What's frightful about my case, is that it isn't precisely her that I regret, for, compared with other women, it's neither the odor of her flesh nor the silkiness of her hair, although it is particularly soft, that haunts me and obsesses me, but the imperceptible, scarcely graspable signs,

1 The first lines of "Les Plaintes d'un Icare," again from *Les Fleurs du mal*.

such as the forgiving and suffering expression of her gaze, the pained fatigue of her smile—in brief, all that is pitiable and the bruised in her wretched existence of a loving and betrayed woman; it's all of that past, about which she never wanted to say a word to me, and which I've discovered entirely since; it's that entire life of dolor and resignation of which I love the reflection in her, and the truth is that it's a soul with which I'm in love."

"But since that soul was another's, it's a fool's game that you're playing, my dear, in attaching yourself to it still. . . ."

"Yes, I know that, but if she hadn't had in her life that first adored lover, would I have known with her the frenzies of passion and tears that have rendered her unforgettable to me? Oh, the first night that she granted me, in that little waterside inn, where we had dined together, with the windows of our room open over the lawns of the park, an old neglected park that we had seen all day, roaming in the shade of its bushes and its quincunxes! How I can still see the kind of *petite mort* that accompanied the spasm; I perceived that I had cheeks moist with tears, like a warm rain that was falling on my face, and the bitterness of which salted our lips and our kisses deliciously. It was her who was weeping silently, her head drowned in her long silken hair, her cheek on the pillow, her two quivering hands leaning on my shoulders, shaken from the nape of her neck to her heels by such anguished sobs that the reverberation, like the tolling of a bell, hammered my heart delightfully.

"I tried to calm her down, but she was still weeping relentlessly: I'd drawn her closer, upon my breast, and while, involuntarily, unconsciously and yet delightedly, I drank her tears one by one, I felt myself invaded by a voluptuous compassion compounded of dolor and pity. She was still

147

whimpering like a child, entirely absorbed in her pain; but there was gratitude in her embrace, and in the manner in which she stammered my name, an imploring adoration such that I was simultaneously faint with sensuality and pride. I've discovered since that all of that beautiful frenzy of sobs and tears was addressed to another, that I was merely the mannequin of her dolor. Amused by a resemblance, she had yielded in becoming my mistress to an unhealthy curiosity, to the desire to relive with a vague double the minutes of anguish and passion of an irreparable past.

"Since then, I've had the explanation of certain expressions, certain gestures; since then, I've discovered the reason for the abruptnesses and caprices suddenly surging forth after indescribable hours of tenderness, almost of ecstasy, the eyes lost in the distance and the hands fastened to mine as if she could see in me and wanted to retain in me a phantom about to escape her. During the eighteen months that our liaison lasted, I had always been someone else for her, whom she loved in me; it was a stranger. It was him, moreover, who took her back after that, and had only to reappear to repossess her. As soon as she saw him, I no longer had any reason to exist; it's as logical and mathematical as amour, which is, fundamentally, something exact and ferocious; but thanks to that other, that anonymous rival who has made a desert of my life, I've known the illusion of love—what am I saying?—I've known love itself, and they're true tears that I've drunk from her lips, and true dolor that I've held against my bosom; in sum, it's a soul, bloody and bruised, whose agony and amorous resurrection I've savored when she sobbed so desperately, her heart against my heart, in that little suburban inn, on that warm and luminous night in July. Oh, that day in the park at Villennes and that night of abandon and tears in that boatman's hotel!"

He had taken hold of my two hands and was kneading them, hurting me, with eyes that had become utterly pale, desires fled from the irises into the corners of the half-closed lids, putting a kind of steely gleam into their fissures.

"If you knew how beautiful it was, that night, and the magic of the moonlight on the tall trees slumbering in the park, the bushes heaping up in great masses of shadow against a sky with the purity of nacre, and, in the distance, the glimmer of the Seine snaking through the meadows. . . .

"Oh, the benevolent humidity that rose from the banks and beneath our windows, like the very respiration of the park; that intoxicating odor of mown hay! We stood for a long time that night, both of us, at the open casement, gazing at the old park of Villennes, the lawns of oats, softly moonlit. There was no wind—I remember it as if I were there again—except in the noisy summit of an old poplar, an entirely white poplar, isolated and glowing, like a candle, in front of the perron of the deserted château.

"Oh, the caress of her cool, bare arms thrown around my neck, the milky brightness of her smile, smiling through her tears, and the soft silk of her hair, having taken on the color of the moon in the luminous shadow of that summer night! I sensed all the warmth of her blood flowing beneath my lips, and, shivering in her bright batiste, she squeezed herself upon me, hugging me and pressing herself against me with all her might, as if she wanted to imprint in my heart the eternal memory of those happy hours. And the fact is that that night, she really did enter into my heart—the liar. . . .

"Never, you see, will I ever be able to forget."

I watched Serge become exalted. A kind of bliss relaxed and transfigured that face, anxious and contracted a little while before. I began to see clearly the kind of morbid amour that he had conceived for that unworthy woman. His psychology—a gross term for which I hold Bourget responsible—finally appeared to me; in him, as in certain elite individuals a trifle world-weary and overly refined, concupiscence was the sister of pity. If he loved suffering it was for the sensual reaction he experienced in his flesh that came to his aid and relieved it; he had betrayed himself in becoming exalted on that passionate night in Villennes, that night made of desperate transports, grateful embraces and kisses steeped in tears, of which he boasted, with narrowed eyes, about the lust of that warm and salty taste.

I finally had the secret of that compassionate and ferociously virtuous soul. Sadness, sobs, regrets and distresses of the heart: that was the atmosphere in which that sensual and delicate cruelty, so easily pitied, thrived.

Cleopatra drank pearls. Why should he not drink the blood of a soul? And the details came back to me of the life that he had led with his mistress for nearly two years, condemning her to the audition of tragically amorous and melodramatic performances, from which the poor woman returned with the distressed gaze of the tortured: the dear friend, acquainted with the unfortunate woman's adventure, took pleasure in making her relive her amorous anguish and the torments of her past.

The case, at any rate, is not the only one of its kind, and these modern Saint Vincent de Pauls of sentiment are numerous enough, always in search of suffering souls, ready for all devotions to cure and console them. That slightly alarming passion for charity is nothing, fundamentally, but a delicate sadism and a refined perversity, infatuated with tortures and tears. Oh, those lovers of suffering! Oh, their tender commiseration! What dilettanti, beneath what lechery!

I looked at Serge intently, and my eyes finally met his. I clapped him on the shoulder and whispered to him, smiling: "Soul-drinker!"

Ophelius

For Marcel Schwob

Claudius ill. Come help me care for him. Urgent.
                                    Comtesse Ethereld.

THAT was the strange telegram, addressed to my pied-à-terre in the Rue Saint-Placid, that I was meditating on the Saturday before Mardi Gras, 1888. I could not explain the illness of Claudius, whom I had left in good health a month before at Mointot, in his little house on the Quai des Pilotes. Even less did I understand the presence with him of Lady Viane, whom I had not seen for nearly two years, since she spent a season at Yport, and I had thought that she was in Spain this winter, attracted there by her recent liaison with the young Marquis de Columbra-Sesto.

I had left the farm, as I always do, after the first fortnight in January. Installed in Paris until the end of June, the time at which I would happily return to my apple trees, and relying on the promise that my friend Aiguor had made to come and join me in Paris for the carnival, I had been expecting for a week to see him disembarking from the train at any moment, my mind a hundred leagues away from the news that telegram had brought me.

The telegram had arrived at a bad time. It would disrupt several projects. Without mentioning the Opéra Ball, to which I had a joyful crew of masked women to escort that same evening, I had my Sunday evening and those of the two following days agreeably filled. But one only has one friend in this world, if one even encounters one, and that friend I had found in Claudius.

I liked him more than he liked me, I think, for fundamentally he was an attractive person, very conscious of his charm, very feminine in that regard, and very egotistical as well, only liking in others his own faults—very captivating faults, however. On that shifting sand we had, however, built a solid amity; those common faults, refined in Claudius as vices, had remained in me within their matrix of primal coarseness and simplicity, and I was often wont to look at myself in the evoked consciousness of Claudius, as in a mirror of polished steel that could reflect my sentiments and tastes, but sculpted in diamond, sharpened and become unhealthy by virtue of refinement.

My health loved that neurosis; I divined his weakness and felt morally constrained to protect him; his seductive nature, gentle, child-like and poetic, adapted marvelously to that quasi-guardianship, but in the foundation of the association, he was the soul and the will—a nervous will, changeable, fleeting, broken by the slightest shock, but once extended, implacable and malevolent: the will of a Catherine the Great, which nothing on Earth could bend.

Lady Viane had nearly killed me during her sojourn in Normandy. On her departure, she had left me in a state impossible to describe, overexcited and nervous, my gaze wandering, in a paroxysm of irritation and feverish excitement sometimes bordering on madness. What game had that cleverest of clever women been playing in leading astray the reason of the unfortunate Aiguor? By what roads had she led him to where I picked him up when she left her famous Moorish villa? The supreme coquetry is in the science of refusal.

An unadmitted hatred, but all the more existent, still simmered dully between Comtesse Ethereld and me. Several times I had accompanied Claudius to the Moorish villa. With what graces had she not welcomed me? Her eyes became soft by dint of being ferocious, she had loved me atrociously; she too was refined, but I had divined her, hence her hatred. Their enigma is the very *raison d'être* of such women.

At any rate, that she-cat crossed with a tigress had a prey between her claws at the time, and it was that prey that I wanted to snatch from her, an aggravation and complication in our hatred. That prey she had left half-dead, but Claudius had recovered his reason. With the blood of his wounds that victim had made a poem, the strange black book of which I still had the manuscript; then time had scarred the wounds that time had cleansed. . . .

She, the artisan of misfortune, the weaver of disasters, had suddenly disappeared without leaving an address—flown, vanished, a woman of the night re-entered into the night.

For two years I had breathed easy, and now she had come to recapture me. While I was in Paris, she was out there, this time triumphant, sure of the work accomplished, since she was summoning me—me, the sole individual that she would have kept away had contest still been possible. The harm was done, irreparable, and she was summoning me to make me the judge of it.

That telegram devastated me.

Was she afraid now, alone in confrontation with her work? Afraid? That was scarcely like her; she was victorious, and she was challenging me.

I was distraught with rage. It was my brother, my friend, almost my child, that the woman was taking from me. In any case, whether it was to defeat me or not, the mere presence of Lady Viane with Claudius constituted a danger, and a most terrible one.

I fastened my suitcase, dispersed a host of small favors in the direction of my crew of masked women, and, at the moment when I should have been climbing the stairway of the Opéra, I installed myself in a carriage on the train to Le Havre, where I arrived exhausted at eight o'clock the following morning.

The same day, at four o'clock, after having stopped at the farm just long enough to give orders, in case it was possible to transport Claudius there, I rang the bell at the little house on the Quai des Pilotes.

Strangely enough, I was sad, and I was cheered up by the sight of all the ships in the harbor, with sails on their yard-arms and pennants on their masts, laden and ballasted, ready to depart for the long haul. Poor merchant vessels with a conquering aspect, thy were arranged there along the docks, bringing a festival gaiety to they quays, like an adventurous flock joyously departing for climes that one imagines to be warmer, more hospitable and bluer than ours because they are so far away, unknown.

The soul of great voyages floating in the topsails was smiling that day, expanding over the old town and the port. Along the jetties, people in their Sunday clothes and mariners already drunk were crowding and jostling.

The thought of Claudius, plaintive and ill in the midst of the gaiety of the locale, so rarely cheerful, was heartbreaking.

I must have rung with a distracted hand, because nobody came in response to my first appeal. The second time, Pierre, his valet de chambre, came to open the door.

"Well then, my poor Pierre . . . ?" And I stopped, impressed, sensing tears in my eyes and a tremor in my voice.

"Oh, Monsieur," he said, and then turned his head, without saying any more. He introduced me into the drawing-room, saying: "Madame la Comtesse is here."

Lady Viane was indeed there, in the drawing-room hung with old tapestries of Claudius' family, the drawing-room that I had known since childhood and where I had seen Claudius' mother personally embroidering all the old silk cushions distributed over the furniture, the pink brocade above the piano and even the petit-point characters of the Louis XVI armchairs: Claudius' mother, a tall blonde young woman who had been known in Mointot as "the lovely Madame Aiguor," a kind of unknown martyr dead at thirty-eight of chagrin and ennui, caught between an egotistical and brutal husband twenty years older than her and an adored son who desolated her, too complicated and too far beyond what she, rectitude personified, was able to comprehend.

The sight of Lady Viane standing in that drawing-room revolted me. How wrong mothers are to depart, especially the mothers of poets. Comtesse Ethereld in the Aiguor house was woe installed in the hearth.

The Englishwoman was not alone; molded in a narrow black dress, a somber sheath brightened at the neck by the white stripe of a little masculine collar, she was standing there talking to Dr. Halmein; I recognized him immediately.

"I was expecting you." And Comtesse Ethereld offered me a hand that I did not take. "I told you," she said then, turning to Dr. Halmein, "that Monsieur Harel would come in response to our appeal. True artists only have one word. Now, Doctor, reassure Monsieur a little regarding the state of our friend."

And the doctor, having coughed three times, explained: "The condition is serious, very serious, but it's necessary not to despair. It's an ataxic typhoid fever complicated by congestion of the meninges; in addition to that, Monsieur Claudius suffers from nerves."

He had already been subject to such crises as a child; an extremely sensitive nature, inherited from his mother, less the energy. Madame Aiguor had died of that energy which her son did not have; by contrast, the son was dying of the imagination that his mother had not had. The patient might be saved, but could his reason be saved? That was the point that worried the doctor.

He added: "That fellow has lived too much apart, too solitary, too self-reliant; he's worn out his brain in crazy conceptions; it's the brain that's under attack today; but with the nervous system one can expect anything, and if a miracle is possible, it's here that it will take place, thanks to this good fairy."

And, with an utterly provincial grace, he took Lady Viane's hand. "Madame has cared for Monsieur Aiguor with a devotion, a kindness and a patience that one no longer finds except in the Sisters of Charity, those outcasts, or mothers, the disdained. If your friend is still alive, thank

157

Madame for it, Monsieur Harel, who has been watching over him for ten days and nights in the contagious and stinking atmosphere of a sickroom."

And having kissed Lady Viane's hand, Dr. Halmein abruptly took his leave.

The grotesque was going. Finally! What ought I to believe? His words were a cruel lie given to my suppositions, but was he not the dupe of some comedy of Lady Ethereld's?

Comtesse Viane, with her back to the fireplace, her elbow on the oak mantelpiece, had a disconcerting expression, both smiling and melancholy. "Would you like to see him?" she said, finally, in a very slow, very sad voice.

I moved closer and, having taken the right hand that she was allowing to dangle inertly beside her, I raised it to my lips and kissed it religiously.

"So, you're no longer holding a grudge against me?" The soft, sad voice said. "If I wished him harm, Armand, in all conscience, would I be here?"

My given name had such a strange resonance in her voice that I was quite nonplussed.

"Yes," she emphasized. "Call me Viane, as I call you Armand. Have we not become brother and sister in the same danger and the same dolor, at the bedside of the same sick friend?" And, taking my hand, she led me out of the room.

Poor Claudius' bedroom: so eccentric, and so typical of him, with it's high sea-green ceiling with oak beams, its walls hung with old pink drapes bordered with silver thistles, and the delicate and savant harmony of the curtain, and the bed in old green silk, an intense and luminous absinthe green, in which old silver braid with rose florets was fading; the poor bedroom of a poet, with its thousand and one meditated, selected trinkets setting their bright or somber patches against the walls. That evening, it appeared to me to be even more crazily somber and strange than all the other evenings.

Above the small Dutch dresser with gilded panels an old cerise lamp was outlined, an item of Venetian glassware—one of Claudius' manias—opalized by reflections, putting a kind of lunar radiation into that corner of the room, a brightness of living gems in the gloom. In the corner of the high mantelpiece, all in cut glass, with twisted columns, and draped with an altar-cloth, was a woman's head, a Renaissance bust gilded on the hair and lips, with enamel irises in a green bronze face, standing on an ebony pedestal, strangely alive in a wrapping of pale pink embroidery with a blue floral pattern, bizarrely coifed with a spangled hennin, from which long silvery gauzes flowed like water: *Dea silens*, the lady of silence, as Claudius called her, because of her golden lips.

The poet had his idols. I had always distrusted that green and pink room, barbaric in its taste and full of a devotion simultaneously mystical and pagan, positively reeking, if not of heresy, at least of frank hysteria.

I found the invalid there, delirious.

An old embroidered screen deployed in front of the four-poster bed hid the patient from sight; at the bedside, a black shadow, a nun, was sitting at a large table cluttered with phials and potions. A rosary in her fingers, she was silent, illuminated from above by the pink glow of a nightlight, the red oil-filled tumbler of a Louis XV silvered bronze church lamp suspended from the ceiling by three slender chains, in front of a Saint Sebastian by Il Sodoma,[1] a marvelous ephebe suffering ecstatically, agonizing in the gleam of that lamp in a thick Louis XIII frame with ornaments laden with ribbons and fruits.

The nun had risen to her feet; at a sign from Lady Viane she disappeared. Comtesse Ethereld had taken my hand again; we were standing next to the bed. She moved aside one of the panels of the screen.

"Behold the man," she said.

And set against the white of the pillows, Claudius' head appeared to me. The face had a green pallor, the head of a beheaded martyr, it had a pinched nose, dead eyes and taut skin, hollow in the cheeks. A dirty beard, a twenty-day beard, mildewed his miserable cheeks. Only his hair and moustache had remained beautiful, bushy and wild, with their tawny color of pale gold or ripe wheat. Between the bruised, blackened eyelids a little of the white of the eye was gleaming: two fissures framed by burnished silver; his gaze was there; the revulsed pupils had disappeared beneath the upper lids.

His eyes were open, and yet he was asleep; a little foam had collected in the corners of his lips, blue-tinted as if putrid. In the illumination of the night-light that foam seemed pink. An odor of ether and chloroform, in which

---

1 "Il Sodoma" was the nickname of the Renaissance painter also known as Giovanni Antonio Bazzi (1477-1549). His most famous depiction of Saint Sebastian is in the Uffizi, but there is another, presently in a museum in Pisa. According to Vasari's *Lives of the Arists*, Bazzi was known as Il Mattaccio [The Maniac], because of his gaudy dress, indecent behaviour and the menagerie of animals he kept in his house. He signed some of his paintings Sodona, which might have been his real surname; "Sodoma" is presumably a corruption thereof, but the author, like the jesters who corrupted it, undoubtedly has other associations in mind.

a fetid odor was dominant—the odor of typhoid fever—
was emitted by those gaping lips and those pinched nostrils.
Lady Viane passed me her flask. "Be careful," she said.
I pushed her hand away. I looked at Claudius. My eyes
were dry. Was he alive, or was he a cadaver? I was overwhelmed.

I felt Lady Viane's gaze weighing upon me. I examined
it in my turn. "Wait," that gaze seemed to say.

I waited.

Suddenly, Claudius appeared to raise himself up; with
one hand he moved his sheet away and parted his chemise,
which revealed his hairy chest. His lips drew back over his
black gums and, with a voice that one might have thought
distant, more like a sigh, he murmured: "Ophelius! Ophelius! Ophelius!"

He pronounced the name three times. Lady Viane had
seized one of the phials placed on the table, and made him
respire it. Claudius' head, which was injected with blood,
fell back on to the pillow, suddenly becoming earthen
again. Lady Viane buttoned the open chemise, pulled the
sheet over the chemise and looked at me.

"Ophelius?" I intimated.

The Comtesse put her finger over her lips; then, having
summoned the nun, she took my hand again and led me to
the back of the room. "Yes, Ophelius," she said, in a very
slow and very calm voice. "That's his malady; he's dying of
that Ophelius." Then, suddenly looking me straight in the
eyes, she said: "Would you like to see him?"

"Who? Ophelius?"

"Yes. Follow me." And she took me into the next room,
which Aiguor had made into his work-room.

After taking time to light a candle, she led me to a tall wrought-iron lectern, the wreckage of some destroyed abbey, which Claudius and I had discovered in the stable of an inn, in the hamlet of Thorp.

A large album bound in the fashion of a missal in Genoa velvet, with artistic metalwork, was placed on the lectern. I knew that missal too. It was a collection of photographs of the paintings of Claudius' favorite masters; with regard to each photograph, he had written with his own hand, on watered silk pages, verses inspired by the subject, or by the painter. Gustave Moreau opened the volume with his *Chimère*, and his young woman bearing the head of Orpheus; there was also his Salome dancing before Herod, the Sphinx, the Young Man and Death, and the marvelous poem of the Sirens, a reverie and a mysticism so elevated that one almost has to be a poet to grasp it and dream it. They were followed by a few Primitives and several Leonardo da Vincis, including *The Virgin of the Rocks*, that painting so closely related to that of Gustave Moreau across the centuries that separate them, Watteaus for the eighteenth century, then two or three Walter Cranes and Burne-Joneses, for the English esthetics.

Lady Viane searched rapidly, the candle in one hand, the other turning the pages . . . finally, she stopped. "Look," she said.

It was a large photograph that I knew already, which Claudius had brought back from Italy: a portrait of a strange and dolorous woman, perversely ideal, if one might express it thus, like a Gioconda penetrated by Ophelia, painted by the best-known of artists: Botticelli's *Primavera*.

In that regard, Claudius had written these lines, which I had not seen before:

In the depths of an old buried Tuscan palace
Is a portrait, sinister by dint of being strange,
An ideal and crazy head with the eyes of a wicked
  angel,
The oval and delicate face of a pale adolescent.

The frail, overly long neck tilts, as if enfeebled,
Under the weight of a high forehead half-veiled by
  a fringe
Of stiff long hair, russet-blonde, almost orange
And pricked by blue irises, signed Botticelli.

Under the photograph, the same hand had written the single word: *Ophelius.*

In what unhealthy and madly imaginative intrigue had I embarked in the wake of Lady Viane? It seemed to me that the rarefied air had become unbreathable; I was afraid of understanding, and did not want to understand.

"I don't know," I said to Lady Viane.

Lady Viane observed me; I felt the gaze of the evil woman penetrating me like an awl.

"Would you like to grasp it?" she said then. And, slowly setting her candle down on a table, "You're afraid—why? Myself, I know everything, and I'm a woman. You're a man and his friend; you ought to know everything."

What was she going to tell me? This time, Lady Viane was scaring me. By means of what horrible secret, revealed, regarding Claudius' life, was she about to kill my esteem and my amity for that poor fellow?

"It's necessary that you know everything in order to care for him in consequence, if I'm summoned to London or Spain. I might have to leave tomorrow, at a moment's notice."

And when she had sat down, with her elbow on the corner of the table, pale and delicate in her black dress, in the light of that single candle in that immense obscure room, Lady Viane began.

And when she had told me the story, in which the honor and morality of my friend foundered, she concluded, pointing at the strange photograph: "Claudius has always had a mania for that face, for that smile and those eyes, which you'll find in the engraving at the head of his volume of verses. It was an obsession, a malady. By that smile and those eyes, when he encountered them in reality, animated by the charm of life, exasperated and impassioned as he was, he was subjugated, defenseless against himself and his desire. That intoxicating face, fatality dictated that it was a man who bore it, whence his strange passion, of which he is dying—but we shall save him, shall we not?"

The Englishwoman had said that coldly, in a slow voice, almost with a smile, svelte and velvety in her somber dress, like a nocturnal sphinx or the black swallow of ruins. She kept her two emerald eyes, which were gleaming, fixed upon me; her calm was exasperating; I sensed that she was lying, and lying brazenly, while conscious and proud of her lie. For two pins, I would have strangled the woman.

"Never," I burst forth, abruptly. "Never will I admit the possibility of such a passion on the part of Claudius.

"How, then, do you explain all the sketches with which this house is filled, all in Claudius' hand and all representing, uniquely and always, the face of this Ophelius, as he called himself—the name written in that album, and those verses on the other side of that page?"

"Monomania! The artist he was might have been fascinated by a type, the character of a rare and strange physiognomy, but I too have drawers filled with studies of the heads of men and boys, and you wouldn't impute, I hope . . ."

"But you're a painter," the Englishwoman interrupted, phlegmatically. "Claudius isn't."

I was afraid. Had I not seen Claudius, during a common sojourn in Paris, become absolutely infatuated with a Great Dane in the Jardin d'Acclimation, to the point of going every day for a week to despoil the merchants in the garden and spend hours there cramming his momentary passion with treats, that magnificent hound sold a month later for two thousand francs to the Sismondo brothers of Vienna, cousins of the Sismondos of Paris? On his part, all extravagances were possible. Nevertheless, I still had my doubts.

"How is it that I've never seen this man you're talking about?" I objected to the Englishwoman.

"First of all, do you ever see anything?" she replied, coldly. "Two years ago, at Yport, you remained for three months in the company of a woman who adored you, without even noticing it. Don't worry," she added, with a malicious smile, "it wasn't me. You've seen this Ophelius a hundred times, but have you looked at him? You haven't even noticed the individual in question—absolutely remarkable, however, with that flaxen hair and that strange smile. I only spent two days here last year, at about this time, with Oscar Grune, the esthetic painter, who had come to obtain authorization from Claudius to illustrate his poem *Le Roi d'Ys*, a commission from Hachette, and we both distinguished this Ophelius, very clearly.

"In any case, Aiguor took care to point him out to us himself; he took us aboard the ship on which the boy was about to leave the following day, the *Saint-Maxient*. He even had him come down from the yard-arms to introduce him to us. 'Isn't he beautiful, that animal?' he repeated. 'Isn't he beautiful, even too beautiful for a man?' During his three-month sojourn on land, that sailor was sometimes his fishing companion, sometimes his model; they manned the same boat together. In addition, Claudius addressed him as *tu*—but you were never there, and if you had been there, you have eyes in order not to see."

"And the boy is dead?"

"A fortnight ago, as I told you. He was found at low tide, drowned in the breakwaters of the jetties. Ophelius! His name predestined him to that tragic end. He had a large wound on the back of his neck. Was he injured in falling? Had someone struck him first and thrown him into the water afterwards? A mystery. The fever took hold of Claudius immediately after the discovery of the body, and hasn't quit him since."

"And you suspect . . . ?"

"No one," replied Lady Viane, with a challenge in her glaucous eyes. "And you, what do you suspect? What do you glimpse in this adventure, bizarre, to say the least?"

"A lie and a treason."

"A lie! Do you think so?"

And as if to give me the lie himself, Claudius' voice rose up in the room next door, bringing us in a gasp, pronounced three times, the name of *Ophelius, Ophelius, Ophelius!*

You see, the green gaze of the Englishwoman seemed to say, in lighting up. *Ophelius!* Abruptly, I picked up the candle, and, having risen to my feet, I approached the mysterious portrait.

Lady Viane had risen to her feet too, following with a cruel curiosity the increasing distress in my features.

The *Primavera* was there, vaguely animated under the vacillating light of the candle, upright beneath her long hair dotted with anemones and branches with ramifications like madrepores, charming with the distant softness of her bleak eyes, and smiling, in the slender oval of her face, her strange, sensual, exasperating smile.

Above the *Primavera*, as thin and pale as her, the obstinate head of Lady Viane was smiling the same enigmatic smile and undulating her winding lips with the same magnetic gaze, drowned in her starry pupils.

"Did the man have that gaze and that smile?" I asked Lady Viane.

"That smile and those eyes."

"Then it's of you and not of him that my friend Claudius is dying—of you, Lady Ethereld, for that portrait is you, and it's impossible that two such perfect resemblances have existed simultaneously, in the same epoch, under the same skies."

"Truly?"

And, very calmly, she leaned over the *Primavera* in order to see better; then, with a sigh: "There is indeed a strange resemblance."

"It's of you that he's dying, believe me, Milady."

"Or of him."

"But if it were him, since it's him, it's you. He has only followed, crazed and dazzled, a vague resemblance; and was not that phantom, always chased but never attained, you, always your living image, unerased and ineradicable in that miserable fellow's sick mind, deranged by you?"

"And how do you know that it wasn't that boy he loved through my resemblance?"

"Oh, that's too much!" I cried, beside myself, at the risk of waking the invalid. "Claudius saw you for the first time in Florence, four years ago—in Florence, from which he brought back that photograph, which one might think is yours . . . and today's Ophelius was then thirteen years old. You can see that it's impossible."

"Everything is possible. We all love, we each pursue, down here, a type, an ideal, through all analogous types, until the day when we believe that we've found it . . . for happiness is a belief. That type, my opinion is that Claudius encountered it in the Ophelius whose name he gasps in his fever. Why does he never invoke that of Lady Viane? That type, assuredly, he loved for a day, for an evening, in me; for one thing, I have only ever pleased the refined, the depraved, the dillettanti—the others, it's almost horror that I inspire in them." And her arm brushed mine insolently. "Then again, I who am speaking to you, have only ever loved a resemblance. Why should Claudius not be like me?"

"A resemblance, you!"

"And yours, yes, that's the way it is . . . for Claudius resembles you. You didn't know that? Oh, don't worry, it was finished between the two of us before having begun. Yes,

168

I loved Claudius before knowing you, because of what he had of you, whom I didn't know: that tawny gold moustache, those dark, ultramarine, questing eyes, that air of adventure and insolence—the ensemble, in a word, of a type that one adores, and of which one dreams; and when I encountered you with him, two years ago, it was to you that my desire went. But men like you don't see. Today, I don't hate you. I'll let you alone, but I wanted you to know everything. With that blue gaze and that hair, such unconsciousness! Oh, you're well-equilibrated, very *together*, as we say in the Three Kingdoms; you, at least, are not a *Primavera* man, not an Ophelius man."

And, with an untranslatable gesture, she added: "And it's really a pity." Then, abruptly: "Good night. It's the eleventh night I've been keeping vigil, and this evening, frankly, it really is your turn."

And, seizing the candle in one hand and lifting up the train of her dress with the other, she plunged into the shadows and vanished.

I groped my way into Claudius' room, guided through the darkness by the luminous embrasure of the door.

I spent the night there with the nurse, reflecting on Lady Viane's singular story and her even more singular confession, in which, arrogantly, with the audacity of a courtesan, she had unveiled herself and offered herself to me, Aiguor's friend, next door to the room in which that friend was dying.

Was it for that reason that she had brought me here? I had avoided the first trap, but the second? What was she still planning against me? She hated me, that was certain, but had she loved me, as she said? Had that confession not been a treason, a bait extended to my vanity? To be my mistress—of me, her enemy, in the invalid Claudius' own house—what a pride and what a triumph for that perverse woman! I feared and feverishly desired the break of day. After the conversation of that night, what would our first encounter, our first conversation, be?

Agitated as I was, vanquished by the fatigue of my previous night spent on the railway, I fell asleep at about four o'clock in the morning. When I woke up at eight o'clock, my stomach tortured by hunger—in my preoccupation with Claudius' condition and Lady Viane's strange stories, I had completely forgotten to dine the previous evening—the valet de chambre brought me a note from Comtesse Ethereld on a tray.

I had recognized at first glance the *sale salax, audax* and the dolphin of the device.

A friend is asking for me in Vienna. Knowing that you are with Claudius, I depart tranquil. Forget. Your Viane.

The strange creature!

"Has she really gone?" I asked Pierre.

"Who?"

"Madame la Comtesse."

"This morning, by the six o'clock train, while Monsieur was asleep. Madame la Comtesse came in to say adieu to Monsieur Claudius; she even wanted to kiss Monsieur on the forehead, in spite of the nurse, who did not want to be the cause of fever; she has no fear of anything, Madame la Comtesse. Madame waited for Monsieur to arrive before leaving; she had announced her departure yesterday to the servants—Madame did not inform Monsieur?"

"Yes, yes," I replied, to cut short the domestic's reflections.

She had lost the game; she had gone—but her flight was a victory, for in departing, she left a poisoned dart vibrating in my heart, and in that heart an open wound that nothing could heal: an agonizing, purulent, profound wound envenomed by a suspicion, and God knows what suspicion, against Claudius' honor.

✳

"And that was that," Armand concluded, planting himself directly in front of me, his eyes shining, as if luminous in the gloom.

Day was beginning to dawn. The lamellated shutters were already striping the opaque black of the casements with gray bars; in the distance, on the plateau of farmland, a cock crowed.

A sudden chill descended upon my shoulders: the chill of the morning and the long sleepless night. I perceived that Armand was quite pale; I took pity on his pallor and, in spite of my curiosity, still illuminated, regarding Comtesse Ethereld, who had disappeared from the story too suddenly for my taste, I stood up, slightly awkwardly, finding nothing to say except a banal remark.

"Terrible, these women of the Anglo-Saxon race, the blonde race. The sharp cruelty of blondes isn't a literary invention. The North is full of Lady Vianes."

"No," Harel replied. "Lady Vianes are everywhere; blonde, brunette or red-haired, Lady Viane is woman, *the* woman, the true woman, the Eve of *Genesis*, Flaubert's Ennoïa, the eternal enemy, the dancer who drinks the blood of prophets, Salome, Herodias, the impure beast, Bestia. When she kills us physically, she's called Debauchery; when she kills us morally, she's called Hatred, and sometimes Love."

Hylas

The tales you tell will be a lie,
The charm will survive having dreamed them.

HE walked for hours along the dusty road, his delicate feet scratched by the pebbles. He had fled the palace as if in a dream; in his haste to follow the negress who had opened its doors to him, in his joy in going down the obscure stairways behind her, which twisted spirally in the damp heart of the rock, he had not paid any heed to the heavy jewels that were now bruising his big toes. Entirely delighted to be free, he had run straight ahead through the flat countryside, the silent and bleak landscape oppressed by the heavy days of August, and now, in the sunlit solitude of the plain, before the monotonous gray somnolence of the olive groves and the vast fields of buckwheat, fear took possession of liberty.

At first he had run, lifting up his hyacinth robes, whose heavy golden fringes flapped over his calves. Now, his face pale and his lips dry, he was trudging rather than walking through the countryside. The sculpted rings around his ankles were clinking, and digging into his flesh continually. Large droplets of sweat were running down his cheeks, and the soaked cloth of his ample tunic stuck to his shoulders, while his long black hair, from which the diadem had fallen, uncurled and soiled, hung down over his eyes, which were astonished for the first time by suffering.

Where was he going? He did not know himself, having never, since his most tender infancy, emerged from the high halls of the palace, paved with mosaics and refreshed with jets of perfumed water. Never, except to go and lean over the terraces on certain evenings, between the gods with the hawks' heads, and from there, under the surveillance of two black eunuchs, to watch the sun setting behind the mountains of Syrenaica.

It was there that he had heard for the first time a marvelous voice rising up in his soul, one evening at dusk, before the melancholy splendor of the sun falling behind the horizon. The sky was the blue-green of turquoise and the sun had sunk behind the high violet wall of the mountains, whose illuminated crests where still shining in the roseate shadow—the same rosy hue as his heels, rubbed with powder—and the voice had spoken of unknown lands and profound forests, cool springs in the clearings of great woods haunted by laughter and voices; and a despair had gripped the child of living thus, imprisoned beneath the painted vaults of the royal castle, as well a reckless desire to see the distant regions that he remembered having known in other times; and since then, he had taken pleasure in listening to the voice.

Woods, green freshnesses where sunbeams, leaf by leaf, picked out large blue flowers, like those exhausted messengers sometimes brought, whose calices, watered night and day, faded slowly in vases, where those blue flowers swayed in garlands around enormous trees in the open air, in the singing perfumed shade of tall chattering reeds, in the mystery of forests haunted by birds and fleeting forms . . . and the visions evoked grew despotically, imposing themselves on the child, returning obsessively at every dusk, at the hour when, emerging from steam-baths, he came to lean over the flat landscape, between the porphyry and jasper columns of the sacred porticos, raising their bronze pilasters bristling with golden palms over the terraces.

With the result that he had fled, joyfully seizing the first opportunity offered, when the negress, one black finger posed over the white enamel smile of her mouth, had slipped into the low room where he was drifting off to sleep, and with a mute gesture had indicated the sandy plains and the distant high mountains, behind the large bay closed by a metal lattice. He had not made any movement of stupor or dread, and, like all intuitive individuals, reassured by the gesture that pointed the way to the land of dreams, and escape, he had got up silently and, with a smile on his lips, he had followed the benevolent messenger of liberty confidently through the subterranean passages and crypts.

Where was he now? He had looked back, but the royal citadel where his childhood had passed had disappeared, swept away, effaced from the horizon like the designs in colored sand traced every morning on the flagstones of the palace by the hands of slaves. Effaced, the citadel and its high walls, where temples were stacked; effaced, the sheer rock with smooth shiny walls, to which the red brick towers of the palace clung like gigantic bats, the one called the Swans' Tower, the one called Heracles' Tower, and Astarté's Tower, where his room was: his room lined with pink and green bricks, shiny and varnished like precious stones, whose large lance-latticed bay overlooked the ravine.

All that had disappeared, melted like wax in the intense heat under the glare of the white sky; ears were cracking in the stubble, and in the silence broken by the chattering of cicadas, the child was still fleeing in the direction of the mountains, exhausted, dusty, his feet bleeding, giving the impression, in his violet robe constellated with jewels and with heavy bracelets on his bare arms, of a little idol escaped from his temple.

Had the voice lied, then, the voice that had promised him bunches of blue flowers and carpets of moss in the shade of great trees?

And the despair of the fugitive, and his growing terror was augmented, at every step, by the incessant retreat of the fleeing mountains of Syrenaica in front of him.

The white sky has become red; an immense fire is setting the crests of the mountains ablaze; the air has cooled. At the feet of the tall silky and noisy reeds, long silvery plumes where the green ribbon of leaves unfurls, the child is lying down; his arms, mortally fatigued, repose on the moss, and soaking in the cold water of the spring, his feet, bloodied all the way to the ankles, have finally become white again; large blue irises, a glimmer in their moist calices, are fluttering like wings in the evening breeze, and a turbulent host of flies is vibrating and humming, like a handful of wheat in a winnowing-basket.

The voice did not lie; the child has his dream and the shadow of the mountain envelops him maternally, like a mantle of coolness.

175

His eyes astonished and delighted, Hylas admires, contemplates and recognizes the landscape glimpsed and divined in his dreams, with the intoxication of a young god finally rediscovering Olympus after exile.

And yet, a regret claws his heart and obsesses him: that of the old palace where, like the son of a king, although a slave, he has grown up, obscurely, in the warmth of odorant steam-baths and the cool solitude of large paved halls with mats extended. Jets of water sang there day and night in fountains, and he, abandoned to the care of eunuchs and master bathers with hands as soft as the hands of women, spent long days half-naked under veils, his elbows on cushions, his eyelids tinted with kohl and his face and arms perfumed; there were Egyptian greasepaints and rare, heady and subtle essences, brought at great expense from distant Asia in silver ewers.

In the evenings, an old mage with the head of a bird of prey came to sit beside him and tell him stories. There was only the question of amours between humans and gods, of heroes as handsome as the dawn riding dragons and crossing the seas in order to rescue nymphs with eyes the color of waves, who were also princesses; the thunderbolt disguised itself as a swan therein, in order to seduce a queen; the moon descended from the sky therein to kiss a sleeping shepherd on the lips, and voices sang under water to entice and bed in death a blond-haired youth named Hylas, like him.

Hylas liked that last story best of all. Did the voice that had called him out of the citadel into the coolness of these unknown places want to drown him in the spring? But the child had so much joy in respiring the open air, far from the high walls where his childhood had languished, a prisoner, that he forgot his vague terrors and could not help smiling; for he was thinking within himself about lessons in music and dance, which he had escaped for the next day, and all the days that followed; for every morning, before he was bathed, perfumed and coiffed like a woman, two Greeks, two captives, had been introduced to his presence, one of whom, under the anxious eye of a eunuch, had taught him to sing verses while playing the lyre, and the other to dance rhythmically, arching his body and lifting his robe like a courtesan.

And the child had a horror of those lessons.

What a strange life was his in that sumptuous and bleak prison—and for what destiny was he being educated thus? Sometimes—once or twice a month, at the most—black men with their hips girdled by a loincloth came into his room like a whirlwind and knocked him down, flattening him with his belly to the ground, before the footsteps of a man of exceedingly tall stature, in the prime of life, who marched over human bodies extended like a living carpet.

He was a very handsome man, strangely pale, with a curly black beard gleaming with essences; necklaces of amber, emerald and jade clinked on his breast; long green tones danged from his ears like teardrops, and beneath his brown eyelids, rubbed with greasepaint, his eyes glittered harshly, full of an immense ennui; a tiara was mounted in his black and wavy hair.

The child was frightened of that jewel-bedecked man, who looked at him for a long time without saying a word, and sometimes caressed him with a gesture of his hand, heavy with rings, pressing on the nape of his neck, and then withdrew, as silently as he had come.

The others called him the King. The King—and there was an anguished expression in their eyes, and their voices trembled with terror—the King who was omnipotent.

That man could do anything.

That was why Hylas had fled.

[Note: In Greek mythology Hylas was a youth who served as Heracles' companion and lover. Heracles took Hylas with him with him on the *Argo*, but during the journey he was kidnapped by water-nymphs, who fell in love with him, and disappeared; Heracles searched for him but could not find him, and the ship sailed on without him.]

Day's End

In memory of Jean Lombard.[1]

THE triumphant mob had traversed the palace, and beneath the high deserted cupolas, illuminated by the yellow and blue light of the stained-glass windows, pools of blood were reddening here and there, damp and shiny, in which feet had slipped, bearing bloody imprints further on and through the galleries.

A great silence weighed upon the Hebdomon, a silence of death interrupted by distant clamors, cries of joy on the part of Greens crushing Blues in some corner of the great city where—who can tell?—the Patriarch was perhaps sitting in Saint Sophia, devoted to the execration of Caloyers.[2]

---

1 The novelist Jean Lombard (1854-1891) wrote some of the most graphic of the lush historical fantasies that were among the pearls of Decadent prose, including *Byzance* [Byzantium] (1890), set in the eighth century, during the first crisis of iconoclasm, when there was a popular rebellion against the worship of "graven images", including Panaghias (icons of the Madonna).
2 Caloyers were Orthodox monks. The Green and the Blues were two of the teams involved in the chariot-races in the circus of Byzantium, and the names were transferred to their supporters, which became significant of different political factions; tensions between those factions first erupted in 532 A.D. in the so-called Nika riots,

Invaded shortly before by an ignoble and variegated crowd of fish-merchants, boatmen of the Golden Horn, street-porters, chariot-drivers from the circus and, mingled with the Orthodox rebels, Syrians, black-clad Jews and even nomads shod in sandals secured around the calf with cords of straw, the palace had escaped pillage. Popular fury had progressed straight to murder, to massacre, and without lingering over the riches heaped up there centuries before by the Justinians and Theodosius, ran through Byzantium, avid for executions, drunk on carnage, ancient rancor and prompt vengeance.

There was, therefore, a sequence of high solitary rooms, some languidly draped with flowery and green fabrics, others painted from top to bottom with holy icons or a monumental Jesus clad in a pink tunic sown with pearly crosses, blessing with a hieratical gesture peacocks, lambs and even unicorns, mingled in strange foliage with pouncing panthers. Further on there were giant Panaghias in the gem-studded dalmatics on Byzantine Empresses, their foreheads starred with emeralds and rubies, with enormous resplendent aureoles behind their rosy faces, both pure and replete; and the sacred image extended all the way to the vaults, under the opaline sparkle of rose-windows, and around the pure Virgin, innumerable heads of Angels and Dominations were heaped up, flocking in a rainbow of multicolored wings, precious mosaics embedded in the cement of the walls, coated with a golden varnish.

---

in which tens of thousands were killed; the Emperor Justinian was almost overthrown but he rallied and fought back; imperial troops led by Belisarius stormed the Hippodrome, slaughtering the rioters. The present story is set in a later, carefully unspecified, period of history; its events do not correspond to any actual historical event.

And everywhere, in the vaulted corridors with falling drapes scarcely brushed by the troubled light of the stained-glass windows, as in the semi-vaulted rooms with ceiling cupolas painted with irradiant evangelical figurations, there were heaps of rare and precious objects with scintillating coruscations, lamps and lamp-stands, metal-encrusted stalls, illuminated gospels bound in nacre and ivory, reliquaries foliaged in silver and gold, and beaten copper coffers studded with gems.

All of that sparkled vaguely in the mystery of interminable rooms that suddenly appeared in the embrasures of tapestries, still sliding on their silver rods. And here and there in the sumptuous abandonment of that palace, which an inconceivable panic had emptied in broad daylight, at the corner of a pillar of jasper and porphyry, or under the altar-piece of some holy icon, a human form was silhouetted, lying in the folds of a chlamys; that was some cup-bearer or maidservant murdered by the rebels, or the two stiffened feet of a eunuch slain in his green robe.

And throughout the Hebdomon, cadavers were strewn, lying one or two in each room, guards in their coats of imbricated mail, servants collapsed in a flood of curtains, all with red patches beneath their necks or armpits, where the blood had flowed; and the moist, shiny red pools were multiplied thus infinitely beneath the high cupolas and the ceiling mosaics. The floor-tiles were pock-marked at intervals by the gleam of a broken sword-blade or the gold-rimmed orb of a helmet; they were the only traces of the frenzied passage of the Blues through the dwelling of the Basileus Autocrator.

Outside, beneath the implacably pure sky of the cities of the Orient, the mob's jeers had fallen silent. The rumors died down, and, gently raising the awning of violet silk, a fresh breeze blowing from the Golden Horn circulated under the porticos and penetrated into the palace, and with it, a heady perfume of laurier-roses and heliotropes: the perfumes of the imperial garden, laid out in terraces facing the sea.

At that moment, a small round and curly head with a black and pug-nose face, broadly illuminated by a white-toothed smile, and as if holed by two large enamel eyes, emerged hesitantly from a pile of fabrics, a flood of decorated silks draped over a large sandalwood box. The head looked around prudently, and the thin torso, patinaed like old bronze, slowly extended, the palms of the hands flat on the tiles, and the child, standing up, searched the sequence of rooms with a rapid glance.

It was a young negro slave employed in the kitchens. During the invasion of the Hebdomon by the populace and the massacre of the servants he had hastily climbed up from the commons to the apartments of the senior domestic staff and had hidden there, lying face down in the corner of the dimly-lit room, where the vertiginous irruption of the mob had spared him. Now, slender and naked, his ears alert, ready to flatten himself on the floor at the slightest sound, the black child moved with infinite care through the silent rooms.

At first the curiosity of a young animal caused him to sniff and palpate each cadaver, but soon he no longer paused, and even avoided them, making detours in order not to bump into their already-cold flesh, and when their rigidity chanced to block a doorway, he braced himself on his little bare feet and leapt over them.

In the distance, Byzantium was still tranquil. By some unexplained mystery, a deathly silence weighed upon the city, and the child continued his solitary excursion through the Hebdomon, his eyes widened by the splendors of the images of Jesus and the Panaghias, already indifferent to the dead.

He arrived thus at a trilobate doorway closed by a high plunging curtain of thick hyacinth brocade with a floral design in gold and mat silver; having lifted it, the child stopped.

This time, it was too much for him.

Illuminated by daylight from a high cupola, a room opened up roundly, with conical depths decorated with magical mosaics; malachite, onyx and sardonyx rose-windows alternated there with immense peacocks of gems embedded in the walls. Here and there, huge cornelian lilies were displayed in sprays, extending toward the vault, and five jasper steps rounded out at the back of the room, in front of a conical niche with ribs covered in a thick layer of nacre. At the top of the steps was a strange chair, very straight, with bronze armrests, a back in the form of a tiara. Around it, there was a cascade of scarlet drapes and violet fabrics, like frozen silver decorated with golden eagles.

And from the threshold of the door to the steps of the throne, this time, there was a carpet of cadavers; the room was full of them. They had fallen so closely adjacent to one another that the child could no longer find anywhere to place his feet.

First, like a harvest of reeds, there was an entire row of eunuchs, fallen there, face downwards, in their long robes of green silk. Then there were the dalmatics, in proudly-colored tapestries representing Biblical scenes, of massacred Hegumens and Archimandrites, and here and there, slipped from their heads, pointed toques with heron-plumes and skullcaps lined with pearls, the head-dresses of the holy anointed and great dignitaries.

They were all scattered, struck from behind, orientated in the direction of the throne, toward which their flight had been aimed, and clots of blood speckled the softness of their flesh—the rubicund or albuminous flesh of gelded prelates or plump freedmen, fat overflowing bellies and the large rumps of eunuchs swelling beneath cloth that a swift kick in passing would have ripped.

Like over-ripe watermelons, those paunchy cadavers were piled up all the way to the back of the room, rising up the steps of the throne. There, such an efflorescence of giant lilies spread an entire hecatomb of slain candidates and cubicularies, breasts thrust forward and heads titled back, in a rigid tangle of long lances and broad golden blades. They had fallen while fighting in serried ranks around the throne, their rude faces striped with tawny moustaches, their eyes wide open beneath the golden orbs of helmets, their oozing reddened breast plates still proclaiming loudly the heroism of their demise.

Above all that butchered flesh, beginning to stink, in the stifling gloom of that mysterious mute room, with vague scintillations glinting here and there, the throne offered the amazing spectacle of its emptiness.

At that moment, an enormous clamor erupted around the Hebdomon: an atrocious clamor of triumph, as if departing from every quarter of Byzantium. It was prolonged and reverberated by all the echoes awakened in the galleries, and the black child, having rushed instinctively out of the room to one of the bays of the external portico, saw and understood why the throne was empty in the room beneath the high cupola filled with the motionless cadavers of eunuchs, hegumens, bishops and soldiers with lions' muzzles.

Down there, way down there at the foot of the Hippodrome, raising the oval of its walkway, perforated by columns and populated by statues, over the blue of the Golden Horn, there was an open area, swarming with a howling and variegated crowd, incessantly pouring forth from the corners of streets and the quadrangles of squares, and everywhere, from the terraces of the houses, and the perimeter of the domes of churches to the nine domes of Saint Sophia, crouching like a colossal sentinel at the foot of the walls of the Grand Palace, innumerable heads, scarves and raised arms were undulating in apotheosis in the blond amber of the dusk, and thousands of shrill cries fused to the rhythmic accompaniment of applause.

From the edge of the quays of the Golden Horn, extending like a sea of lapis to the luminous horizon, to the terraces of the neighboring houses, stacked in crude gray cubes at the foot of the gardens of the Hebdomon, intoxicated people were swarming and howling, a crazy admixture of men, women and children hoisted and shoved up to the entablatures of ledges above the heads, bristling chaotically with banners and crosses; and all those eyes were gazing at the Hippodrome, and all those hands were applauding, extended toward the site of the Games.

A man of the people with the face of a tiger had just scaled the marble pedestal of the equestrian statue of Justinian. His arms steeped in blood to the elbows, like a butcher, the man was now climbing the gold-plated boots of the bronze emperor, and, other bloody hands having handed him from below and enormous cup in which a strange flower was floating, the man with the bestial face raised that cup above his head against the blue of the sky and, laughing, offered it to Justinian.

And the crowd exhaled a great cry; and the black child clutched the silk of the awning in order not to stumble.

In the cup, offered thus to the founder of the Slavonic dynasty, the mouth gaping disdainfully and tugged at the corners by a superhuman dolor, he had just recognized the exsanguinated head of the Augusta.

Disheveled and bleak, she seemed to be weeping in her blood, still haloed at the temples by the sapphires and sardonyxes of the Imperial Sarikion.

The Legend of the Three Princesses

For Mademoiselle Marguerite Moréno.[1]

THEIR names were Tharsile, Argine and Blismode. All of them had different mothers, but they resembled one another and were reminiscent of one another by virtue of the long slenderness of their feet, the almost disturbing delicacy of their fingers and the nacreous transparency of their skin—a skin as if infiltrated with pale azure by the blue of their veins—characteristics appropriate to a race of old Viking kings, former pagans now baptized, of which they were the last flowers in full bloom.

Tharsile was, however, distinguished by wide blue eyes, very dark, and heavy brown tresses always anointed with essences, and her immoderate love of perfumes. Argine, on the contrary, had the gray and piercing eyes of an eagle beneath delicate eyebrows, as if drawn by a pencil; her hair was a blonde so pale that one might have thought her crowned with faded old gold, always sparkling with rubies and carbuncles; she walked as if weighed down by the

---

1 Marguerite Moreno (1871-1948) was the stage-name of the actress, born Marguerite Monceau, who married the Symbolist writer Marcel Schwob in 1900, five years before his death. She subsequently became a successful film star.

bulk of strange and barbaric jewels—that was her caprice. Meanwhile, the last, Blismode, with chestnut-red hair and large violet irises speckled with pink beneath fluttering pupils with long lashes, only took pleasure in flowers and among the swans with gold-circled necks in old parks.

Tharsile liked sumptuous brocades and silken drapes woven with argyrose and pearls. Argine preferred red fabrics, crimson satins and scarlet samites, and also long green robes in which the troubled reflection of waves seemed to be mirrored. Blismode, on the contrary, only appeared draped in supple and soft white silks, sparsely decorated with fine golden arabesques. None of the three, brought up severely by an aged and suspicious warrior king, had ever quit the palace, where, passive and haughty, they each awaited the royal fiancé that their father had chosen, either reciting old Latin prose at the lectern or embroidering hennins for the Virgin or altar-cloths, in the long winter evenings.

During the long days of summer, the three princesses had the custom of going to sit in their father's orchard and going to sleep there in the shade of a large apple tree, snowy pink in April and golden green in August. The orchard, situated at the extremity of the park, was surrounded by high walls; the grass there was brilliant with violets and jonquils, and among the corollas, to the murmur of the air vibrant with the hum of bees, Tharsile, Argine and Blismode slept.

They slept with their heads posed between the roots of the tree, and the distant flower-beds, replete with yellow lilies, giant angelicas and hollyhocks, sent them delightful dreams on the gusts of the wind, born of the souls of flowers. Guards watched over them from without the walls, but none of them knew the faces of the princesses; blind pages served them and, except for those stony faces, the King's three daughters had never seen the face of a man.

No, not quite none, since the wrinkled face of the old gardener of the royal domain was familiar to them. He was a poor individual, broken and curbed by the years, half fallen into second childhood, and whose presence the King's indifference tolerated in the sacred enclosure. He lodged at the extremity of the orchard in a wretched cabin backed up against the wall, and not far from his dwelling there was an old well with an overgrown rim and a little slate roof ornamented with ironwork, whose strangely cold and pure water often attracted the three princesses. They made a game of maneuvering the old well's buckets themselves, making the pulley and the chains screech, and when they had drunk deep of the ice-cold water, they sometimes stayed there for some time, leaning over the hole and anxiously awakening its echoes. Then they ran away with a loud rustling of skirts and hid behind the rugose trunks of the apple trees, and the old man, brought out of his humbled lodgings by their cries, thought he had been dreaming.

On one June evening, warmer than the others, they had a singular encounter beside their well. An unknown young man, almost still a child in his youthful slimness, was standing there, leaning against it. Almost naked in the rags of cloth that covered him from his waist to his knees, he dazzled Tharsile, Argine and Blismode simultaneously with the radiance of a triumphant beauty. He was tall and slender with muscular bare arms, which he was holding crossed over his breast, and his shirt of coarse cloth was gaping, unfastened over a powerful neck. A young athlete . . . his flesh, bitten by sunburn, was downy and gilded everywhere.

Nonchalantly, he crossed the most beautiful legs in the world, and, as proud as a young animal, inclined toward the three princesses a blond tousled head, with a delicate face, and eyes molded by malice but nevertheless penetrated with an adorable languor.

The three princesses blinked in confusion before the gaze of his profound emerald irises. With a charming intuition, he maneuvered the cable of the well, brought up the bucket and offered them a drink. Then, a voice having called to him from the cabin, he bowed, still without saying a word, smiled, and disappeared. He left three freshly-cut flowers on the edge of the well: a blue iris, a red poppy and an asphodel.

Tharsile took the iris, Argine the poppy and Blismode the asphodel.

The following night, each of the princesses had a dream, and in that identically bizarre dream, each of them was walking in a mysterious illuminated garden and encountered, leaning lightly against the bronze bowl of a lively fountain, an unknown man of divine grace, as naked as an Eros—an Eros with blindfolded eyes and two peacock feathers oscillating over his shoulders in the guise of wings—smiled at them and offered them flowers.

The next day, Blismode, Argine and Tharsile returned to wander in the paternal orchard, and, toward evening, chanced to direct their footsteps toward the old well—but they did not find the stranger there. He was a great-nephew of the old gardener who had come on foot from the remote depths of the countryside to enroll in the royal militia, and the King's soldiers had come at dawn to collect him, and had taken him away with them.

Tharsile, whose corsage was embalmed by a blue iris, fell into a mortal languor.

As she deteriorated from day to day, the King was worried, and on the advice of seers, decided to send the Princess to a region of woods and mountains. Argine and Blismode accompanied their sister. An old citadel, half demolished, overlooking thirty leagues of forests and fifty leagues of mountains, became their place of exile. A torrent roared with a noise like a forge under the arches of a bridge spanning a ravine, and a noisy pine-wood quivered like an organ two hundred feet above the crenellations where the beauties came to lean their elbows in the evening. On the horizon were glaciers, blue- and red-tinted by turns, ardently ablaze or as cold as steel.

The dark-haired Tharsile with the languid blue eyes grew paler by the hour, and did not want to be cured. One night, when insomnia tormented her more than usual and she was meditating, leaning on her window-sill gazing at the stars with a void in her heart, she suddenly shivered at the sound of singing, guzlas and violas far away in the forest. It was the music of some bohemians on the march, and among all those voices repeating vague refrains in chorus, there was one that attracted her, delightfully pure and sad, which she had never heard before but which she recognized nevertheless. The voice had been extinct for some time while she was still listening for it; the cold of the dawn surprised her, attentively leaning over the larches in the ravine.

The next day, the Princess interrogated her sisters adroitly about the music she had heard. Argine and Blismode looked at her in amazement, but some time after that, a chance remark having informed the princesses that the gardener's great-nephew, the handsome youth glimpsed in the park, had deserted from the King's army in order to join the bohemians, Tharsile no longer doubted for a moment that she had not dreamed the voice she had heard. Her melancholy became more profound; and then, one morning, on going into her bedroom, her maidservants and her sisters did not find her.

What had become of the dreamy invalid? All searches proved futile; she had vanished like smoke.

Thus disappeared Tharsile, the dark-haired eldest daughter of the old King.

Argine and Blismode protested their innocence in vain; they could never disculpate themselves in his eyes.

The two disgraced princesses were sent to a distant convent in the provinces, a cloister of Poor Clares situated at the extremity of the realm, on the high plateau of cliffs bordering the sea. It was a harsh and barren land, all heaths of gorse and briars, whose dismal expanses were perpetually swept by the westerly wind, and upon which the low gray clouds weighed down like a lid: a land where the sun rarely shone, and as if haunted by specters in the mist and the wind.

The only distraction the two exiled princesses had, in between so many masses and prayers, was to go for walks escorted by processionary nuns through the gorse and the briars. Sometimes they went as far as the edge of the cliff, and looked over, three hundred feet below them, at miserable convict laborers occupied in extracting marl and hollowing out a difficult channel in rock hardened by the sea.

Seen thus, the men appeared no taller than their little fingers; they toiled in the foam and the mist, with arms and torsos bare, and the two princesses thought vaguely about the nudity of the beautiful young man they had once encountered in the orchard, and it was necessary almost to drag them away from the melancholy spectacle.

One summer's day, when they had come to parade their ennui above the channel, they were greatly surprised no longer to see the crew of workmen, but in their place, scattered among the rocks, groups of men with hard white limbs, evidently barbarians drying their nudity in the sun. Others emerged, half-engulfed by the waves, and by the effort of their muscular arms, raised their dazzling torsos above the surface. A line of ships was immobilized at sea; the pirates had dropped anchor and were indulging themselves in the delights of bathing.

The frightened nuns wanted to go back to the cloister in all haste, but Argine and Blismode could not tear their eyes away from the beautiful naked barbarians. Argine, especially, thought that she recognized one of them: the sleekest and most handsome of them all, with his long mane displayed to the sun—evidently their chief.

The next day, when the indignant superior went into Argine's cell, she no longer found the Princess there. Like Tharsile, Argine had disappeared.

As for Blismode, recalled in all haste to the presence of her father the King and shut away in the highest tower of the royal castle, she was agitated by strange presentiments. A bold pirate, it was said, had set out on campaign, and was marching rapidly toward the city, to which he intended to lay siege with an innumerable army of pagans. He was bringing in his war chariots, it was said, two princesses, captive and glad to be, two royal lovers who had betrayed their fatherland and their race for him. Their names were not pronounced, but Blismode had a presentiment that they were her sisters, just as she had divined that the handsome pirate with the russet mane was the divine blond adolescent of the bouquet of the asphodel, the poppy and the iris.

In fact, the tents of the enemy camp soon surrounded the ramparts of the city, and Blismode, captive and etiolated, spent her days at the top of the tower appealing for the defeat of her own people, and fearing at the same time a victory of which she knew that she would be the trophy.

But the siege dragged on. The city, resupplied by means of secret tunnels, laughed at famine, and, on one fine autumn evening, Blismode died quietly in the arms of her maidservants, her enlarged eyes gazing toward the barbarian camp, pressing to her heart the dried asphodel of the barbarian Enemy.

A Bohemian Tale

For Aurel.

AS April approached, the rumor spread throughout
the land that a strange singer, an invisible and mysterious musician, had established himself in the forest of
Ardennes. He lived there in the densest thickets with the
birds and beasts of the woods, and since his arrival, among
the ravines, the clearings and the green shade of the paths,
there had been an effervescence of lilies of the valley and
primroses, a frenzy of unslaked lust and such a joy in living that from dawn to dusk, there was an audible delirium
in the nests in the branches, and the red deer were belling
every night by the light of the moon.

As a rising tide of sap and desire unfurled henceforth
in the leafy forest, exasperated gasps agonized in the air
that covered the region. In the heavy and storm-laden atmosphere, the guitar and voice of the strange musician
could be heard. His song rose up in the coolness of mauve
and roseate dawns, and in the blazing sadness of evenings,
infinitely sweet and pure, and also infinitely sad, while trills
and pizzicati sparkled, fused and spilled, scintillating and
pearly, under the guitarist's fingers.

The accompaniment was all mocking, scornful and satirical gaiety, while the ardent tenderness of the voice was imploring and tearful, and the mockery of the loquacious guitar over that passionate and poignant appeal was one melancholy more.

In the suddenly-invaded forest, clumps of asphodels and digitalis surged forth, beside pathways that became impenetrable for weeks beneath an unprecedented growth of vines and creepers; there was an overflowing of life, hectic grass and blooming flowers in the midst of an enamored concern of reckless nightingales. The thirty leagues of forest sang, laughed and loved, suddenly enchanted; the voice of the musician was always lamenting there.

A fever took hold of the entire land. By night, especially, the voice of the invisible singer took on unexpected, delightful, intoxicating sonorities. One could no longer take a step in the countryside without falling upon tax-gatherers and good-for-nothings lying in furrows or roadside ditches; they came in bands to surround the forest and lay in wait until dawn, attentive and charmed. Young women ran away from villages and cowherds from farms to come and listen at closer range; young soldiers deserted; the tocsin sounded until daybreak in the convents to recall souls in peril to God, and aged monks blanched by fasting and prayer suddenly stopped by night in the depths of cloisters in order to dissolve in tears, thinking about the past.

A great trouble agitated all hearts. A surge of stupor and adultery was unleashed in all the towns. Women abandoned their homes to go with travelers; one no longer found anything along the hedgerows but entwined couples; agricultural laborers prey to vague sadness left the fields fallow; artisans from the towns spent days wandering through the countryside; and the roads were no longer safe because there were so many vagabonds scattered around the province.

That damnable musician had bewitched the whole region, sowing laxity and sloth among the rabble, distress and mourning among the nobility and the bourgeois—so much and so thoroughly that the Duc de Lorraine, in his good city of Metz, was upset, and made the decision to rid his people of the accused singing sorcerer. No one had ever seen him. He was, it was said, a very young bohemian estranged from his tribe, and who, during the last passage of the Lords of Egypt through the marches of Lorraine, had settled in the Ardennes, and was singing there despairingly day and night. Perhaps his nostalgic appeal would be heard one day by one of his own people. As feral as a wild beast, however, and surely a past master in the art of spell-casting, he had thus far hidden from all gazes. Besides which, a superstitious dread protected his retreat and, since he had been singing in the florid forest, no one any longer dared to go into it.

That went on for months.

One beautiful night in May, the Duc de Lorraine set forth on campaign with a large party of cavaliers. He brought with him the Bishop of Nancy and twelve members of the chapter, in case there were charms to break and exorcisms to perform. They marched for two days, and reached the edge of the forest on the second day.

Since dawn they had encountered no one on the road but pilgrims in procession and foolish young women wandering along the hedgerows with amorous gazes. Then, in the dusk, a soft and pure voice sang, and the Duc and his companions bowed their heads and lowered their lances involuntarily over the necks of their horses, which had stopped suddenly. One might have thought that the marrow was melting in their bones, and a delightful chill gripped their hearts.

But the Bishop of Nancy recited the prayer of Saint Bonaventure and, having made the sign of the cross, the Duc and his men-at-arms entered the forest. They wandered all night beneath a rising moon, distracted and charmed by the voice that sometime sang to the left, and then resumed to the right, and seemed to wander hither and yon; the blossoms of the wild apple trees embalmed the air, nocturnal vapors floated before their eyes like robes; sometimes bare feet appeared on the moss; sometimes silky contacts touched them; but they were illusions that the prelate of Nancy soon scotched.

The sad and pure voice of the unknown singer was still mourning and imploring, but now more distinctly and closer at hand; and through the thickets, bathed in quicksilver, through the suddenly enlarged forest they marched, bizarrely disturbed, beneath and odorous shroud of petals, with the precautions and gestures of mounted falconers.

Suddenly, the voice broke into a kind of laughter, as limpid as water, and the stupefied cortege came to a halt.

The bohemian was there!

Standing on the edge of a spring, he was leaning over foolishly under a cold ray of moonlight, and, his guitar in his hand, was looking at his reflection in the water, intoxicated by his own image, as if drawn forward and bent over the water by the weight of his hair, a chimerically long flow of yellow silk, and the joyous arpeggios sparkling beneath his fingers.

The Duc's cavaliers fell upon him as if on a prey, tied him up before he had uttered a cry, and threw him, bound hand and foot, over the rump of a horse. The Bishop of Nancy had picked up the guitar.

At daybreak, the Duc and his retinue emerged from the forest and returned to Metz by way of side-roads. During the three days of the journey, the captured bohemian did not say a word. From time to time, a gourd was raised to his lips and he was made to drink, and as his prestigious beauty might have intrigued passers-by, he was covered by a mantle. At the third dawn, the little troop reached Metz and the ducal palace.

The strange musician lived there for two months, immured in a grim silence, almost free under the surveillance of three guards, his gaze bleak and absent, deflecting all conjectures and troubling men and women alike with his quasi-divine beauty.

He was a slim youth, seventeen years old at the most, with slender arms and muscular legs, imposing with his supple stride and agile movements the idea of a proud and dangerous animal; long blond hair hung down to his waist, and a kind of rictus drew back his lips at times in a slightly bestial fashion; but the abyss of his eyes was astonishing.

The Duc, simultaneously alarmed and charmed, had conceived an amity for him; he was one more work of art in the ducal castle. The bohemian wandered from room to room all day long, his arms folded without unclenching his teeth; sometimes he stopped before an open window and gazed at the clouds for a long time, and then resumed his restless march, observed from a distance by the eyes of the courtiers.

He had been dressed in the richest garments, and his guitar had been returned to him, but he scarcely seemed to recognize it, and the mute instrument was trailed through all the rooms, within the reach of his hand, without him deigning to honor it with a glance; so the Duc wasted his effort and the courtiers their trouble. The intoxicating song that he had once sung recklessly for the vagabonds of the roads and the poor, the accursed bohemian refused his master and the grandees of the court. The sad and pure voice had fallen silent forever, and the Duc's daughter, who was consumed by the desire to hear it, became melancholy, and fell into a languor.

In a towering rage, the Duc had the diabolical musician thrown into a dungeon along with his guitar, and then left Metz for his château in the woods, for the summer was advancing and it was very hot.

Some time after that, on a stormy night in August, one of the jailers in the city prison heard an infinitely soft and sad voice rising up from the dungeon. A tumultuous music accompanied it, quivering, strident and also joyful; it was like a melodious tide rising in the tower and beating the walls: a poignant music, in truth, made of bursts of laughter and tears, and the jailer, who had never heard it, recognized the voice of the bohemian.

He went down the stairs at a gallop and, shoving aside the sentinels, who had all come running to hear the voice and were sobbing with anguish, sitting on the steps, he ran toward the barred judas-hole of the damnable musician's cell.

The prisoner, standing up in his cell, was singing recklessly, his hands clutching his guitar. An enormous, strange golden yellow moon was shining through the barred window of the cell, cutting out a kind of mirror of water in a large bowl placed on the ground, and, leaning over the reflection of the star, the bohemian was mirroring himself therein, and singing wholeheartedly, enveloped from head to toe in the yellow sheet of his hair.

He sang all night before the eyes of his guardians, who were heaped up, shivering, at the judas-hole in the door; and in the square at the foot of the prison walls, a mob of poor people waved their fists at the sentinels, tore out their hair and fainted amorously.

The bohemian sang all day, and toward evening a great rumor went up in the surrounding region, and the governor of the citadel, having climbed up to the watchtower, saw that the fields were black with crowds, processing slowly toward the city; one might have thought them an army on the march.

They were coming from all points of the horizon. They were the vagabonds of the roads and barefoot peasants, the entire legion of the poor, running to the appeal of their singer. They had finally found him, and had been traveling since dawn, drunk with anger and joy, and the dusk was full of terrible threats; pikes and scythes were brandished under the pink sky. A breath of panic swept over the countryside, and the city-dwellers, gathered on the ramparts, listened fearfully as the clamor grew and came closer.

The bohemian was still singing.

The Duc, hastily warned, reached the rebel camp at the gates of the city in two days; the garrison made a sortie and the ill-clad and poorly armed vagabonds were easily crushed.

It was an atrocious, pitiless slaughter; more than thirty thousand dead remained on the terrain, women and children among them, for the unfortunates had come in couples and in families, as if on a pilgrimage, and the countryside around Metz was red with blood.

The Duc slept in his city that same night, where the mob was still grumbling, but when someone went to fetch the bohemian in order to torture him and hang him, his cell was empty. He had disappeared.

A few days later, however, as the superior of the Brothers of Mercy was wandering over the battlefield with some of his followers in order to gather together and bury the dead, a captious music suddenly burst forth above the charnel-house, and, having raised his head, the monk perceived a young and slender boy who was singing and laughing, his guitar in his hands, standing on a mound encumbered with cadavers.

A blazing golden sky was bloody at the horizon. Draped to the waist in flaming hair, the musician mingled vibrant bursts of laughter with his song, and, leaning over a pool of blood, looked at his reflection.

And the gravedigger monk recognized the bohemian, the bohemian Amour who sings in the woods for the disinherited and the vagabonds, falls silent in palaces, mirrors himself in Death, and loves no one but himself: Amour, as free and wild as solitude.

Princess Ottilia

THE young woman raised herself up mechanically between the pale silk cushions where she was reclining on her elbow, dreaming, and, having gone to the large open window, looked out over the shade of the royal park for a long time in the direction of the city.

In the vast room hung with silken tapestries, several maidservants were tormenting the strings of the orbs and great archiluths, filling the entire octagonal courtyard with a vague and delicate murmur that the young woman did not hear, for the Princess Ottilia had been both mute and deaf since birth, as almost always happens in these tragic cases; and, immured in her infirmity, she had already been living for twenty-five years retrenched from life, without any other communication with her fellows but a few vague gestures at length adopted by those who served her. She was sad, in the long garments of sky blue brocade patterned with golden flowers, or her heavy sheaths of violet silk fabric embroidered with green dragons, two shades of which she was fondest of all; she was so sad that no one had ever seen her smile; and her large eyes, the color of dead water, devoid of dreams and thoughts, shone beneath her beautiful eyelids with the dull gleam of fake gemstones.

She was the oldest daughter of the King of Sicily, a poor infirm creature issued from a marriage between cousins, a bleak political marriage, and her birth had caused her mother to be repudiated.

The King did not love the princess with the absent gaze, whose immobile and placid beauty was never animated. He had had her brought up in an isolated part of the palace, forbidden thereafter to the personnel of the court; and the profound shade of the private park surrounded and hid the tower of pink marble in which the gentle Ottilia had grown up and had slowly begun to fade away, in the midst of an idle troop of maidservants.

The tourneys and amorous courtships, and for want of such gallant festivals, the ever-new spectacle of the sea and its horizons, the movement of the port, the exit and entry of gliding galleys, and the turbulence and gaiety of the common people along the jetties and the channel, might perhaps have distracted the sorrowful Princess, but the King was ashamed of her infirmity; she dishonored his family. And, confined to her marble tower and her obscure garden, the pale Ottilia only went out rarely to witness some royal ceremony from the throne, where her prestigious beauty impressed the people.

On those days, the King consented to look at his daughter. Seated in a hieratic pose, in the midst of sacred music, the fluttering of banners and the splendors of metal and silk of warrior corteges, she appeared truly regal; the immobility of her face was merely one glory more. She seemed born to be enthroned under an awning, in the midst of incense fumes and the floods of flowers of liturgical festivals, beneath the high vaults of cathedrals, and the proud monarch deigned to recognize her beneath the gold, precious stones and heavy ermines of ceremonial garb.

But those were rare moments of short duration. All of the King's heart was devoted to his son, the Prince that he had obtained from a second marriage after the disgrace of Ottilia's mother, a proud and handsome dauphin already aged twenty and who, whimsical, hot-blooded and impetuous, filled the city and the kingdom with the scandal of his caprices, amusing the people and alarming the bourgeois with the ostentation of his mistresses and his favorites.

Princess Ottilia saw that younger brother even more rarely. Not caring to go and shut himself away with the mute with the phantom gaze and dreamlike gestures, the dauphin declared that he preferred the living to pictures painted in frescos. That eternally grave sister frightened him, and the poor abandoned young woman had scarcely any other pastime than leafing through the heavy illuminated pages of old missals, making illustrative tapestries or receiving visits from weavers of fabrics and jewelers who came to submit to her plans for designs and colors, or models of clasps, bracelets and necklaces; they were the rare bright hours of her solitude.

In the gynaeceum darkened by stained-glass windows, the maidservants, who were dying of boredom, played music quietly in the attempt to distract themselves, or sometimes pinched one another in corners in the fashion of amorous virgins, but whether they were giggling with laughter or scraping the strings of their instrument, the royal deaf-mute did not hear them.

She was still standing at the window, both hands leaning on the marble sill, but her distant gaze was no longer seeking to discern the domes and bell-towers behind the high crowns of the palm trees and cypresses. Princess Ottilia was now gazing, with singular attention, at the foot of the tower, in the midst of the starry clumps of clematis and jasmine.

Three men had just come into the garden—three young men, all unfamiliar; a lord and two musicians. There was a flute-player and a viola player—a particular viol whose vibrant and penetrating sounds were only exhaled under the bow, known as a *viola d'amore*.

The young lord, having sat down on a circular bench, unrolling a parchment manuscript that he had in his hand, made a sign to the other two, and the Princess, who could see all three of them clearly from her window, as if they were at the bottom of a well, in retreat and singularly pale in the blue shade of cypresses, saw the flute-player raise his instrument to his lips, and the other musician balance the viola on his shoulder.

The young lord moved with the rhythm, oscillating his upper body and, leaning forward, indicated the resumptions, following the movement, with his mouth wide open, evidently singing, nodding his head to words that she could not hear.

They were rehearsing some ballad, some gallant concert destined for a beautiful lady adored by the young man with the manuscript. They had chosen that solitary spot in order to repeat in complete security their serenade of amour, and, to judge by the intoxicated face of the lord, his moist eyes and his ecstatic expression, everything, words and music alike, must have been his own composition.

And more cruelly than ever, the Princess regretted not hearing sounds, or seizing the delicate meaning of words. Everything about the young stranger—his passionate attitude, his ardent pallor, even his supple slimness and his remote gaze—attracted her; she would also have liked to have known the lady of the court to whom that tender epithalamium was addressed, for there could be no question for her of any aubade or song; and the gallant knew perfectly well what he was doing in choosing the solitary garden of the deaf-mute Princess to rehearse his work.

Deaf-mute! An anguish gripped her heart.

One of her maidservants, having approached the window at that point, saw the three men leaving the garden, and recognized the young lord.

It was Beppino de Fiesole, the Prince's present favorite, and who, it was said, was accumulating all the employments of the court, including that of the lover of the heart of the beautiful Duchess Catarina d'Aydagues, the Dauphin's current mistress.

The following night, Princess Ottilia saw in a dream the handsome unknown and the two musicians from the garden; but a novelty that had something miraculous about it—sweet sonorities filled her ears, a delightful music invaded her entirety, which plunged her into a joyful stupor—thrilled her with ecstasy and caused her simultaneously to faint and recover consciousness, with a sudden warmth and then frissons of agony, in her finally blossoming flesh.

The next day, at about four o'clock, a sensation of tenderness and softness she had not experienced before brought her suddenly to her feet and drew her, almost unconsciously, to the window that overlooked the park.

The three men of the day before were already there, the handsome Beppo de Fiesole already sitting on the bench and the two musicians standing in front of him. The flute and the *viola d'amore* were playing the tune of a languorous ciaccona, and, to the simultaneously ardent and mannered rhythm, Signor Beppo was exhaling suppliant words, criticism and praise mingled in honor of a lady; and the royal deaf-mute, understanding the meaning of it, felt saddened in her soul, because the verses and music were addressed to someone other than her; and her heart, abruptly initiated to life, divined that it was an amorous request.

The Florentine lord's verses celebrated the silken and solar hair of an insensible beauty with ambered flesh as transparent as grapes; those verses celebrated the moist and fresh rosiness of the lips of a lady with steely eyes like daggers. And without knowing the meaning of the words, Princess Ottilia knew that she had shiny black hair, a mat complexion, and that eyes as blue as faded turquoises smiled back at her from the depths of her mirror

She had just instinctively picked one up from a table within arm's reach, and contemplated herself within it. When she plunged her eyes into the garden again, she saw that the young man had raised his head, and was looking at her. In her turn, Princess Ottilia felt herself blushing, and stepped back.

She came back nevertheless the following day to lean on the window-sill. Signor Beppo and his two musicians were already installed in the cypress arbor, and the *viola d'amore* and the flute were sighing languorously.

Miraculously, however, the music was not the same. It was imploring more persuasively and more tenderly, and the deaf Princess understood that; the verses had changed too. They were no longer celebrating the gray eyes of a redhead with an amber complexion, but pale dead-water irises of a lunar beauty, and dark hair.

The singer was singing with his eyes fixed on her, and the intoxicating Princess no longer consulted her mirror.

That night, her dreams were full of delirious visions.

✳

Some time after that, one evening when Prince Alexandre was lying on quilts of Genoa velvet and Scutari carpets, moving his long hands nonchalantly through the silky tresses of the beautiful Catarina, the Duchess asked him, indifferently: "What's become of our Signor Beppo?"

The hereditary Prince of Sicily, his tongue thickened by drunkenness, replied: "Our Beppo must have some folly in mind. He's neglected us a great deal lately, don't you think?"

"Why should he take the trouble to pay court to us? Is he not the favorite, Your Highness's cherished darling? You've made him a Count, and governor of Sardinia; he draws from our coffers with full hands and can aspire to anything. Has he not dreamed of making me his mistress?"

"What! He has dared . . ."

"And for an entire week he has kept to himself. Is he not, after you, Milord, the most accomplished horseman in the realm? But our Florentine has higher aims; he is making the deaf hear and the mute speak."

"What do you mean by that?"

"Nothing, Milord, that the entire court does not know, except for His Majesty and you. Go take a stroll tomorrow, then, with your people, at the hour of the siesta, in the Princess's private garden."

"Ottilia, my sister? Beautiful Duchess d'Aydagues, my darling Catarina, it's the ax for you if you're lying."

✳

Two nights after that, Princes Ottilia had a frightful nightmare. The handsome Comte de Fiesole, assisted by his two accompanists, was singing her his daily ballad. The song rose up, ardent and passionate, and she, leaning out of the high window, was drinking him in with her gaze and fainting with joy at hearing him this request for amour . . . when, all of a sudden, the handsome singer appeared utterly pale in the sudden darkness of the cypress. He tottered and paled even further, and his voice fell silent; the viola had become mute too, or else she had become deaf again.

And the Princess woke up, utterly cold, with a great anguish in her heart.

The next day, when she got up, a page in the King's livery asked to be introduced, and deposited, for her, in the hands of her maidservants a curious Venetian box enriched with gems and enamel. The Princess opened it in great haste and found therein, placed on a silken cushion, the head of the Florentine Beppo, still warm, with the eyes revulsed.

At that sight, a powerful fever gripped her, which carried her away in the evening.

Thus died Princess Ottilia, for having listened to the song of the *viola d'amore*.

The Marquise de Spolête

Cajoling minstrels
With sweet songs
And harmonies
Weeping fountains
In the flowery orchard,
The horn-players
And cupbearers,
All those, in sum, who once
Passed by in marvelous décor
And will pass again. . . .

The varlets who will die
Imprisoned in towers,
And the servants of amour
All come in turn
With flowers and smiles
And Timor roses,
And then the knights,
And the cavaliers of Tyr
All those the round has brought,
And will bring back again . . .

But you,
Your lips and hair,
And your rosy fingers,
And your confessions
At dusk by the fire,
But you,
And the May evenings,
The beloved evenings,
All that is finished now
And will never return.

Tristan Klingsor[1]

BARTHOLOMEO GIOVANNI SALVIATI, Marquis de Spolête and Duc de Ventimiglia, of the old Salviati family that furnished doges to Venice and governors to Florence, was already fifty years old, widowed for fifteen years of Maria Lucrezia Belleverani, of the Naples Bell-veranis, related to the ducal families of Modena and Parma, and even the house of the Medicis, when he married for a second time, although already old and bald, a beautiful young woman of twenty in the full flower of a dazzling puberty, Simonetta Foscari.

Simonetta Foscari, Florentine by race and instinct, of the blood of the old Foscaris, so terrible in their own homeland—the Foscaris of riots, conspiracies, tragic

---

1 "Tristan Klingsor" was the pseudonym of a Symbolist poet, painter and composer associated with a group of *avant garde* musicians who called themselves Les Apaches; he had been born Léon Leclère (1874–1966), the names being borrowed from a Wagnerian hero (from *Tristan und Isolde*) and a villain (from *Parzifal*). His first collections of poetry were *Filles-Fleurs* [Flower-Girls] (1895) and *Squelettes fleuris* [Flowery Skeletons] (1897). Lorrain could not know that Klingsor would still be writing in the 1960s, the last survivor of the Decadent Movement.

amours and treasons, a line of criminals and sensualists, in which the men, as handsome as courtiers, and the women, as beautiful as archangels, furnished poppets to Castel Sant'Angelo and popesses to the Vatican—was not made to belie a proverb popular in Italy regarding the insolent beauty of the members of her family. The quasi-sacrilegious saying: "The Foscaris, so beautiful that they would tempt God," was blasphemed then and is still blasphemed today throughout Tuscany.

An anonymous portrait by a pupil of Leonardo da Vinci, which might well be that of the Foscari of this story—for the catalogue of the Uffizi Gallery titles it "Portrait of the Marquise de Spolête"—has transmitted her perilous beauty to us. Relegated to a small obscure room of the museum, only hazard or a well-informed determination can discover the precious canvas, but I challenge anyone who has once contemplated that arrogant little head ever to be able to forget it.

From the swelling of the forehead to the violent neck, it is a curt, imperious, obstinate little head, a willful little head which would almost be wicked without the languor of the eyes, with their overly heavy lids: two long shadowed eyes whose irises, strangely set back beneath the supercilious brows, with their brown gaze of burnt topaz; a sinuous mouth with sculpted lips; a narrow, short nose with dilated nostrils; the planes of the face pronounced and sharp, as if carved from hard stone. It is the mask, both imperious and tenacious, of a young adventuress and a sensual princess, a head of a youth and ardor frightening in their intensity.

The head-dress is the kind made of heavy torsades, interlaced with pearls and green-tinted gems, with which the school of Tuscany helmed all women's faces. The neck, very feminine, almost viperish in its long gracility, in which determination is tangible, springs like a stem from a deeply-cut corsage adhering to the shoulders: a saffron damask that harmonizes very well with the rusty tint of the eyes and the hair. The mat complexion, with green-tinted transparencies in the light, evokes both the softness of wax and the hardness of metal—and yet the painting is rather poor. The face, in which one merely senses resemblance, is spoiled by the conventional details and routines of the school, such as the overly long neck and the russet hair, for the woman, so pale, must have been brunette, and that curt head with its moist eyes must have rested on a swollen neck. . . .

But such as the centuries have bequeathed it to us, that face obsesses you and troubles you, and pursues you through the other paintings in the catalogue, and by virtue of the anonymity of the painter and the model . . . a pupil of da Vinci? who was that pupil? Marquise de Spolête? who was that Marquise, and what was her life? . . . obsessing most of all because of the tangible enigma of a beauty that one senses deliberately diminished. . . .

I am inclined to identify that Marquise de Spolête as the heroine of the following tragic story.

Simonetta Foscari, espoused for her regal beauty and triumphant youth, brought into the rude little court of the Ventimiglias the refined elegance, liberal mores and sumptuousness of a Florentine princess.

There were in that little frontier town, previously more accustomed to the soldiery of a garrison, throngs of poets, performers and musicians, a whole series of artistes, illuminators of missals, modelers in wax and even speakers of pretty trivia, rhymers of sonnets and improvisers of ballads, such as were then pullulating in Lombardy and Tuscany in the pay of the rich and the powerful. All of them came in the wake of the new duchess, slaves of her fortune, some in fief to her beauty and the majority to her largesse. The old fortress filled up with the sound of laughing voices, the rustle of silk and the chatter of instruments, where nothing had once been heard but the breaking of goblets and the clinking of halberds, and during the long evenings, the rattle of dice and blasts of cornets.

Henceforth, from dawn to dusk, and especially from dusk to dawn, there were the pizzicati of mandolins, the sobbing and moaning of guitars and the verses of poets, sometimes cadenced and sometimes babbled in ecstasy by caressant voices swooning with amour. There were decamerons in the old low rooms, previously reserved for men-at-arms; the bare walls were ornamented with frescos. The young Duchess brought painters from Fiesole and sculptors from Romagne, and her image, sometimes in the features of a nymph, sometimes those of a canonized saint, embellished the corridors and courtyards of the palace.

Andrea Salviati, the son of the Duc and Maria Lucrezia Belleverani, the child of his first marriage, abandoned the paternal court resentfully. He was a thin and puny adolescent, rather graceless in his person and taciturn by nature; he obtained that haughty and chagrined humor from his mother. He had beautiful dark green eyes, and that was the sole charm of that tormented face of a runt.

It was those eyes that the proud and nonchalant Simonetta encountered, in Vinitimille, on the day of her arrival; the gazes of the Neapolitan's son and the Florentine met like two épées, but no spark sprang from the collision.

Politic, like all those of her race, the young Duchess tried to win the son of the foreigner to her cause; she made herself maternal, coaxing, even tempting, but she could not bend Andrea's increasing hostility. Then weary in advance of a futile struggle, she disdained that fleeting conquest and returned to her pleasures.

There was, in the midst of a court of musicians, painters and poets, the absolute reign, voluptuously despotic and whimsical, of a queen of amour. The infatuated Duc allowed it free rein. Deaf to all observations, passionately blind, he responded to all malevolence with a single phrase: "She's a Foscari," and the fact is that all the handsome young men, all Florentines like her, were to Simonetta more like domestic animals, playthings and clowns, than creatures of her race: her pride protected her against the heat of her blood, and her caprices succeeded one another without pause: one day's favorite was in disgrace the next. When one of them had ceased to please her she expelled him or married him to one of her maidservants. Guillaume de Borre, a Provençal troubadour strayed to Ventimiglia and heaped with honors for two months, had to flee by night and reach the frontier at a forced march, in order to avoid marrying an old Piedmontese woman employed in the kitchens, whom a whim of the Princess had suddenly imposed on him. The suddenness of her fantasies defied all suspicions.

Andrea Salviati had quit Ventimiglia resentfully to take to the sea and hold in check the pirate vessels that were then devastating the coast from Messina to Aigues-Mortes; moved by braggadocio and filial rancor, he had entered the service of the King of Sicily, a relative and enemy of his father.

The old Duc, increasingly subjugated by his young wife, now lived confined to the old part of the castle, in the company of astrologers and alchemists, creatures of the Duchess, devoted body and soul to her cause, and who—so popular rumor had it—led the old Duc's reason astray as they desired in the perilous research of accursed sciences. It was necessary now to occupy Bartholomeo's attention, to blind the amorous old eagle; in sum, to conceal from him the deportment of the "greyhound bitch"—as the slim and supple daughter of the Foscaris was known in Ventimiglia—in the midst of her pack of Genoese mastiffs and Tuscan hounds, lap dogs and stud dogs.

For the scandal was now public; worse than that, it had crossed the frontier, and was spreading joy in Provence as well as Italy: the Duchess was a debauchee. It was a courtesan who now ruled the court of the Salviatis, and among so many favorites, small fry that were expedited on a weekly basis by the strangler's cord or the alchemists' poisons, three Italians allied in the same interest of their salvation and their credit, shared the ducal favors.

Beppo Nardi was a poet raised in the Court of Avignon and a composer of sonnets of the Petrarchian school, a slim and delicate cavalier with the profile of a cameo, a glabrous and arrogant visage always hooded in scarlet velvet, whose muse, as supple as his spine, celebrated the glorious youth of Simonetta every morning.

Angelino Barda was a player of the mandolin, a composer, at times, of languorous canzoni, which he accompanied with a youthful voice, Neapolitan by birth, as dark as an olive with large pale blue-tinted eyes and ardent dry lips: feverish and voluptuous lips, the violet-tinted black of mulberries. It was said that the Neapolitan Angelino was singularly inventive in modes of pleasure.

Finally, Petruchio Arlani was a sculptor and painter in the manner of Michelangelo, a superb brute, muscled like an athlete, with the thick curly black hair of a head of Antinou. Petruchio Arlani was a former goatherd, it was said, descended from Abruzzo to the studios of Rome, where he had posed as a model, a legendary stallion of great Roman ladies, whom an irony of the Vatican, the drunken whim of the Pope at the end of a supper, had sent to the court of Ventimiglia with two legates and a nuncio as a specimen of Roman art. The lad being very handsome, the Duchess had kept him. His talent as a sculptor, at any rate, did not extend beyond wax figurines. He had already wrought, modeled on La Foscari, three busts of Pallas Victrix, which the duchess had, each time, pitilessly devastated and demolished; but as the rascal had a neck like a bull and powerful loins, Simonetta still kept him with her in the hope that a masterpiece might one day be born under his fingers, those of a domesticated brute.

And the Florentine continued to domesticate the shepherd of Abruzzo, in the company of Nardi the poet and Barda the Neapolitan. Guitar tunes, sirventes and sonnets, painted wax busts: such was the atmosphere of savant sensuality and joyful languor of the court of the beautiful Duchess, on the shore of the blue sea, sparkling and swooning between the laurier-roses and palm trees of the strand, before the grandiose and vaporous décor of the valley of the Roya.

And Bartholomeo Salviati allowed it. The seers and the physicians took possession of the Duc and of that fine intelligence, that sure and prompt will, of all the character of decision and audacity of the old captain, once so terrible to the enemies of the Italian fatherland, nothing remained but an old man, prey to the most dangerous entourage, a man returned to infancy, or very nearly.

That was what the young duchess had wanted. Ten years had sufficed for Simonetta to capture the old eagle and make a laboratory owl of him. Now, he no longer quit the crucibles and the retorts in the midst of which the beautiful Foscari had confined him, and when, by chance, he emerged from the part of the palace that he had adopted, it was to witness, in response to his young wife's plea, some fête, comedy or ballet organized by her, and thus consecrate with an august presence the luxury and license installed in his court.

And, sure of impunity, the favorites became bolder, and the audacity of the Duchess dared even more. Intoxicated by flattery and incense, the "greyhound bitch" had the mania of scandal; she wanted to affirm and advertise in splendor her adultery and her lovers. "A woman infatuated with her body is soon denuded of sense."

And, forsaking all prudence, counseled by who knows what evil genius, the adventuress Simonetta resolved to do nothing less than appear on the stage herself before her entire court, along with her three favorites, who would take roles beside her, in a comedy or ballet composed for the occasion, which would affirm the talent of each of them.

That was the bravado of a woman drunk on power, defiant with pride and loudly infatuated, and yet, the project was settled and the piece elaborated for a long time. The Duchesse de Ventimiglia ordered the play from Nardi and the music from Barda, but imposed the subject on them. Petruchio d'Arlani the painter and sculptor at her orders, was responsible for costumes and sets, still under her direction. The Florentine did not hand over to anyone; she inspired, faithful in that to the traditions of the princesses of her nation; and the most sublime artists would only have been obscure collaborators in her hands.

That was neither the case of Beppo Nardi, a rather mediocre poet, nor that of Angelino of Naples, a perfect musician but a paltry composer; as for the rascal Petruchio, he was devoid of taste and ideas, having looked after his goats on the slopes of his native mountains—but the Duchess had imagination and ingenuity enough for three, and when Nardi and Barda brought her, finally concluded, *The Death of John the Baptist*, which they had had been commissioned to produce, Simonetta proclaimed it a masterpiece, for, through the conceits of a poetry that was all assonance and preciosity, she had recognized her original idea, and the insipid melodies of the Neapolitan did not diminish overmuch the beautiful horror of the drama that had tempted that tragic soul.

The Duchess threw a gold necklace around the neck of Angelino and put the large ruby of a ring on Beppo Nardi's finger, and both of them, enthused, kissed Her Highness' hand. The poet, like the musician, had respected the plan given by her; her favorites had obeyed her.

The death of John the Baptist—the beheading of the Precursor, the legend of lust and blood of which the entire Italian Renaissance was as if obsessed, Herod and Salome, the terrible figures that had tempted all the painters of the epoch, of whom the museums have bequeathed the dangerous haunting to us—was the subject toward which the voluptuous and tenacious Foscari had been directly drawn. Among all the heroines of the Bible and Fable, Salome had summoned her most of all; and it was the immodest princess of Judea that she, born a princess of

Florence and a duchess and marquise by marriage, took pleasure in evoking, incarnating and living for an evening before her people.

The little girl who danced stark naked before an old libertine king and obtained an enemy head by means of the mysterious offering of her sex: that was the character she wanted to be. It was the realization of that chimera that delighted her perversity; and who can tell whether the Italian woman's curious imagination might not have been seduced by a similarity between the advanced age of the legendary Herod and the anticipated old age of her husband?

It was the *mise en scène* of the senile weakness of Herod, but reduced by the brain of a woman to the vengeance of a spiteful little girl. The Duchess had conceived it in three tableaux. The first was the encounter of Salome and the Precursor in one of the corridors of the palace, the saintly prisoner between two guards, the Princess perhaps not so much pitiless as curious, first offering him a drink and then holding out a flower to the ascetic; the saint's disdainful refusal, and, Salome persisting, the prophetic fury and anathema of John summoning the fire of Heaven upon his temptress. The second tableau showed Herod on his throne, in the midst of his dignitaries and his court, and Salome, on his order, having been introduced and asked to dance, the bloody bargain struck between the tyrant and the little Princess; then, the murderous dance once executed, the third showed Herod keeping his promise and the executioner bringing the saint's head on a platter.

La Foscari distributed the roles. Beppo Nardi, the poet, would take that of Herod. Angelino of Naples, with his ardent emaciated head, would be the Precursor; his

221

thinness and his gleaming eyes designated him to incarnate the grim eater of locusts. As for Petruchio d'Arlani, his tall stature and enormous musculature indicated his role well enough: he would be the executioner. He it was who would stand motionless, scimitar in hand, behind the kneeling saint during the entire dance; he it was who, seizing the prophet by the shoulders, would lead him off stage; he it was, finally, whose muscular arms, extending from behind a pillar, would place the bloody head of Saint John on the platter. . . .

And, with the child-like joy, the febrile passion and the science of details that women bring to those kinds of things, the Duchess, immediately occupying herself with the costumes, the scenery and the decoration of the hall, went in quest of Oriental fabrics and precious velvets.

Scribes, on her orders, wrote to Venice; Jewish merchants were summoned from Genoa to submit Damascene carpets and Tyrian silks to her choice. Dancers were hired from Bergamo at high prices, who regulated the tempo of Salome's steps and taught the Duchess to move and undulate on the spot, shaken by brief frissons from nape to heels, and then to dare torsions of the hips and sudden swellings of the breasts, like an almah from Barbaric lands.

The court orchestra was reinforced by fifteen musicians. The old Salviati family tapestries, representing the life of the Virgin, emerged from the camphor-wood chests where they were conserved, for they were inestimably valuable and were only taken out for great fêtes, the marriages of the Ducs and the baptisms of first-born male children.

The Duchess did even more; she wanted the interior courtyard of the palace as an arena for the spectacle and, even sculpting the ramparts of the citadel, she had twenty meters of wall overlooking the sea demolished. The pikes and pickaxes bit into the old blocks of granite that Umberto the Strong had placed; a great bay was opened up, luminous and blue, over the infinity of the gulf, to a height of twenty meters, in the wall itself; that was the theater.

The marvelous Salviati tapestries were draped around the platforms, piled up in the courtyard in the shadow of the keep and the watchtowers . . . and the day of the spectacle finally arrived.

Simonetta had chosen the very day of the anniversary of her marriage for the sumptuous scandal. A brocade canopy in the ducal colors was set up facing the stage, in the exact center of the platforms, reserved for old Bartholomeo and his retinue of scholars.

The spectacle was announced for three o'clock and the crowd, aggregated on the steps, all dark heads and bright clothing, was impatient and restless, but the Duc's place remained empty. After waiting for three-quarters of an hour the crowd became exasperated, stamping their feet; the orchestra struck up a concerto of viols and flutes, and the curtains of the bay drew apart.

Duc Bartholomeo had sent word to the Duchess that she was not to wait, and that she would have to start without him. Having suffered a fit of weakness as he was leaving his apartment, he asked for ten minutes to collect himself, and would certainly arrive, in a quarter of an hour at the most, to witness Salome's dance; he had a keen desire to admire the Duchess in that dance, to admire her and applaud her.

And the spectacle commenced, in slight anguish, because, in truth, the beautiful Simonetta had never pushed audacity so far.

On the stage, standing against an old Flanders screen of verdure simulating the frescoes of a corridor, draped in heavy Asiatic fabrics, enturbaned with long blue-tinted veils, there was the delicate and curvaceous silhouette of the Duchess as the Princess of Judea.

She held out to Saint John, by turns, a rose and then a cup, and enveloped him amorously and lasciviously with the nudity of her beautiful arms. . . .

Then the tapestries fell back again . . . and in the improvised hall, the Duc had not yet appeared. Now there were indiscretions whispered in women's ears regarding the surprise that the second tableau reserved: a frightful head of wax modeled by Ardali on Barda himself, the musician's resemblance painted and colored with the blood of the execution and the lividity of death, which the Duchess would offer to everyone at the end of the tableau, triumphantly held up on a platter.

And, the tapestries having been raised, there was, against the blue of the sky and the blue of the gulf filling the whole courtyard of the palace with light, the vision of Herod, of Nardi heavily clad in crimson and coiffed with a miter, installed on a throne with, round him, clearly outlined against the sky and the sea, an entire row of lords and slaves. The tall stature of the almost-naked sculptor dominated them all: d'Arlani superb in the display of his muscles and his torso, girded solely in a white loincloth. . . .

And to the pizzicato of mandolins, to a light and leaping rhythm, reminiscent of little bells—a strange music, in truth, mingled here and there with the call of flutes and the languorous chords of guzlas, Salome made her entrance. . . . A Salome—which is to say, the Duchess Simonetta—clad in a tight sheath of green silk, shiny and spangled silk, like the skin of a snake, with enormous jet black rose-designs blossoming here and there.

A narrow band of emeralds and sapphires enclosed her breasts, and her bare shoulders and arms sprang like flowers from that blue-tinted sheath; each of her movements revealed her armpits and each of her steps the tops of her bare legs, for the tight green dress opened up, split to the hip, fortunately weighed down by thick golden fringes.

The face, with the eyes magnified and blue-tinted by kohl, had the pallor of death beneath the greasepaint, as hallucinatory as a mask; heavy pendants trembled over the forehead, which appeared very narrow beneath the hair coiffed in a tiara, a cone of darkness heightened with blue powder, and constellated like a firmament with golden stars.

She advanced stiffly, as if rigid within her adornment and her jewelry, and from an opal, placed between her breasts, suspended from the end of a strong of pearls, lower than the navel, almost level with her vagina, hung a large enamel flower.

She danced, and in her large staring eyes, in her mute smile, something akin to fear rose up; and, following the direction of her gaze, all the members of the audience, who were drinking her in with their eyes, turned their heads.

The Duc had just taken his place. Old Bartholomeo had come to sit beneath his canopy, and beside him, standing in a respectful pose, his fist on his hip but his eyes full of menace, was Andrea, Andrea Salviati, the outlaw, the exile, the son fallen into disgrace, the enemy returned.

He it was who was gazing at Simonetta. Herod on his throne, Saint John kneeling behind the dancer, and the executioner standing beside his victim, had lowered their heads.

Her eyes staring directly ahead, as if hallucinated, Simonetta danced, but when, following her role, the dance eventually concluded, she turned to Herod to ask him for the head of the blasphemer, a great cry sprang from all breasts, but the Duchess, her mouth wide open, could not find an exclamation in her throat.

The Duc had just risen to his feet, one hand on his son's shoulder, the other had made a sign . . . and three severed heads lay at Simonetta's feet.

Soldiers, posted among the mute actors, had carried out the order precisely; a triple stroke of the ax had decapitated Saint John, the executioner and Herod; a similar punishment had struck Nardi, d'Arlani and Barda.

"They are repaid," were the only words the Duc spoke as he retired.

On the evening of the same day, a woman woke up, recovering consciousness in the vacillating gloom of a cell illuminated by candles: a cell whose door and windows had been walled up; for the condemned woman who was lying there inert was never to emerge therefrom.

At her feet, three bloody heads were heaped on a platter; three heads of young men with eyes revulsed and hair bristling as if straightened by fear; three heads livid beneath their greasepaint; and as the woman, still scintillating with jewels and silk, made an instinctive movement of recoil, she caused a parchment sealed with the Salviati arms to slide from her dress.

And Simonetta Foscari, having taken the manuscript that had fallen to the ground in her hands, opened it and read the old man's adieu:

You loved them alive, Madame; love them dead. It pleased you to live with them and for them; it will be pleasant for you to die with those whose death you have caused.

And the Duchess, having turned the page, found these consolatory lines:

And I too have loved you, Simonetta; I remember that and I pity you. Your lips are poisoned.

The Princess Under Glass

S HE was a delicate and beautiful princess with slender limbs, as pretty as those of a wax figurine; her transparent skin was so tender that one might have thought it animated by a vacillating candle-flame, extinguishable by the slightest wind, and, beneath her thick chestnut-colored tresses, the little Princess gave such a gripping and cold impression of whiteness that to her name, Bertrade, the appellation "the Pale" had been added by the common folk, while her father, a bellicose old king always occupied in making war on the pagans in the Northern Marches, had baptized her "his little Christmas rose." Bertrade did indeed have the morbid fragility, the frail charm and the placid gleam of white hellebore, as if deadened by winter.

She had had a somewhat gloomy childhood in a castle in a region of woods and marshes where her father had had her brought up by governesses with stern faces, far from the tumult of the court.

Her mother, a princess of Occitania who had never been able to console herself for having quit her kingdom of golden sands, had died a few months after her birth, and that precocious mourning had darkened with permanent melancholy the royal childhood confided henceforth to mercenary hands.

She was born so puny and pale that it had been feared for a long time that she might not survive her mother. Espoused almost without contribution for the great beauty of her milky flesh and her large, slightly wayward eyes, the greenish blue of turquoises, that Emperor's daughter had scarcely arrived in Courland than she had fallen into a strange languor; an incurable regret undermined her, it was said, for the horizons of masts and sails that she had had before her eyes back there, at the foot of the terraces of the imperial palace, in the city interminably decorated with the pennants and standards of her father the exarch. She had not been brought up with impunity on the shore of the sea, and the rumors of the ocean, the cries of departing sailors; the thousand and one clamors of a port were lacking for that beautiful marine flower, who, transplanted into dismal and flat Courland, all peat-bogs and forests, had been rapidly faded by nostalgia, and etiolated by regret.

Her horror for the horizons of fir-trees and ponds of her new kingdom had become so intense that in the last months of her life she had had the mullioned windows of her bedroom walled up to half their height. She only left that bedroom of brocade and tapestries again with her arms folded over a crucifix and her feet stiff, in a coffin; and the mournful days of the last phase of her pregnancy and the bloody hours of her churching she had spent in the half-light of the darkened room, her eyes fixed on a large mirror placed very high, opposite the half-condemned windows, which only reflected the errant clouds and the changing appearances of the sky.

Her reverie, thus voluntarily abused, allowed her to believe that she was still in Occitania, beneath the firmament swept with clouds with nacreous fractures, on the shore of the sea.

That obsession of the exile had cut short her days—at least, that was the rumor credited by the people; but among the nobles there was talk of a deadly beverage and the hatred of a princess of the blood, once honored by the favors of the King, who had dreamed of sitting on the throne; the young Queen had paid with her life for the rancor of a rival. The poison that had been administered to her ought to have killed the child with whom she was pregnant too, but, either because the doses had been miscalculated, or because Heaven had taken pity on those two cadavers for one coffin, only the Queen had died, and Bertrade had survived. The court of Courland was, at any rate, a sufficiently sinister court full of strange stories. While Bertrade was growing up delicate and frail in the hands of governesses in the calm of the Castle in the Woods, the King had a nephew brought up at court, the son of an elder brother, the same brother whose throne he occupied, who had died rather singularly in a hunting accident.

The Black Prince—that was what Prince Otto was called by the people—was a rather taciturn young man five years older than Bertrade, whose incoherent and bizarre conduct authorized more than one nasty rumor.

As pale as his royal cousin, but supple and robust in his slenderness, he paraded in the palaces of the high city as well as the taverns of the old port the slim body of a squire, always sheathed in black drugget. He passed from the worst debauches, those which one can scarcely mention, to the most ardent practices of piety; acts of almost divine charity were credited to him, alongside deeds of savage cruelty, and he was simultaneously the most frantic libertine in the kingdom and the most gentle of young monks, illuminators of manuscripts, in all the provinces; for in his inexplicable savagery, he sometimes retired for long months to a cloister, where he led the life of a postulant.

His gaze, fixed and hard, as cold as onyx, revealed his violent soul well enough. No poisoned beverage had been poured for him, but a popular rumor claimed that he was expiating in his fashion a bohemian vengeance. A zingaro whose mistress he had confiscated one night, on a whim and whom he had then—such are the games of princes—soundly beaten, had sung him some time afterwards a singular aubade. Insinuating himself no one knew how into the Prince's apartment—there is always devilry in tales of bohemians—the wretch, instead of planting his dagger in his enemy's heart, had sung him the airs of his homeland all night, accompanying himself on a maleficent violin, or a guzla, whose strings were made from the hair of a hanged man. The soul of the victim of execution, some bandit of his tribe, suspended from the wood of justice, had tortured the Prince's sleep all night, and since that nightmare, Otto's reason had sunk into the unknown.

The old King, overwhelmed by so many disasters, shrugged his shoulders and let rumor run its course, but he had been obliged to renounce any project of union between the Prince and his cousin. He had nurtured for a long time the design of uniting the handsome Otto with his little Christmas rose, but it would have been cruel to deliver the delicate and delightful Bertrade to that maniac and unpredictable madman.

The Princess was then in her sixteenth year. She had not only inherited from her mother the slightly suffering oval of the face where the blue veins were transparent under the skin, and the sloping shoulders, and the poignant gaze of distant irises, sea-green in the dead woman, amethyst violet in Bertrade; she had also inherited from the Queen a kind of anxious melancholy that made her seek, in preference to conversations at the window and walks in the open air, the half-light of bedrooms and vague soliloquies before mirrors. Her favorite pleasure was to shut herself away for long hours in some high-ceilinged room hung with tapestries, whose characters of wool and silk ended up becoming insensibly animated under her gaze. If she looked at the sun, it was through the bezel of one of the rings with which her slim fingers were charged, and she had often been seen in the moonlight, amusing herself by making the sparkling gems of her necklaces stream in the radiance.

In all of nature she only seemed to love reflections. Water also attracted her, and the only flowers whose presence she could tolerate were the iris and the nenuphar; she loved to linger at dusk on the icy edges of springs and in the feverish mist of ponds, but to everything else in the world, she preferred interminable and silent pauses before the fixed silvering of looking-glasses; the soul of her mother seemed to her to be retained there, returned from the darkness to the equivocal surfaces of mirrors.

It was then that, without anything having permitted that precious end to be foreseen, Princess Bertrade was extinguished—or, rather, went to sleep—in the arms of her maidservants. She was in the sixth month of her sixteenth year, and had spent the day before in a convent of Clarists, where the nuns had made a great fuss of her. On her return, in the burning gold of the sunset, she had stopped her litter in the midst of the ripe wheat-fields in order to listen to the voice of a reaper who was singing. The next day, she was dead.

In the absence of the King, who had been notified by courier, the tearful governesses bathed the pure white cadaver and perfumed it with essences; then, having combed and braided the shiny silk of her hair, crowned her with roses of pearl and the pith of reeds, as one sees on statues of the Madonna, they joined her little hands, sparkling with rings, over a great lily of gold filigree, placed fur slippers on her feet and, prostrate beneath a double row of candles, waited in great dolor.

But when the King, weighted down by chagrin and years, penetrated into the mortuary chamber, accompanied by Bishop Afranus, with his crosier, mitered in gold with a crimson dalmatic over his shoulders, with a cortege of archdeacons and physicians in mourning in their wake, it was discovered that the one that had been thought dead was only asleep—but what a strange and lugubrious sleep! Nothing could recall her to life: neither the prayers of the priests not all the efforts of the master seers and physicians.

For three days she remained exposed on a large scaffold draped with white velvet in the middle of the cathedral; for three days masses were celebrated without interruption by the bishop and his clergy; for three days, the songs of Easter were intoned by all the people with the thunder of organs; but the Princess did not wake up.

Rose petals piled up, like a rising snowdrift, at the foot of the platform, the pearly orient of her necklaces shone upon the white of her neck; around her there was the light of thousands of candles, and the vapors of incense unwound their blue-tinted spirals, but distant, as if inaccessible and seemingly dreaming behind their moving mists, the Princess lay motionless, still asleep in the midst of brocades, illuminated candles, psalms and flowers.

She was neither alive nor dead.

It was then that Bishop Afranus had an inspiration from Heaven. Who could tell whether the sun, the open air, the wind and the rain, the very force of the elements, might not contrive what the Church and its liturgical chants had been unable to obtain? For that tender body fallen into lethargy, therefore he had a long, narrow coffin of glass constructed, with its eight corners decorated with sculpted silver lilies; the sleeping Princess was laid therein on a bed of padded silk, and the old prelate decided that that every day that God provided, Bertrade should be paraded on a stretcher through the villages and the fields, with pauses at all the chapels and all the convents in the realm; a long cortege of penitents and the faithful, in prayer, would always follow the royal body. Perhaps God would eventually take pity on their dolor; by night the traveling reliquary would repose in the choir of a church or the crypt of a cloister.

Then there was an interminable series of processions through the saddened realm. All that one ever encountered on the roads henceforth was deacons in surplices and monks in hoods, chanting lamentations; on the edges of fields and at the entrances of towns, there was nothing but ardent eyes and ecstatic faces, clasped hands and bare feet: women of the people, artisans, rustics and laborers come running in great fervor as the Princess passed by.

Through fields yellow with crops, as along the flowering April hedgerows, long hooded silhouettes suddenly appeared at crossroads; great banners of soft silk, hung like high sails above the crops; odors of myrrh and incense mingled on earthen pathways. In the midst of incense-burners and lighted candles, the royal reliquary was passing by.

White in the pallor of her brocades and silks, her eyes closed beneath her crown of pearl roses, one might have thought her an immobile Our Lady of Tears, all silk and filigree; and the limpid walls of the hexagonal bier glistened in the August sun like frosty water. In November, it happened that the candles were abruptly extinguished beneath the rain, the tall silver crosses tottered in the swollen hands of the carriers, the wind inflated the banners, and before the white coffin, crackling under the hail, noblewomen and peasants knelt pell-mell in the mud of pathways, and in every season, the knell tolled relentlessly over hallucinated regions.

From one end of the year to the other there was an uninterrupted sequence of slow and sumptuous pilgrimages; all the churches and all the convents in the land were visited. The royal reliquary was only returned to the capital twice a year, the week before Christmas and the one before Easter, great Church festivals in which an opinion credited by the people claimed that Bishop Afranus gave communion to the enchanted Princess. By means of the miraculous host, it was said, he sustained the lethargic and gentle cadaver, the bloodless and royal body of the virgin who could neither revive nor die; but that was popular rumor.

The Princess Under Glass, as Bertrade was now called, remained exposed to the veneration of the faithful in the middle of the cathedral choir, from Palm Sunday until Easter Tuesday, and the entire week preceding Christmas, but the bishop was never seen to approach the august reliquary. Once a year, only, on Palm Sunday, six Ursulines chosen from among the youngest in all the convents of the realm, were allowed to touch the royal coffin and to change the crown of pearls and reed-pith on the dead woman's head.

When the festivals were over, the Princess and her cortege resumed the course of their peregrinations under the sun and the rain.

It was already the fifth year of those futile pilgrimages. In spite of the archbishop's previsions, the Princess Under Glass had no more moved the stiffened silk of her eyelids than the cold ivory of her beautiful hands.

The old King, her father, fallen into a species of dull torpor, having become almost indifferent to grief, had abandoned his frontier camp to cloister himself in the Castle in the Woods: the castle built in the middle of the marshes, where the Princess of Occitania, Bertrade's mother, had died more than twenty years before, and where Bertrade, his little Christmas rose, had fallen asleep so singularly sixteen years and six months later.

The old monarch lived there henceforth, in the gloom of high-ceilinged rooms with walled-up windows, alone in confrontation with the past that sometimes surged forth from the dead water of mirrors, scarcely emerging from his retreat to witness, twice a year, the exhibition of the Princess Under Glass in the middle of the cathedral.

From there he went back to his castle, to his oblivion; ministers reigned in his stead.

As for Prince Otto, he too had disappeared almost completely. Following a bizarre accident, the burning of one of his summer residences, where the most beautiful courtesans in the realm had all perished horribly, his humor had become even grimmer; and half out of remorse and half out of terror of the popular hatred that accused him of having set the fire himself, he had retired into the forests of the West, amid the wooded solitudes of the frontier, the ones that neighbored the north of Swabia and the marches of Bohemia.

The fire that an odious rumor accused him of having lit in the course of a fête offered to the heir to the Dukedom of Livonia, in which the most beautiful women of the age had found death, had completed the disarray of his reason. Taking refuge in the depths of impenetrable woods with a handful of rogues, it was said that he lived the life of a bandit chief—that, in sum, of the noble barons of the century—robbing travelers, killing birds in the air, pillaging Jews and merchants, forcing beasts in their lairs and peasants in their hovels; and all the poor people trembled before the Black Prince who had become the Red Prince.

One last exploit of Otto's completed the measure.

In the course of one of his armed expeditions, an ambush or hunting party—no one knew exactly, since he was accompanied by his dogs—the Prince had encountered on the edge of a wood the slow cortege of candles and crosses that accompanied the Princess. The sight of the lighted candles awoke in him the memory of his crime, or perhaps the bohemian's spell was exasperated by liturgical chants.

A sudden access of fury seized him, and with foam on his lips, vociferating anathemas, he had suddenly fallen on the pious escort, with his pack and his men, knocking over monks and novices, trampling women and candle-bearers, Christs and banners, pell-mell beneath the rearing horses.

There was an atrocious panic, a terrified stampede through the consternation of the fields; the terrified stretcher-bearers precipitately abandoned the glass reliquary, which shattered, and Bertrade's delicate body, half-projected from her coffin, slid away from her bed of pale silk into the sticky mud of the road. It remained there all night, exposed to the November rain.

It was recovered the following day, at dawn, in the midst of silver candlesticks and long banners thrown down by the fugitives along the road, motionless and pale beneath her crumpled brocades and the dusty fragments of her crown of pearls.

Prince Otto, bewildered by horror, had fled from his sacrilege; the fragile body of the Princess Under Glass had therefore remained abandoned for twelve hours. When the King's men, notified in all haste, came running to the place in order to pick up the reliquary and return the Princess to the palace, they recoiled in fear. Two streaks of blood had moistened and stiffened the silk of her dress; her thin arms, which had been folded the day before, over a gold filigree lily, were now two dangling, formless stumps on which blood was clotting.

The ferocious animals, the Great Danes and mastiffs of the cruel Prince Otto, a pack worthy of its master, which had been unleashed on the priests, women and children during the hunt, had been offered a portion of prey that the Black Hunter would not have disavowed, and had devoured the hands of the Princess.

The halloo had earned its reward.

And the blood was flowing, warm and red, in spite of the closed eyes and the blanched face; the Princess was still alive.

At that news, an indignation rose up throughout the realm. The old King finally emerged from his torpor and decreed in an edict that there was now a price on the Prince's head. The Archbishop obtained a brief from the Pope forbidding water, bread and salt to the sacrilegious Otto and his companions. Gibbets were set up at all the crossroads; the accomplices of the Black Prince, pursued and tracked down, swung their cadavers there; only the Black Prince escaped, having left the country, a refugee in some unknown retreat, vanished, disappeared forever.

The Princess Under Glass was reintegrated, never to emerge again, into the narrow nave of the cathedral. Hoisted high above the main altar, at the very foot of the great Christ opening his two pierced palms over the stalls of the choir, she remained henceforth offered to the veneration of crowds in a reliquary sealed into the wall: a reliquary made, this time, entirely of rock crystal, with corners enriched with opal anemones, and which glittered, ablaze with reflections, with rainbow spectra, in the multicolored light from two stained-glass rose-windows.

The candles burned their flames beneath her, and beneath her was suspended, like an enormous bird, the great lamp of the choir. From a distance, vertiginously, she seemed to the faithful to be a dazzling point of light, a living corpse retrenched from life and already on a level with eternity, already so close to the beams of the vault, already so far away in the heights.

Her poor mutilated hands had been covered by a golden cloth, and, henceforth hidden up to the chin beneath that sumptuous shroud, one might have thought her truly dead rather than a sleeping princess; and people were afraid when, during the offices, their eyes encountered her little waxen head posed on the cushions, outside the splendid mass of fabrics.

The punctured feet of the Christ seemed to be weeping the blood of their wounds over her.

A long time ago, now, the old King had died.

And the years passed, and other kings died. Another dynasty reigned over Courland, distant collaterals of the old King, who had never known Princess Bertrade or wild Otto, vague strangers for whom the royal martyr, enclosed in her aerial reliquary, was only a stranger, a vague heroine of a folktale. Very old people remembered having seen her in their childhood at strange ceremonies, but the misdeeds of Prince Otto were unfortunately associated with those recollections, obsessing the memory of the people, and the reigning family, then in all the glory and insolent pride of a Courland united and pacified, decided one day that the dead woman, perched in the midst of the banners of the choir, had saddened the hosannas of triumph with her specter for too long.

The Princess Under Glass darkened the cathedral; it always seemed, beneath that funeral reliquary, that people were attending a mass for the dead, and that cadaverous face apparent in the half-light of the vaults changed the most beautiful *Te Deum* into a *De Profundis*, and then again, had she not frightened the towns and villages long enough while the old King was alive, with the somber pomp of her mournful corteges, the Princess Under Glass always wandering the roads and by-ways?

After sixty years of repose, hallucinated Courland had not yet recovered from that nightmare; why eternalize forever in the mind of the crowd the abominable memory of a court of lunatics and maniacs, of ensorcelled queens and criminal princes? The memory of such a tragic reign could only harm the prosperity of other reigns; the day when the enchanted coffin was no longer there would be a deliverance for everyone.

What the Emperor wants, the Pope blesses; what the King wants, the priests approve.

One night, the crystal reliquary in which Bertrade reposed was brought down from the vaults. Poor Bertrade the Pale; Bishop Afranus was no longer there to defend her. He too had been asleep for a long time under the flagstones of the choir, in the company of other prelates ranged, crosier in hand, on high sarcophagi in the cathedral crypt.

In the same place where the scintillating Princess Under Glass had floated above the faithful, the arms of the reigning family were displayed between the standards and trophies of war, and the people applauded the heraldic blazon, overwhelming with the gold of its crest the divine tabernacle and the prayer of the candles.

A lateral chapel had received Bertrade's reliquary. She grew old there in the shadows, an object of the devotions of a few old women, survivors of the former reign, who gradually came no more. A saint devoid of miracles, who did not cure lepers or paralytics, she soon fell into abandonment; the petty clergy charged with maintaining the lamp before her spectral splendor also became negligent; the crystal walls became dusty, the opals at the corners tarnished; spiders spun their webs there, and it was as if a second shroud were woven around the Princess Under Glass by silence and forgetfulness.

The silks that touched her yellowed; the flowers of pearls lost their petals, and in the damp and dilapidation of the poor chapel an anguish grew around that apparent phantom, reminiscent of a wax doll beneath a gilded shroud and stiffened gauzes. In all seasons, a long ogive with unpolished windows shed a bleak wintry daylight over the altar-cloth, and, placed on the retable, the glass coffin glistened sadly, like a block of ice in which a cadaver had been frozen.

The candles were never lit, no deacon ever celebrated mass there, and the devotees lingering at some neighboring altar were afraid, once darkness fell, to go past the chapel, because of the dead woman and because of the wound beneath the shroud, which might perhaps be bleeding still.

And as bad priests, to please reigning princes, spoke of sorcery and cited stories of vampires found fresh and plump in their graves, eyes closed like those of the Princess, and, like her, apparently asleep, the high clergy became troubled and resolved to hide the daughter of a king from popular suspicions. It was also necessary to return the suspect chapel to worship as soon as possible.

A scruple gave the chapter pause, however; that lethargic body which had perhaps not ceased to live could not be interred without sacrilege; so it was decided to deposit the royal reliquary in a boat and confide both to the current of the river and the mercy of God.

The reliquary was transported one moonless night to the bank, in the midst of the osiers that extended behind the cathedral. There, the Princess was furtively embarked on a flat-bottomed boat under the eyes of the bishop, assisted by two deacons. Holly foliage and pine branches formed a bed of verdure around her, for Christmas was approaching, and holly and pine keep the Evil Spirit at bay. Then the bishop gave her a final absolution and the boat was pushed into the current of the river. The exiled corpse began to move slowly downstream.

They followed it for a long time with their eyes, and when they finally thought that it was out of the city, they hurriedly went back into the church and celebrated a low mass there, which put their conscience to rest.

In the distance, far away, toward the Castle in the Woods, under the cold nocturnal wind, the Princess Under Glass descended the slow stream that snaked idly through the marshes.

She floated thus for league after league between banks desolated by winter; the dry reeds rattled in a melancholy fashion in the bitter wind; large gray clouds fled recklessly across the sky, and on starry nights great black shadows rose up heavily over ponds; they circled momentarily with plaintive cries above the boat, and then fled into the distance as if in great distress; and there was nothing above those pale waters more sorrowful than the calling of those wild birds.

The Princess Under Glass continued to glide along the river, indolently, between banks swollen by frost. No one came to salute the passage of the one whose pilgrimages had once excited the entire country. The dense fog of the dusks and the frost of the dawns bathed her by turns, and under the rain, the wind, the ice and the snow, the crystal reliquary, washed and shiny, recovered the splendor of old.

The ancient Castle in the Woods of her early childhood saw her wander thus, for an entire long day, through the marshes that surrounded it, but the old guardian, the only one who might have recognized her, had gone blind; the thick shutters of the casements were no longer opened because of his lost sight, and the Princess Under Glass passed the shadow of its towers without a salute.

And the banks recommenced, even bleaker, flatter and icier as they plunged northwards; there were expanses of hardened wood where innumerable reed-stems were undulating as far as the eye could see, and not a single thread of smoke rose into the sky.

She reached thus, on Christmas Eve, a dazzling frozen solitude, all peat-bogs and pools; and there, among the brown osiers and vast fields of yellow sagittaria, the waters of the river began to lose impetus, and the boat was stopped by floating ice.

An infinite distress weighed upon that landscape, whose air seemed frozen and mute; it was Christmas Eve, but no sound of bells vibrated over the plain, although the roofs and the belfry that protruded above the curtain of reeds not far away were surely the roofs and the belfry of a convent.

A strange monastery, in truth, was that convent of men numbed by the winter in that bleak and dismal landscape, and whom no ringing bell or liturgical chant awoke from torpor on the eve of the great festival of the Church, the eve of Christmas.

A strange convent! For more than forty years now, the bells had no longer been rung there, psalms had no longer been sung, and, as if plunged in lethargy, it was silent in the midst of the silence of the marshes. Such was the formal will of its prior, a most strange old man with an entirely white beard, who was soon going to die.

A somber legend claimed that in other times, while the preceding abbot was alive, an outlaw, an unknown with the face of a bandit had come to request sanctuary in the monastery, then sonorous with orisons and angelus. The man, taken in, made great penitence, edifying the brothers and novices by the austerity of his fasts and the ardor of his flagellations. On his deathbed, the previous abbot had designated him as his successor; the vote of the monks had ratified his choice. But since then, in the choir as in the belfry, all voices had fallen silent; the prose of canticles was read in hushed voices, and for forty years, the bells had been mute.

The new abbot had imposed silence on the community; the rule that was already strict had redoubled its rigor under him; and in the exact observance of that rule, in fasts and vigils, in prayer and poverty, the present prior—a great sinner, some said; a great lord, said others—waited to die for the motionless bells to ring out in space; for the day when the bells sounded would be for him the day of mercy and his past would be forgiven him.

That night, under the snow that was beginning to swirl in the courtyards, the monks quit their cells one by one and went to the choir for the midnight mass; it was now a low mass devoid of hymns of joy, devoid of chants of welcome. The prior was the last to come down, so old, so broken, so burdened with chagrins, remorse and years that two monks were required to sustain him; he came in, his eyes extinct, his face so pale and drawn beneath the flow of his white beard that one might have thought him a cadaver in the hands of the two monks; but scarcely had the three of them arrived under the porch than a clear and joyful sound of bells saluted them from above. All the bells were sounding a carillon in the tower, and all the monks felt an exquisite surprise in the depths of their hearts.

They all emerged in great haste from the enclosure of the cloister, and spread out joyfully along the river bank to see what angel of the Lord had descended into the tower. The dazed prior followed them, leaning on his aides, his two hands in front him, groping.

The bells were ringing by themselves, at full tilt, but in the middle of the river, stopped by the ice, the Princess Under Glass was radiant, sparkling with a supernatural light; around her floated soft, slow snowflakes, and beneath the translucent crystal of the reliquary, her transparent forehead was crowned with Christmas roses, no longer artificial but freshly blooming.

Her blissful body had thrown off her shroud, and, with a smile on her lips, her eyelids closed, she was asleep, holding between her hands—her poor hands, once devoured by dogs, which had become pure and beautiful again—an enormous sheaf of red roses, the same red as the blood of her wounds.

And the prior, having fallen to his knees, understood that Bertrade was dead, that she had forgiven, and that he too was about to die.

To him, her cruel torturer, to him the wild Otto, the sinister Black Prince who had become the Red Prince, today a monk and repentant, she had come as a sign of absolution, bringing the dazzling vermilion bouquet, the symbolic roses born from her wounds, the flowers of her blood.

He tried to have the boat brought to the bank, but the ice broke under the feet of the lay brothers, harpoons fell into the water, and it was impossible to reach it. All night long Prince Otto stayed there, in prayer, kneeling on the bank, under the falling snow; the monks ranged around him sang *Hosannas* and *Misereres* by turns. Above the convent in festival, the bells were still ringing.

At the first light of dawn the ice melted; the marvelous boat moved slowly downstream, and then disappeared around a bend in the river.

The Mandrake

WHEN it was known that the Queen had given birth to a frog there was consternation in the court; the ladies of the palace remained mute, and no one any longer ventured into the high vestibules except with sealed lips and heart-rending gazes that spoke volumes. The master-seer, who had supervised the fine operation, could not bring himself to take the news to the King; he hurriedly took to the fields via the postern of the commons and was not seen again. As for the Queen, at the sight of the little monster issued from her entrails, she fainted.

When she recovered consciousness, it was to see the King at her bedside, his brows furrowed and more frightening in his silence than in the heart of the battle when, at the head of his troops, he crushed the turbaned miscreants of Egypt and Syria, all looters, lechers and pagans; his appearance was so terrible that the poor Queen felt faint again, but she took control of her senses, with a view to her salvation.

"You've struck a hard blow there, Madame," he said, looking into the depths of her soul. "It's the first time that frogs have been seen in my family; you must have been ensorcelled, unless you've slept very profoundly on the edge of some pond; in that case, it's a matter of questioning all the castle guards charged with watching over your person, and a few others."

And he raked her, this time, with a stare so cruel that the poor Queen fainted unwittingly, in the midst of her blood—on seeing which, he left the royal bedchamber, thinking that he had said enough.

Five years before, the Queen had given him a beautiful little prince, as seductive as his father and mother, for Queen Godelive was one of the most marvelous creatures of the time, and the two of them formed the most handsome royal couple among reigning monarchs. So the pot-bellied frog with the thin legs, emerging suddenly in the midst of the family, cast a great chill into the soul of King Luitprand, and the Queen had to reckon herself very fortunate to have given birth five years earlier to such an adorable dauphin.

That son, of whom the King was very fond, was, however, as vicious as a one-eyed horse; he terrified his governesses by gluing their hair with pitch, or slyly nailing the hems of their dresses to the floorboards; he liked nothing better than inflicting cuts and bruises, and his greatest pleasure was to crucify living bats to the panels of doors, or to sit little monkeys with shaven behinds on the red hot ovens in the kitchen. The child was already promising to be a greater burner of heretics in later life.

In favor of the charming dauphin the King wanted to pardon the Queen, but he ordered the immediate death of the frightful little monster.

When the Queen recovered consciousness it was to learn about the horrible sentence; she greeted it with dry eyes and without overmuch regret, for she was proud of the beauty of her family members, and even more so of her own, and her ulcerated vanity could not be consoled for having given birth to a monster. She therefore went to sleep at the curfew peacefully enough.

In the middle of the night, however, she was woken up by vague sounds. A child was whimpering in the next room and the voice of an old woman was singing a nursery rhyme; the Queen felt a vague presentiment grip her heart. Although still very weak, she found the strength to drag herself out of her bed in the high room, among her sleeping chambermaids, and to open the door.

In the center of a well-lit room, the oldest of the midwives who had assisted her was sitting next to a crib, while around the walls, huddled maidservants were asleep. In the crib, under a canopy of white silk with pearl fleurs-de-lys designed for royal heirs, with eyes wide open—enormous, somnambulistic eyes—the hallucinated frog was asleep. Its two little webbed forepaws were holding a green sprig from a box-tree on its breast.

The old midwife was gently rocking the cradle with her foot and quavering, to a very ancient tune, these mysterious words:

> *Your own have disdained you,*
> *And you're dying of love*
> *Will your great bleeding eyes*
> *Ever be able to laugh?*

> *They all think you ugly,*
> *My darling beauty;*
> *Whom a little bounty*
> *Might have made adorable.*

Your sound eyes that weep
Fill them with fear;
For life is a lure
And the heart a chill.

Your own have disdained you,
And you're dying of love,
Will your great bleeding eyes
Ever be able to laugh?

And the frog's golden eyes were varnished with tears.

And the Queen, who knew she was to die, uttered a scream and fell down.

When her chambermaids brought her round, the equivocal vision had disappeared; in the next room there was no crib and no frog; the King's orders had been carried out to the letter; the monster's head had been crushed between two stones and the flaccid remains had been thrown to the castle moat.

The Queen never recovered from that childbirth; she remained lying henceforth in the half-light of her bedroom, prey to a strange languor.

Henceforth, there was a strange presence close to her. She could no longer remain alone; there always had to be lighted candles in her room, and maidservants keeping vigil; they worked hourly shifts, terrified and mute, slowly bewitched by the Queen's fearful obsession. The entire castle was haunted by funereal rustlings and innumerable crawling sounds; a wind of folly blew through it; something frightful was prowling there, born of Godelive's hallucinated anguish. Sometimes, she sat up very straight in her chair and uttered a loud scream, and then fell back, with sweat on her temples, inert. At night, equivocal nightmares visited her.

Sometimes, she saw herself repudiated by the King, traversing the deserted streets of the city at a slow pace, alone, holding the insidious frog by the hand, already grown and dressed as a little princess—for in all her dreams the frog was always there beside her, very much alive, and in her dreams, her horror for the monster diminished day by day; her large eyes circled with gold had pupils so human, and her little cool and sticky paw held her hand so tenderly!

At other times she saw herself transported on warm and moonless nights to the middle of sinister plains, where pale grass undulated at the foot of high gibbets; then a large black greyhound followed her. She wandered, full of anxiety, beneath the heavy beams of the gallows, a carrion pestilence weighed in the air, and in the sulfurous night streaked with orange gleams, phosphorescent vertebrates became visible; the frog had disappeared, and she, an exiled and fallen Queen, wandered like a she-wolf at the foot of the gallows in order to find and dig up the terrible root that grows in the midst of carrion: the mandrake, the obscene and hairy root whose fibrils affect the form of thin limbs twisted around the wide-eyes head of a gnome, if one can call a gnome something with a swollen belly and an obscenely gaping sex. . . .

And she, Godelive, the Queen repudiated by the throne of Thuringia and the daughter of the Kings of Courland, the very Catholic and very Christian Queen, wandered at midnight in those solitudes, in the middle of those dismal plains, her eyes keen and anxious, stopping at the foot of each gibbet, where sometimes, something warm, like a tear of wax, but strangely reeking, fell upon her cheek. . . .

And the long pale grass, as white as the bones of the dead, rustled softly around her, so softly that one might have thought it the sound of distant voices, or some obscure whimpering. . . .

And the feet of the hanged men were outlined, black and dislocated, level with her temples; sometimes a soft big toe brushed her, the odor then rising more forcefully, and the beat of wings greeted her in the night, of birds of prey that she had awakened in passing. . . .

And Godelive continued to wander in the midst of the carrion and its pestilences, exhausted and weak but hallucinated by her obsession, reanimated continually by the frightful hope that she had in her heart; and with her feverish hand she sought the black greyhound walking in her shadow, and reassured herself by stroking its flanks; it was beside her, anxious and sniffing, attracted like her to the feet of the gibbets by the horrible odor, and sometimes a muffled sound of chewing notified the Queen that the dog had found what it sought.

And she, who had not found anything, pursued her agonizing round beneath the disgusting fetid dew of the gibbets, in the midst of the whispering grass, like the plaints of infants.

And the Queen, through the oppression of her dream, remembered, very lucidly, what atrocious rites the Kabbalah imposes on those who want to take possession of the magic root: to attach a living dog to one of the fibers of the accursed plant, and while the choking animal struggles, uprooting a little of the coveted plant with every movement, to keep watch surreptitiously in the darkness, in order, when the mandrake is scarcely out of the ground, to fall upon the breathless beast and stripe it with thrusts of a knife. The life of the slaughtered animal then passes into the hideous root and animates it with the breath necessary to prompt and sure incantations.

And the Queen woke up, bathed in cold sweat, knowing perfectly well why a black greyhound followed her.

Now, in fact, she surrounded herself with mages and necromancers; an invincible attraction drew her toward the occult sciences; one might have thought that she wanted to free herself from a spell, that she was in haste to break the stifling circle of a curse. Far from curing her, however, all those tenebrous consultations exasperated her illness; her curiosity to know was sharpened, becoming feverish and morbid, and nothing any longer satisfied her. The Evil One, now that she was half-given to him, refused her desire, and the frog still obsessed her.

Another nightmare tormented her too; it seemed to her that she was living, having been in retreat for years, in the middle of a wood, in the depths of a melancholy manner; the people and the King had forgotten her, and in her solitude florid with hawthorn in April and snow in winter, she led an effaced and almost happy existence accompanied by the frog, as attentive and affectionate as the gentlest of daughters.

She had ended up accustoming herself to her repulsive ugliness. In her high room hung with old tapestries she lived, without complaint, with the monster with the almost human gaze, always coquettishly crowned with meadow-daises, whose little viscous paw had at length acquired infinite softness. Her shame at having been able to engender such a monstrous creature had attenuated with the years, and on sunny days, she sometimes went walking with the poor creature in the meadows, and sometimes took pleasure in it.

In the course of one of those sunlit walks, as they were going through a wood snowy with apple-blossom and flowering almonds, as they emerged into a clearing they happened upon a cortege of noble ladies and peasant women all going, in their festival clothes, to the chapel of a nearby monastery.

They were all happy mothers or fortunate grandmothers, taking their progeniture to receive the Lord's blessing, for they were each holding by the hand some pretty child with long hair, crowned with roses; some even had three or four brats clinging to their dresses, girls or boys with complexions the color of the dawn and laughing eyes.

At the sight of those women, the Queen's heart broke, less out of dolor than of shame; she blushed with all her being at the pitiful garlanded frog who was hopping at her heels; abruptly, she drew her toward her and covered her with her cloak; her instinct hid her from all gazes. A sudden distress warned her at the same time of an immense misfortune; moistened by shame and moistened by fear, she nevertheless held the cloak closed over her.

When the cortege had passed, the frog was no longer there, but a large bloodstain soiled the lining; her incurable pride had killed her daughter for a second time.

And the nightmare saddened her life all the more because it was now mingled very strangely with reality. She had left the court and, effectively repudiated by the King, finally alarmed by a Queen prone to bestial pregnancies and more preoccupied with magic than the mass, she had been obliged to cede her place to a less perilous and younger mistress; and, half-condemned by popular opinion and that of the clergy, she lived henceforth in a small royal fief situated on the frontier.

She grew old there alone, visited at distant intervals by her son, the pretty child with eyes already cruel, now become a young man; he lived on bad terms with his father, conspired clandestinely, and came once or twice a year to spend twenty-four hours with the exiled Queen, less out of filial respect than to irritate the King; those rare meetings between Prince Rotterick and Queen Godelive had the gift of exasperating old King Luitprand to a towering rage.

The Queen, moreover, had become disaccustomed to giving a good welcome to a son whose every visit was followed by the departure of one of her maidservants, for Prince Rotterick was as debauched as he was ferocious; he loved evil for evil's sake, taking pleasure in the suffering of bodies as in the dolor of souls; above all, he liked to corrupt, and, served by the marvelous beauty that he had inherited from his mother, he attacked lazily, sure as he was of victory, all the candors and all the modesties that he encountered in his path. At court, they were the ladies of the palace, in the town, the daughters of the burghers, in the fields, the goose-girls and the laundresses; in his mother's house, they were the maidservants.

Queen Godelive had seen the departure, one by one, of the few noble daughters that remained faithful to her misfortune; thanks to her sin, she was reduced to being served by none but woodcutters' daughters, whom she cleaned up as best she could, on condition of putting the gynaeceum under lock and key when Prince Rotterick was signaled by the watchman. When the buzzard had gone, the poor Queen released her doves and went back to her needles and her spinning-wheel in the midst of her slightly disappointed women.

And that was her life, between maidservants with little imagination and devoid of conversation, more or less adroitly decked out in the cast-off clothing of the royal house, with the abrupt irruptions of her son, as rare as fine days and as maleficent as hail, each of which visits filled the vast corridors of the forgotten manor, as if lined by silence, with a squall of threats and screams. And the poor Queen's solitude was great.

In the early days of her sojourn, she had been strongly tempted to distract herself by devoting herself to magical practices, but, deprived of the help of her usual astrologers, carefully tracked and proscribed by royal decree, she had been groping in the dark and had ended up, in consequence, with a personal experience that had cured her of it forever.

One evening in June, an equivocal pauperess had presented herself at the postern of the manor and there, with a mysterious air, her eyes flamboyant beneath her hood, had left for the Queen a coarse canvas sack, bizarrely sealed.

"If the object displeases her," the beggar-woman had added, "the Queen only has to have it returned tomorrow, at nightfall, to the third step of the calvary of Riffauges, at the intersection of three roads. If, on the contrary, it pleases her and she keeps it, it's three hundred gold pieces that it's necessary to leave in the same place, at the same hour; but in any case, the object or the money in the same sealed bag; the treasure can defend itself."

The Queen had kept the object; it was a kind of fibrous and hairy root affecting the form of a monstrous toad or a stillborn child. She had recognized, tremulously, a mandrake: the mandrake that her previous dreams had revealed to her. The soul of a dead man inhabited that root; she knew that from a reliable source and knew all the rites prescribed for the cultivation and development of that soul.

God, or perhaps Hell, was perhaps rendering her thus the real presence of the murdered frog. She therefore devoted herself to the culture of the mandrake. Enclosed in a jar of dark glass, the root with the human form floated there, bathed in a nameless liquid; a death's head sniggered beside it, and a large sand-glass, inverted hour by hour, poured out the continuous trickle of its sand.

After a week, the oil of the liquid had become a kind of red mud, the color of blood. By night, the Queen got up in order to expose the jar to the rays of the moon, and by day she kept it carefully far from the sunlight, in an obscure redoubt, the key to which she always carried on her person. Twice a week, strange mendicants brought her herbs collected in the country, and from day to day the head of the mandrake became rounder, as if eyes were hollowing out in the flat surface, and little palmate hands were visibly palpitating at the ends of its hideous fibers; the charm was working.

By night, the Queen left the door of her room open in order to listen while she slept, for at night, the mandrake, inert during the day, became animated and snored like a man.

It was during one of those nights that the Queen struggled in the grip of the most frightful nightmare; she dreamed that an improbably enormous frog, almost human in stature, was crouching on her chest and slowly stifling her with its weight; she felt its icy palms posed on her shoulders, and the chill of its viscous belly adhering to her breast.

The nightmare lasted two hours; she only awoke at dawn, but the awakening was worthy of the dream; the mandrake, sticky with its oil, had slipped furtively out of its jar and was clinging to her, embracing her with its thin arms; and its hideous mouth was sucking at one of her nipples.

She had only screamed once and, terrified by horror, had seized the long-limbed root by one leg and had thrown it convulsively out of the window; it had fallen in broad daylight into the shiny water of the moat. That same evening, a peasant's child had been found drowned there, his little hands entangled in the tresses of a root unknown in the region.

Since then the Queen had occupied herself with prayers, and never with magic. Her ordeals were, however, not over.

One winter evening, there are cries and torches, rumors and the clink of weapons at the door of the manor. It is Prince Rotterick. He has asked for supper and shelter for himself and his escort, but this time, his audacity surpasses all bounds; he is carrying behind him, on the rump of his horse, a debauched woman whose brocade dress shines strangely in the night—a debauched woman, unless it is some girl abducted by force, some prey of lust for whom he is demanding a warm bed and supper.

The Queen, who listens to her steward giving her an account of the visit, is utterly pale in her high-backed chair; outside, the horses are whinnying and the riders are becoming impatient. The Queen, motionless and cold, cannot decide to give the order to raise the portcullis.

"The girl is wounded and dying; she has blood everywhere, on her hands and on her dress; it's a coffin and a shroud the Prince is asking for, rather than sheets and a bed."

The Queen stands up, she has precipitately given orders, has descended the staircase of the tower, her heart in great anguish, and comes into the low room. Prince Rotterick is already there; his men, helmed, masked and gauntleted in iron are arranged along the wall. The Prince inclines his head slightly toward his mother, showing her a heap of clothes thrown across the table.

"I found her crucified to a tree," he says. "She's in danger of death. Please help her."

On the oaken table lies the most delightful creature, a tall and pale young woman with thick, scattered hair as black as ink; her cleavage, throat and legs are naked; the glaucous green brocade of her robe is shiny, reflecting the light of the torches. Motionless, her teeth clenched, she rolls her terrified gaze around her, holding in her clenched fingers wisps of her hair with which she is trying to cover her breasts, but the palms of her poor hands are bleeding, cruelly pierced, and the flesh of her bare feet is bloody too, dolorously transpierced.

The Queen spent the whole night beside the unknown woman. She had washed and bandaged her wounds, and installed the poor bruised body in her own bed, but the injured woman, her eyes wide open, had looked at her without saying a word, without any thanks. The woman crucified in the forest had spent the entire night in a troubling and bizarre posture, folded up on herself, not so much lying as crouching in the middle of the bed, and that tragic face had not uttered a single plaint, not a single sob; and the Queen had ended up being afraid of that mute, whose gold-circled pupils were enormously dilated, improbably luminous in the dimly-lit chamber.

Downstairs, the incessant striding of the Prince filled the night with a rising sound of footfalls. Frightful images loomed up before Godelive from the depths of the tapestries: they were the same woven noble characters, squires corseted in breastplates and ladies in hennins, but deformed and all regressed to batrachian types; and the Queen sensed herself sinking into madness, dizzied by vertigo. At about four o'clock in the morning, however, she fell asleep.

When she woke up, it was broad daylight; the rays of a roseate winter sun, setting the window ablaze, bathed the large four-poster bed in which the unknown woman lay with an amber light, but in the same place where a woman had suffered all night long there was an enormous frog, an almost human frog, and all the more monstrous for it; and that frog was the young woman, for she had her four paws delicately bandaged with linen, and beneath the membranous eyelids of the beast, the Queen recognized the gold-ringed pupils that had terrorized her two hours before, pupils now singularly softened.

She finally recognized the frog of her dreams, the one that obsessed her and that she had regretted throughout the long nightmare of her life.

At the same moment, the Prince knocked on the door and asked to come in.

The bloodied frog fixed two large imploring eyes on the Queen; a tremor of fear shook her entire body, and the Queen, replying through the door, having asked the Prince to wait for her downstairs in the armory, Rotterick went downstairs muttering.

There, before all the Prince's assembled men and all the manor's servants, when the Queen, remembering the entire history of her life, had recounted her frightful child-birth and her dolorous nocturnal nightmares, those of her churching and those of her exile, including the sinister and recent ordeal of the mandrake, as all of them kept silent, prey to horror, and Rotterick, foaming with lust, grew impatient and sniggered, the Queen, having beckoned to him to follow her, went back up to her bedroom, opened the door wide, and led the Prince to the bed.

And Rotterick, having entered, felt his hair standing on end and a cold sweat pearling on his temples. Rotterick was afraid to comprehend, because he, too, recognized the frog. He had pursued and tracked her on horseback, and, for the sake of derision and ferocity, once the beast was captured, he had crucified her himself to the trunk of the birch where the martyred monster had been bleeding for a year.

And, in the russet red of the October forest, he saw once again the gesture and futile leap of the monster when, amid the brambles and ferns, he had surrounded it with his dogs. The alerted beaters had been able, this time, to draw the beast far way from ponds and, forced by the pack, the bleeding frog had been attempting vainly to climb the trunk of a tree, when Rotterick had burst into the clearing like a whirlwind, at the head of his men.

His chestnut horse had stopped as if dead, and the basset hounds and even the Great Danes had not dared approach, their chops drawn back from their fangs, sniffing and hesitant to bite; the fluid green beast was repugnant to them. Then Rotterick had had her seized by his men, stretched, palpitating along the birch, and while the huntsmen sounded their horns he had nailed her to the tree personally, with four arrows from his quiver, driven into the bark, amid the blood and the tears.

And it was that ensorcelled beast that his infamous desire had pursued today; it was that princess of the marshes that his lust coveted; like her, he was of the accursed race, and like her, surely bewitched by a horrible charm, since they had both emerged from the same entrails, issues of the same blood. Then, enveloping the frog and his mother with the same hateful glare, he drew his sword and, with a burst of savage laughter, launched it across the room at the bleeding monster.

The Queen, with a loud scream, threw herself in front of the bed. The sword traversed the room like a streak of light, and plunged into the large window, which shattered into smithereens; but in passing, the blade had touched the Queen on the shoulder, and Godelive collapsed at the foot of the royal bed, her dress stained with blood.

All the witnesses, dazed by horror, had fled. The Prince remained alone for a moment, standing before the two quivering bodies; he suddenly uttered a loud scream, and whirling around, ran head-first into the wall, groped fearfully, finally found the door. He disappeared.

The manor was now deserted, panic had emptied it; and under the arches of the posterns and under the vaults of the porches, left wide open, the snow, which had been falling all morning, mute and slow, piled up against the ornamental scrolls of the stone colonnettes, and the figures in relief on the capitals of the pillars. In the bedroom, already crepuscular, the two bodies lay limply, but both of them were still alive.

Through the shattered window, the snow penetrated the room from outside, covering the silken bedsheets, shiny with shards of glass, with a velvety down; and under the chill of the snow, the unconscious Queen slowly recovered consciousness.

A little icy hand squeezed hers convulsively, and in the dark room, where the shadows were accumulating, the Queen gradually felt the cold little hand that was clutching her fingers warm up. The Queen felt herself penetrated by an exquisite tenderness, but she kept her eyes closed and remained nonchalantly limp, because of her wound, the pain of which she was afraid of reawakening, and because of that little hand with its human warmth.

And that had lasted for hours, or centuries, when strange little distant voices—no, muffled, rather—drew her gently from her torpor.

And those voices said:

"Princess Ranaide is going to die."

And others responded: "Is Queen Godelive pardoned?"

And the voices resumed: "Blood washes away blood. Suffering absolves; dolor purifies. The snow is a soft shroud."

Then other voices, as if emerging from the thickness of the walls, said in a strange colloquium, one after another: "It is thus that the pride of a race is expiated. Heaven hates the superb. The hearts of the great are hard. Pity flourishes among the humble. Excessive arrogance engenders monsters; but the snow is a soft shroud."

And like a refrain, all the voices repeated: "Princess Ranaide is going to die."

And in the night of her eyelids the slumbering Queen saw all of her life again, and now understood the meaning of her nightmares; it was life itself that she had lived and led with her daughter. If she had been able to defend her in the cradle against death, what crimes and what misfortunes might she not have avoided! But the friction of wings vibrated softly above her head, odors of incense floated intoxicatingly, the caress of a little hand warmed her own, and the Queen almost no longer regretted the past.

Suddenly, the sound of bells rang out in the night; a larger cluster of snowflakes came to land on her face, and the Queen suddenly opened her eyes, remembering that it was Christmas Eve.

She looked around curiously. The room was brightly lit; there were candles everywhere, and they were all held by wolves, foxes, and even moles and weasels, all the forest animals curiously gathered around her. Here and there, in their ranks, a silhouette loomed up of a shepherd or a woodcutter, hooded against the cold, and beasts and humans alike were murmuring prayers, but the Queen was not astonished by that, knowing that the beasts could talk on Christmas Eve.

On the bed, the delightful creature of the previous night, the white Princess Ranaide, was dying, a smile on her lips. The tapestry hanging on the wall now represented the Nativity of Christ. Through the open door, more animals were still arriving.

Queen Godelive felt two tears moistening her dry eyes. A little hand wiped them away gently, and a child's voice whispered: "My mother!"

The following day, the two women were found dead.

OTHER SNUGGLY BOOKS YOU WILL ENJOY . . .

BLUE ON BLUE
by Quentin S. Crisp

A SUITE IN FOUR WINDOWS
by David Rix

NIGHTMARES OF AN ETHER-DRINKER
by Jean Lorrain

DIVORCE PROCEDURES FOR
THE HAIRDRESSERS OF A METALLIC AND
INCONSTANT GODDESS
by Justin Isis

BUTTERFLY DREAM
by Kristine Ong Muslim

GONE FISHING WITH SAMY ROSENSTOCK
by Toadhouse

METROPHILIAS
by Brendan Connell

CPSIA information can be obtained
at www.ICGtesting.com
Printed in the USA
BVOW03s0808261216

471813BV00001B/144/P